OF THE STANDARD OF TASTE

And Other Essays

The Library of Liberal Arts

OSKAR PIEST, FOUNDER

The Library of Liberal Arts

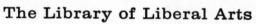

OF THE STANDARD OF TASTE

And Other Essays

David Hume

Edited, with an Introduction, by

John W. Lenz

Professor of Philosophy, Brown University

The Library of Liberal Arts
published by
THE BOBBS-MERRILL COMPANY, INC.
A Subsidiary of Howard W. Sams & Co., Inc.
Publishers • Indianapolis • New York • Kansas City

David Hume: 1711–1776

Contents

Contents

Introduction

As a philosophical critic Hume has few peers. No one has challenged more sharply rationalism's central thesis that matters of fact can be known without recourse to experience; nor has anyone revealed more clearly the severe problems raised by insisting that all factual claims be empirically verified. Holding that without experiential support beliefs are arbitrary, Hume attacked the rationalists' allegedly intuitive "truths" about God, spiritual substance, and immortality. Arguing, on the other hand, that common-sense convictions about the future, the external world, and the self cannot themselves be experientially confirmed, Hume showed that unrestricted empiricism leads to thoroughgoing skepticism. In his *Treatise of Human Nature* Hume posed a dilemma—between dogmatic rationalism and skeptical empiricism—that continues unresolved to this day.

As a constructive philosopher, Hume is also of major rank. In the first place, he brought out the problems inherent in empiricism only because he so thoroughly worked out its implications. Moreover, he was the first philosopher to formulate its tenets with precision and purity; the still popular view, originated by Reid, that Hume simply reduced to absurdity the empiricist principles already stated by Locke and Berkeley is clearly mistaken. In the third place, despite his own dissatisfaction with them, Hume's solutions to particular problems have proven highly suggestive. Whatever their ultimate tenability, his regularity view of causality, phenomenalistic analysis of physical objects and persons, and formal interpretation of mathematics are important contributions to the empiricist tradition. Such views, moreover, often utilized other original ideas—particularly an associationist psychology stressing the primacy of feeling—that have proved highly seminal.

The essays here collected form a significant part of Hume's thought. For one thing, they help us better understand Hume the man. Some were undoubtedly written to win critical acclaim; others, almost suppressed, manifest a fierce intellectual independence. They best reveal, therefore, the deep tension that dominated Hume's life and explains so much about all his writings. This theme will be pursued more fully in the brief biographical sketch offered in the next section.

Secondly, the essays display Hume's early and continuing mastery of this genre. Section II of this Introduction will discuss Hume's perfect adaptation of the English essayists' form and style to his own literary and philosophical purposes.

Thirdly, precisely because of their "popular" tone, the essays are an excellent indication of what Hume deemed most central in his own thought. His basic principles stand out all the more clearly there for being applied, as he said, to "less abstruse subjects." Three such tenets—his empiricist methodology, emotivist theory of valuation, and naturalistic view of man—will be discussed below.

Most significantly, the essays are our major source of Hume's views on art, about which, despite his lifelong interest, he wrote comparatively little. *Of Refinement in the Arts* traces the moral effects of art; *Of the Rise and Progress of the Arts and Sciences* considers the cultural conditions conducive to it; *Of Tragedy* analyzes the psychological appeal of that art form; *Of Eloquence* studies the rhetorical function of art; *Of Simplicity and Refinement in Writing* offers practical criticism; and *Of the Standard of Taste* tackles the difficult problem of the "objectivity" of aesthetic evaluations. Important in their own right, some of the above views also aid our understanding of other parts of Hume's thought. The particularly crucial *Of the Standard of Taste* will be examined later, for it not only presents a subtle analysis of aesthetic evaluations but also sheds a great deal of light upon Hume's influential theory of moral sentiment.

Hume's Life and Writings

Born in Edinburgh, Scotland, on April 26, 1711, David Hume grew up at Ninewells, the family estate in the nearby countryside. In 1723 he entered the University of Edinburgh, where great intellectual ferment was occurring: Locke's "new way of ideas" and Newton's mechanistic physics were challenging traditional modes of thought in philosophy and science; the controversy between ethical rationalists (such as Cudworth, Clarke, and Wollaston) and moral sense philosophers (such as Shaftesbury, Butler, and Hutcheson) was stimulating renewed interest in ethics. Three years at the University undoubtedly helped shape Hume's later thinking; by the time he left he had formulated his plan to apply the scientific method to the study of man.

His modest means, however, led him to decide upon a career in law, and, though his subsequent preparations proved abortive, he did acquire extensive legal knowledge. In 1729 he suffered an emotional collapse, perhaps attributable to his over-conscientious practice of the stoic regimen of self-questioning and self-denial; to enter upon "a more active scheme of life," he briefly took a merchant's post at Bristol. His health restored, he finally decided to risk a literary career, and in 1734 set off for France, settling at La Flèche, where Descartes had composed his revolutionary *Discourse on Method*. In three years, at the age of twenty-four, Hume had substantially completed an equally pivotal work, his *Treatise of Human Nature*.

Its fate was to affect Hume's life deeply. Today it is universally recognized as one of the most decisive of philosophical writings, but at the time of publication it was coolly received; what attention it won in England and on the Continent was unsympathetic and uncomprehending. Hume was keenly disappointed, and having published the *Treatise* anonymously he later acknowledged authorship only to repudiate the work once and for all.

Concluding that he had gone to press too early, Hume blamed the demise of the *Treatise* on its "manner rather than on its matter." A more felicitous way of presenting his ideas, he decided, was needed. The two volumes of *Essays, Moral and Philosophical* published in 1742 are Hume's first such "literary experiment," and were successful enough to restore his confidence as a writer. With the exception of four works —*Of Tragedy, Of the Standard of Taste, On Suicide*, and *On the Immortality of the Soul*—all the essays contained in the present volume are taken from them.

In 1744 Hume vainly sought the chair of moral philosophy in the University of Edinburgh. In the eyes of the conservative presbytery that controlled the school, the *Treatise,* far from dead, branded him as a free-thinker, unfit to teach the young, and he became tutor to the virtually mad Marquis of Annandale. In 1746 Hume gladly accepted an invitation from General St. Clair to serve as his secretary, first during an ill-fated attempt to invade the coast of Brittany and later in the military embassy to Vienna and Turin. These posts brought the financial independence which enabled Hume from then on to pursue his writing without distraction; they also helped develop in him those humane and urbane qualities which in later years inspired the title "le bon David."

The fourteen years of Hume's life from 1748 to 1762 were enormously productive. The *Philosophical Essays* (later titled *An Inquiry concerning Human Understanding*) and the *Inquiry concerning the Principles of Morals,* elegant revisions of the first and third books of the *Treatise,* appeared in 1748 and in 1751; the *Political Discourses,* the most immediately influential of his writings, in 1752; and *Four Dissertations,* including two contained in the present volume—*Of Tragedy* and *Of the Standard of Taste*—in 1757. (*On the Immortality of the Soul* and *On Suicide* were originally scheduled for inclusion in the 1757 volume but, because of various pressures, were omitted.) From 1754 to 1762 Hume also successively published the six volumes of his *History of England,* wherein he remains the student of human nature, explaining events in terms of forces internal to man and society. The success of his writings, though somewhat mixed and not always immediate enough to suit Hume, was such that by 1757 he was generally regarded as one of the leading literary figures in Great Britain.

These fruitful years, however, were not without disappointments and difficulties. In 1751 Hume was again refused an academic appointment, this time to the chair of logic at Glasgow University. Despite the ardent support of men such as Adam Smith, the opposition of the influential clergy, now further nettled by Hume's attack upon miracles, remained overwhelming, and once more he had to settle for a lesser post, that of Keeper of the Advocates Library in Edinburgh. By 1756 the religious clamor against him had become so enormous that an attempt was made to excommunicate him from the Scottish church. Though frustrated by its liberal members, the attempt helps to explain Hume's decision to have the inestimably great *Dialogues concerning Natural Religion* published posthumously.

As a Scotsman in insular-minded England and freethinker in church-dominated Scotland, Hume was never entirely accepted in either place. It was different in cosmopolitan and liberal France, the center of the Enlightenment, to which he returned in 1763, as Secretary in the British Embassy. His fame, even greater there than in Britain, brought him into the company of *philosophes* such as d'Alembert, Buffon, and Diderot, and his ready wit and engaging simplicity of manners made him, much to the surprise of visitors from England, the hit of the Parisian salons.

After returning to London in 1767 to serve for two years as the Undersecretary of State for Great Britain, Hume retired to his native Edinburgh, intending to spend his remaining years quietly editing and perfecting his writings. In 1775 he was stricken by an illness that was to prove fatal. Realizing he was dying, Hume remained firm in his philosophical convictions and retained his customary good humor and detachment. Even the nagging James Boswell, unable to believe a skeptic could approach death with equanimity, did not succeed in ruffling Hume's philosophical calm. Hume died in his native city, Edinburgh, on August 25, 1776.

The Form and Style of the Essays

Hume's frank admission in his autobiography of a love of literary fame has been taken to reflect not only on his character but also on the quality of his post-*Treatise* writings. An examination of the essays, however, will help refute the charge that he distorted his ideas to win popular acclaim.

After the *Treatise* Hume explored various literary forms: the *Enquiry concerning Human Understanding* is a set of interrelated essays, while in the *Dialogues concerning Natural Religion* Hume employs the genre perfected by Plato. The works collected in the present volume utilize the short essay form made so popular in eighteenth-century Britain by the periodical writers, particularly Addison and Steele. Hume's essays, however, differ in important respects from the *Tatler* and *Spectator* papers. It is not simply that Hume's are often lengthier and treat more difficult subjects. More significantly, whereas Addison and Steele state their views as "one man's opinion," Hume marshalls evidence in support of his contentions. Whereas the formers' essays tend to be delightfully rambling and discursive, Hume's are usually tight arguments whose rigorous logical structure is artfully concealed. In short, Hume adapted the form and style of the periodical essayists to his own literary purpose.

That purpose is clearly stated in his own *Of Essay Writing:* to improve communication between men of thought and men of affairs.

> It is with great pleasure I observe, that men of letters in this age have lost in a great measure that shyness and bashfulness of temper, which kept them at a distance from mankind; and, at the same time, that men of the world are proud of borrowing from books their most agreeable topics of conversation. It is to be hoped that this league

> between the learned and conversible worlds, which is so
> happily begun, will be still further improved to their mu-
> tual advantage; and to that end, I know nothing more ad-
> vantageous than such *Essays* as those with which I endeav-
> our to entertain the public.[1]

Acquaintance with the reflections of the learned, Hume believed, would add depth and significance to the thought and
conversation of men of the world. At the same time, men of
learning would gain from presenting their ideas to general
mankind; their writing would become more tasteful, their
thought more "relevant."

> On the other hand, learning has been a great loser by
> being shut up in colleges and cells, and secluded from
> the world and good company. By that means every part
> of what we call *belles lettres* became totally barbarous,
> being cultivated by men without any taste for life or man-
> ners, and without that liberty and facility of thought and
> expression which can only be acquired by conversation.
> Even philosophy went to wrack by this moping recluse
> method of study, and became as chimerical in her con-
> clusions as she was unintelligible in her style and manner
> of delivery. . . .[2]

Hume is here undoubtedly speaking about the author of the
Treatise of Human Nature.

In his essays Hume achieved the intelligible and tasteful
style he sought. They well illustrate, as a matter of fact, the
contention of his own *Of Simplicity and Refinement in Writing* that in good prose these factors are nicely balanced. The
writing is free of the technical terminology that so often makes
philosophical prose opaque. It is nicely literal; metaphors are
used sparingly, and then mainly to summarize and emphasize
points rather than to establish them. The readily apparent
elegance of Hume's prose comes not from the baroque adorn-
ments that he so much scorned, but from its very economy
and precision. It achieves its chief appeal to the imagination,

[1] P. 39.
[2] P. 39.

as Hume thought it should, from the novel and important ideas it expresses.

The Experimental Method of Reasoning

At the beginning of *On the Immortality of the Soul* Hume reiterates the main epistemological point of his Treatise: abstract a priori reasoning cannot by itself decide questions of fact; appeal to experience is necessary. Matters of fact, that is, must be known either directly, through sense perception or memory, or else indirectly, through causal inference. For example, one can sense warmth, one can remember having done so, or one can infer its existence upon observing its cause, say fire. Hume further held that the causal laws utilized in such inferences must themselves be established empirically, by observing the constant conjunction of individuals of two kinds, as in the case of fire and warmth.

Hume thought of this theory of knowledge as espousing the experimental method of reasoning used so successfully by physicists such as Boyle and Newton. Eschewing unverifiable hypotheses, the latter explained a particular motion (for example, an apple's falling to the ground) by subsuming it under a general law that simply states perceived regularities in the behavior of bodies. By conjoining such laws with present conditions Newton was, moreover, able to infer events as yet unobserved, whose existence he could later confirm through perception. That in Newton's hands the experimental method was a potent instrument of both explanation and prediction was undoubtedly Hume's major reason for advocating it.

In the essays, as in the *Treatise,* Hume seeks to extend the range of Newton's method by using it in investigating what he called "moral" (that is, social and psychological) phenomena. In *Of the Rise and Progress of the Arts and Sciences* he attempts, through a rather broad reading of historical evidence, to discover those conditions under which these aspects of culture flourish; in *Of Tragedy* he seeks to discover experimentally the cause of the pleasure which men, almost paradoxically, derive from watching drama that portrays horrifying events. Perhaps Hume's most daring—and problematic—use of the experimental method is in ascertaining aesthetic standards. In *Of Simplicity and Refinement in Writing*, for example, he attempts to arrive at the canons of good writing by isolating those factors common to works that have won wide critical acclaim. This method has been much criticized, for it is not at all obvious that its supposition—that good art is that which has won lasting praise—is correct. *Of the Standard of Taste*, however, contains a defense of this procedure.

Despite his advocacy and use of the experimental method, Hume was not unaware of the difficulties it raised. In the first place, our necessary reliance upon it severely limits human knowledge. Men's experience is often restricted by accidents of time and place, though, as Hume points out in *Of the Study of History*, it can be broadened by examining the past. More crucially, since some objects of thought are beyond any possible experience, beliefs about them cannot in principle be justified. As *On the Immortality of the Soul* brings out, ascription of human purposes to a deity is a paradigm case. One cannot perceive God directly; and because, a fortiori, one cannot observe any constant conjunctions between his activities and the natural world, one cannot establish the causal laws necessary to infer his intentions.

In other writings Hume showed that the experimental method itself presupposes a factual belief that cannot be justified empirically: namely, that nature is uniform in the sense that what has been constantly conjoined in the past will continue to be so conjoined in the future. We cannot, Hume claims, know this principle through perception or memory, and any attempt to argue that because nature has been uniform it will continue to be so begs the very question at issue. Thus, Hume radically deepened his skepticism toward men's claims to know. Such doubts are mitigated only by the utterly natural character of experimental reasoning. As we shall see, forces within human nature make it impossible not to believe that what has gone together in the past will continue to do so in the future, and, hence, any skeptical admonition to the contrary is simply beside the point.

Evaluations as Feelings

A second tenet of both the *Treatise* and the essays, that moral and aesthetic evaluations are expressions of sentiment, attacks the rationalist contention that one can by means of "intellectual intuition" know what is good or bad. But Hume's view cuts even more deeply, contradicting any claim that goodness or beauty are descriptive properties whose inherence in objects is knowable either a priori or empirically. As he says in *The Sceptic:*

> A man may know exactly all the circles and ellipses of the Copernican system and all the irregular spirals of the Ptolemaic without perceiving that the former is more beautiful than the latter. Euclid has fully explained every quality of the circle, but has not, in any proposition, said a word of its beauty. The reason is evident. Beauty is not a quality of the circle.[3]

Hume's view is that in finding something to be good or bad, beautiful or ugly, a person is reacting emotively to it; that in saying something is good or bad, beautiful or ugly, a person is expressing his feelings of approval or disapproval.

> . . . the case is not the same with the qualities of *beautiful* and *deformed, desirable* and *odious* as with truth and falsehood. In the former case, the mind is not content with merely surveying its objects, as they stand in themselves. It also feels a sentiment of delight or uneasiness, approbation or blame, consequent to that survey; and this sentiment determines it to affix the epithet *beautiful* or *deformed, desirable* or *odious*.[4]

Because Hume is sometimes careless in his way of putting it, his position can easily be misunderstood. His view is *not* that in finding an object worthwhile, a person is *describing*

3 Pp. 124–125.
4 P. 124.

or *stating* how he feels toward it. Were this his view, goodness or beauty would be empirically discoverable properties,
namely of arousing, or having the capacity to arouse a favorable sentiment in the judger. Were this Hume's view, he
would find it difficult to account for the obvious fact that
men do disagree in their evaluations; for if one man in finding a painting good and another in finding it bad are merely
stating how they feel toward it, their judgments are equally
correct and hardly in conflict. Hume's view—that the two men,
in feeling differently toward the same object, are *therein*
evaluating it differently—allows for what may be called a
conflict of sentiments.

Hume's support for his analysis of evaluations is essentially
twofold. First, Hume claims that whenever we evaluate
objects we do find ourselves with feelings of approval or disapproval. Secondly, he claims that only if evaluations are
regarded as feelings can we account for the ability of the former to influence our actions—as when, for example, our judgment that cheating is wrong tends to deter us from it. This
latter argument is premised on another doctrine of Hume's:
that only passions can directly motivate actions, conclusions
of reason being unable to do so.

In his emotivist analysis of moral and aesthetic evaluations, Hume again is restating a position of his immediate
predecessors, in this case Francis Hutcheson. Hume reinter-
preted the latter's theory of moral sense and, by drawing out
its implications, revealed the serious problems it presents.
Above all else, it severely limits the role that reason can play
in men's ethical life. If evaluations are feelings, it would seem
that reason can help "establish" them only to the extent of
ascertaining the true character of the objects toward which
our sentiments are directed. (An especially important case
of this is determining whether an action is in fact an effective
means to some accepted end.) Our feelings of approval or
disapproval toward some object can be "unreasonable" in the
sense that we have not discovered its true nature, but given
a correct understanding of it, there seems no further sense in

which one emotional reaction toward it is more reasonable than another. As Hume says in *The Sceptic:*

> To diminish, therefore, or augment any person's value for an object, to excite or moderate his passions, there are no direct arguments or reasons which can be employed with any force or influence. The catching of flies, like Domitian, if it gives more pleasure, is preferable to the hunting of wild beasts, like William Rufus, or conquering kingdoms, like Alexander.[5]

This statement, however, must be supplemented by what Hume says in *Of the Standard of Taste.* When we examine that essay later, we shall find that Hume recognizes a sense in which the reasonableness of evaluations can be assessed.

Deterministic Theory of Belief and Passion

Just as physical forces control the motions of bodies, so, Hume held, analogous powers govern men's desires, feelings, and beliefs. It is not by chance or by choice that men seek pleasure, sympathize with those in pain, feel moral indignation toward brutality or infer that because fire has warmed, it will continue to do so. Such mental events occur in necessary accord with general forces within human nature.

Hume's theory of universal determinism is very explicit in his essay *On Suicide,* where he argues that since all events are causally necessitated—a man's decision to kill himself just as much as the calamities that lead him to make it—none can be contrary to "natural" law. And although it is less explicit there, Hume's determinism is absolutely basic to his sketches of perennial philosophical attitudes: *The Epicurean, The Stoic, The Platonist,* and *The Sceptic.* The epicurean, stoic, and platonist are determined by their internal make-ups to react as they do; each fails to realize that someone with a different mental constitution will of necessity have a divergent outlook. The skeptic has at least one advantage over the others: realizing that each reflects a dominant pas-

5 P. 130.

sion, he can take a detached attitude toward them, while at the same time giving the proper weight to the insights of each. With the epicurean, the skeptic can extol pleasure and happiness, for he realizes they are, of necessity, the end toward which men direct their actions; with the stoic, he can recognize that industry and virtue are the best means to abiding satisfaction; and with the platonist, he can recognize the importance of rational thought even though he restricts its scope. In short, the skeptic's knowledge of human nature can enable him to live better.

Of all the internal forces explanatory of mental phenomena, Hume was proudest of his having discovered the "gentle force of association." Analogous in the psychological sphere to gravity in the physical, it serves to associate ideas and feelings (as, for example, when the picture of a loved one spurs us to review his qualities and awakens our feelings toward him) and to transfer the vivacity of one perception to another related one (as, for example, when the intensity of our love of our children intensifies our pride in their achievements). In his essay *Of Tragedy*, Hume explicitly uses his theory of association to account for the seemingly paradoxical pleasure men take in viewing such drama. Hume argues that the very intensity of one's emotional response to scenes of horror and destruction only heightens the usually calmer aesthetic pleasure one receives from the drama. In many of the other essays Hume's theory of associations is more implicit. Thus, in *Of the Delicacy of Taste and Passion* Hume contends that cultivating the former will serve to dampen the latter; the softness of the sentiments comprising taste will be transferred to the passions, lessening their violence.

The force of association also explains men's sympathizing with their fellows. Because we resemble others, the thought of their pleasure or pain is transformed into feelings of pleasure or pain of our own. In this way, sympathy gives rise to our feelings of moral approval of what aids the happiness of mankind, or disapproval of what detracts from it. Inasmuch as such sentiments arise "naturally," Hume says in *Of the*

Standard of Taste that it is impossible to deny their "reality"; that is, there is no point in demanding that we stop making moral judgments, for, given our nature, such a demand cannot be obeyed. In this respect, Hume's ultimate "justifications" of moral evaluation and causal reasoning are similar; both rest upon the primacy of natural feeling.

Of the Standard of Taste

In *Of the Standard of Taste* Hume not only raised the extremely important problem of establishing aesthetic standards, but also brought all three of his major tenets to bear upon its solution; thus it is appropriate that this introduction conclude with an examination of that essay.

It begins with a clear statement of the problem: men's critical appraisals vary tremendously and, being expressions of sentiment, seem equally valid. Nonetheless, it is antithetical to common sense to think that no evaluation is better than any other—that, for example, finding Shakespeare's poetry beautiful is no more defensible than finding doggerel sublime. The problem is to establish standards of excellence with reference to which appraisals can be shown right or wrong.

Hume's solution rests on the claim that while men react variously to an aesthetic object and, thus, evaluate it differently, their common human nature will assure their agreeing that certain critics are best able to judge it. Emotively approving of critics possessing the qualities described in *Of the Delicacy of Taste and Passion*—impartiality, broad acquaintance with art, and extensive experience in judging it—men in effect agree that the evaluations of such critics are correct. Hume does not say so explicitly, but presumably he thought that such "qualified critics" would always agree among themselves; his deterministic theory of the passions certainly implies that where the internal make-up of men is identical, their sentiments will be so too.

It is easy to see why, on the above view, Hume believes that standards of taste can be established empirically. By abstracting features common to objects of which qualified critics approve, one discovers those properties which determine aesthetic value. Ascertaining which critics have those characteristics that mark them as qualified, discovering of what objects such critics approve, and isolating the common properties of such objects can all, according to Hume, be done empirically.

Evaluative disputes, it follows, are themselves resolvable empirically. If one man approves of an object while another disapproves, they can decide who is right by appealing to standards of worth upon which they both can agree. Or, if such standards are not available, they can at the very least ask what judgment a critic, whom they both accept as most qualified, either does make or would make of the particular object in question.

It may seem that at times Hume puts forward in *Of the Standard Of Taste*—and uses in *Of Simplicity and Refinement in Writing*—an alternative criterion of correct appraisals, namely, their having withstood the test of time. In my opinion, however, this is simply a corollary view. Judgments that endure are regarded as correct only because the succession of generations acts as a kind of ideal critic. In the long run, the temporary effects of insensitivity, ignorance, and partiality on critical judgment are eliminated.

In any case, it is clear that Hume consciously likens moral and aesthetic evaluations to perceptual judgments. A ripe tomato may look brown to a color-blind person, yellow to someone with jaundice; but both would agree that the tomato *is* red because it looks that way to someone with normal vision. Similarly, one man may feel approval toward an object, another disapproval; but both would agree that the true worth of the object is determined by the reaction of the qualified critic. In his view, too, Hume is recognizing two distinct "levels" of appraisal. At one level, finding an object worthwhile consists in reacting favorably toward it; at another level, finding an object good consists in believing that an ideal critic either does or would feel approvingly toward it, *and* in feeling approval toward such critics and their judgments. The second type of appraisal, we will note, has a "cognitive" component, namely, a belief as to how a certain kind of man does or would react, whereas the first does not. But we must remember, too, that the second does have an "emotive" element, namely, a feeling of approval toward a certain kind of critic and his judgments. It is this component which, consistent with Hume's general emotivist analysis of evaluation, gives the appraisal its normative force.

Many questions can be raised about Hume's procedure for establishing standards of taste. Do all men agree that critics possessing certain qualities are best able to judge art? In any case, are those qualities—consider delicacy of taste—empirically discoverable? Is there a significant analogy between perceptual judgments and evaluations; granting that someone with jaundice can say, "This looks yellow to me but is actually white," can one inexperienced in judging art say, "This seems good to me, but it really is not"?

Whatever weight we give to these criticisms, one thing must be remembered. Hume is one of the few philosophers who, having given an "emotivist" analysis of evaluations, try nonetheless to explain in what way appraisals can be correct or incorrect. In confronting this problem squarely, Hume has presented us with a subtle theory of evaluation that repays our most careful study.

JOHN W. LENZ

Selected Bibliography

Hume's Works

A Treatise of Human Nature, Books I and II (1739) and III (1740)

Essays, Moral, Political, and Literary (Vol. I: 1741; Vol. II: 1742)

An Enquiry Concerning Human Understanding (1748)

An Enquiry Concerning the Principles of Morals (1751)

Political Discourses (1752)

History of England (1754–62)

Four Dissertations (1757)
1) *Natural History of Religion*
2) *Of the Passions*
3) *Of Tragedy*
4) *Of the Standard of Taste*

Dialogues Concerning Natural Religion (1779)

Editions of Hume's Works

The Philosophical Works of David Hume, edited by T. H. GREEN and T. H. GROSE. London: Longmans, Green, 1898. Volume I of the *Treatise* contains the highly influential introduction wherein Hume is interpreted as having reduced British empiricism to absurdity.

An Abstract of a Treatise of Human Nature, edited with an introduction by J. M. KEYNES and P. SRAFFA. Cambridge: The University Press, 1938. Hume's own summary account of the *Treatise.*

Hume's Treatise of Human Nature, edited by L. A. SELBY-BIGGE. Oxford: The Clarendon Press, 1941. Contains a very useful analytical index.

Hume's Enquiries, edited by L. A. SELBY-BIGGE. Oxford: The Clarendon Press, 1902. Also contains an index.

An Inquiry Concerning Human Understanding, edited with an introduction by CHARLES W. HENDEL. "The Library of Liberal Arts," No. 49. New York: The Liberal Arts Press, Inc., 1955. The best edition available.

An Inquiry Concerning the Principles of Morals, edited with an introduction by CHARLES W. HENDEL. "The Library of Liberal Arts," No. 62. New York: The Liberal Arts Press, Inc., 1955. The best edition available.

David Hume's Political Essays, edited with an introduction by CHARLES W. HENDEL. "The Library of Liberal Arts," No. 34. New York: The Liberal Arts Press, Inc., 1953.

Hume's Moral and Political Philosophy, edited with an introduction by HENRY D. AIKEN. "Hafner Library of Classics." New York: Hafner Publishing Co., 1948. A very important introduction.

Hume's Dialogues Concerning Natural Religion, edited with an introduction by NORMAN KEMP SMITH. "Library of Liberal Arts," No. 174. New York: The Liberal Arts Press, Inc., 1964.

The Letters of David Hume, edited by J. Y. T. GREIG. Oxford: The Clarendon Press, 1932.

The New Letters of David Hume, edited by R. KLIBANSKY and E. C. MOSSNER. Oxford: The Clarendon Press, 1952.

Books on Hume

BASSON, A. H. *David Hume.* London: Penguin Books, 1958. Emphasis is on critical assessment of Hume's views.

BROILES, R. DAVID. *The Moral Philosophy of David Hume.* The Hague: Martinus Nijhoff, 1964. More specialized than the title indicates; discusses Hume's views on respective roles of reason and passion in moral decisions.

BRUNIUS, TEDDY. *David Hume on Criticism.* Stockholm: Almqvist & Wiksell, 1954.

CHURCH, RALPH. *Hume's Theory of the Understanding.* London: G. Allen & Unwin Ltd., 1935. A very subtle and penetrating treatment.

FLEW, ANTHONY. *Hume's Philosophy of Belief: A Study of His First Inquiry*. New York: Humanities Press, 1961. Successfully relates Hume to twentieth-century analytic philosophy.

GLANTHE, A. B. *Hume's Theory of the Passions and Morals*. Berkeley: University of California Press, 1950.

HEDENIUS, INGEMAR. *Studies in Hume's Ethics*. Uppsala and Stockholm: Almqvist & Wiksell, 1937.

HENDEL, CHARLES. *Studies in the Philosophy of David Hume*. "Library of Liberal Arts," No. 116. New York: The Liberal Arts Press, Inc., 1963. An enlarged edition of a thorough rendering of Hume's thought.

KYDD, RACHAEL. *Reason and Conduct in Hume's Treatise*. London: Oxford University Press, 1946. An imaginative account of Hume's views on the function of reason in the ethical life.

LAING, B. M. *David Hume*. London: Benn, 1932.

LAIRD, JOHN. *Hume's Philosophy of Human Nature*. London: Methuen, 1932.

LEROY, ANDRÉ-LOUIS. *La critique et la religion chez David Hume*. Paris: Alcan, 1931.

———. *David Hume*. Paris: Presses Universitaires de France, 1953. In this writer's opinion, the best book on Hume's total philosophy. Unfortunately not translated from the French.

MACNABB, D. I. C. *David Hume, His Theory of Knowledge and Morality*. London: Hutchinson's University Library, 1951. A clear introduction for the beginner in philosophy.

MAUND, CONSTANCE. *Hume's Theory of Knowledge*. London: Macmillan, 1937.

MOSSNER, ERNEST C. *The Forgotten Hume: Le bon David*. New York: Columbia University Press, 1943.

———. *The Life of David Hume*. Austin: University of Texas Press, 1954. A remarkable biography; instructive and enjoyable.

PASSMORE, J. A. *Hume's Intentions*. Cambridge: The University Press, 1952. An excellent book, both at emphasizing major themes in Hume's thought and at relating them to later developments.

PEARS, DAVID. *David Hume: a Symposium.* London: Macmillan, 1963. Contains popular talks by Stuart Hampshire and others.

PRICE, H. H. *Hume's Theory of the External World.* London: Macmillan, 1940. A penetrating critical study.

ROSS, W. G. *Human Nature and Utility in Hume's Social Philosophy.* Garden City: Doubleday, 1942.

SHEARER, EDNA ASTON. *Hume's Place In Ethics.* Bryn Mawr, Pennsylvania: Bryn Mawr College, 1915.

SMITH, NORMAN KEMP. *The Philosophy of David Hume.* London: Macmillan, 1941. Perhaps the most influential of the recent books on Hume. Stressing Hume's "naturalism," it constituted a much needed broadside against the traditional Reid-Beattie-Green interpretation of Hume as a complete skeptic.

STEWART, J. B. *The Moral and Political Philosophy of David Hume.* New York: Columbia University Press, 1963.

Books Partially Devoted to Hume and Articles

Aristotelian Society Supplementary Volume XVIII ("Hume and Present Day Problems"), 1939.

ATKINSON, R. F. "Hume on 'Is' and 'Ought': A Reply to Mr. MacIntyre," *Philosophical Review,* LXXX (April 1961), 231–238.

BROAD, C. D. *Five Types of Ethical Theory.* Paterson, New Jersey: Littlefield, Adams, 1959. Chapter 4.

FLEW, ANTHONY. "Hume's Check," *Philosophical Quarterly,* IX, 34 (January 1959), 1–18.

HUNTER, GEOFFREY. "Hume on 'Is' and 'Ought,' " *Philosophy,* XXXVII (April 1962), 148–152.

LAMPRECHT, STERLING P. "Empiricism and Epistemology in David Hume," *Studies in the History of Ideas,* II (1925), 221–252.

LENZ, JOHN W. "Hume's Defense of Causal Inference," *Journal of the History of Ideas*, XIX, 4 (October 1958), 559–567.

MacINTYRE, A. C. "Hume on 'Is' and 'Ought,'" *Philosophical Review*, LXVIII (1959), 451–468.

McGILVARY, E. V. "Altruism in Hume's Treatise," *Philosophical Review*, XII, 3 (May 1903), 272–298.

MOORE, G. E. "Hume's Philosophy," Chapter 4 of *Philosophical Studies*. London: Routledge & Kegan Paul, 1922.

———. *Some Main Problems of Philosophy*. London: Allen & Unwin, 1953. Chapters 5 and 6.

POPKIN, RICHARD H. "David Hume: His Pyrrhonism and His Critique of Pyrrhonism," *The Philosophical Quarterly*, I, 5 (October 1951), 385–407.

PRIOR, A. N. *Logic and the Basis of Ethics*. Oxford: The Clarendon Press, 1949.

RANDALL, JOHN H. "David Hume, Radical Empiricist and Pragmatist," in *Freedom and Experience*, edited by S. HOOK and M. KONVITZ. Ithaca: Cornell University Press, 1947.

RAPHAEL, D. DAICHES. *The Moral Sense*. Oxford: The Clarendon Press, 1947. Chapter 3.

REID, THOMAS. *Essays on the Intellectual Powers of Man*, edited by A. D. WOOZLEY. London: Macmillan, 1941. Especially Essay 2.

SMITH, NORMAN KEMP. "The Naturalism of Hume," *Mind*, N.S. XIV (1905), 149–173 and 335–347.

STEVENSON, CHARLES. *Ethics and Language*. New Haven: Yale University Press, 1941. Chapter 12.

VON WRIGHT, G. H. *The Logical Problem of Induction*. New York: Macmillan, 1957.

Note on the Text

The present edition of these essays is reprinted from the first edition of Hume's collected philosophical writings, *The Philosophical Works of David Hume,* published in 1826 by Adam and Charles Black. That text is based upon the edition of Hume's works published in 1777. I have compared this text with the one edited by T. H. Green and T. H. Grose, published by Longmans, Green, and Co., 1898, and have in a few cases, where the former is clearly mistaken, changed it. All such changes have been extremely minor.

The editor of the edition of 1826 stated that he had compared the edition of 1777 with former editions, and "where any alterations were discovered, not merely verbal but illustrative of the philosophical opinions of the author, to add these as notes to the passages where they occur." Such notes have been gathered into an Appendix (pages 171–183), along with a key to letters designating the various editions.

The notes I have added are enclosed in brackets. In Hume's own notes, bibliographical references have been completed where necessary, and standardized to conform with modern usage.

OF THE STANDARD OF TASTE

And Other Essays

Of the Standard of Taste

The great variety of Taste, as well as of opinion, which prevails in the world, is too obvious not to have fallen under every one's observation. Men of the most confined knowledge are able to remark a difference of taste in the narrow circle of their acquaintance, even where the persons have been educated under the same government, and have early imbibed the same prejudices. But those who can enlarge their view to contemplate distant nations and remote ages, are still more surprised at the great inconsistence and contrariety. We are apt to call *barbarous* whatever departs widely from our own taste and apprehension; but soon find the epithet of reproach retorted on us. And the highest arrogance and self-conceit is at last startled, on observing an equal assurance on all sides, and scruples, amidst such a contest of sentiment, to pronounce positively in its own favor.

As this variety of taste is obvious to the most careless inquirer, so will it be found, on examination, to be still greater in reality than in appearance. The sentiments of men often differ with regard to beauty and deformity of all kinds, even while their general discourse is the same. There are certain terms in every language which import blame, and others praise; and all men who use the same tongue must agree in their application of them. Every voice is united in applauding elegance, propriety, simplicity, spirit in writing; and in blaming fustian, affectation, coldness, and a false brilliancy. But when critics come to particulars, this seeming unanimity vanishes; and it is found, that they had affixed a very different meaning to their expressions. In all matters of opinion and science, the case is opposite; the difference among men is there oftener found to lie in generals than in particulars, and to be less in reality than in appearance. An explanation of the

terms commonly ends the controversy: and the disputants
are surprised to find that they had been quarrelling, while at
bottom they agreed in their judgment.

Those who found morality on sentiment, more than on
reason, are inclined to comprehend ethics under the former
observation, and to maintain, that, in all questions which
regard conduct and manners, the difference among men is
really greater than at first sight it appears. It is indeed obvious, that writers of all nations and all ages concur in applauding justice, humanity, magnanimity, prudence, veracity;
and in blaming the opposite qualities. Even poets and other
authors, whose compositions are chiefly calculated to please
the imagination, are yet found, from Homer down to Fenelon,[1] to inculcate the same moral precepts, and to bestow their
applause and blame on the same virtues and vices. This great
unanimity is usually ascribed to the influence of plain reason, which, in all these cases, maintains similar sentiments
in all men, and prevents those controversies to which the abstract sciences are so much exposed. So far as the unanimity
is real, this account may be admitted as satisfactory. But we
must also allow, that some part of the seeming harmony in
morals may be accounted for from the very nature of language. The word *virtue*, with its equivalent in every tongue,
implies praise, as that of *vice* does blame; and no one, without the most obvious and grossest impropriety, could affix
reproach to a term, which in general acceptation is understood in a good sense: or bestow applause, where the idiom
requires disapprobation. Homer's general precepts, where he
delivers any such, will never be controverted; but it is obvious, that, when he draws particular pictures of manners,
and represents heroism in Achilles, and prudence in Ulysses,
he intermixes a much greater degree of ferocity in the former,
and of cunning and fraud in the latter, than Fenelon would
admit of. The sage Ulysses, in the Greek poet, seems to de-

1 [François Fénelon (1651–1715), French prelate and writer, was appointed by Louis XIV as tutor to his grandson, the Duc de Bourgogne;
Hume refers to Fénelon's *Télémaque*, composed for his pupil's instruction.]

light in lies and fictions, and often employs them without any necessity, or even advantage. But his more scrupulous son, in the French epic writer, exposes himself to the most imminent perils, rather than depart from the most exact line of truth and veracity.

The admirers and followers of the Alcoran [2] insist on the excellent moral precepts interspersed throughout that wild and absurd performance. But it is to be supposed, that the Arabic words, which correspond to the English, equity, justice, temperance, meekness, charity, were such as, from the constant use of that tongue, must always be taken in a good sense: and it would have argued the greatest ignorance, not of morals, but of language, to have mentioned them with any epithets, besides those of applause and approbation. But would we know, whether the pretended prophet had really attained a just sentiment of morals, let us attend to his narration, and we shall soon find, that he bestows praise on such instances of treachery, inhumanity, cruelty, revenge, bigotry, as are utterly incompatible with civilized society. No steady rule of right seems there to be attended to; and every action is blamed or praised, so far only as it is beneficial or hurtful to the true believers.

The merit of delivering true general precepts in ethics is indeed very small. Whoever recommends any moral virtues, really does no more than is implied in the terms themselves. That people who invented the word *charity,* and used it in a good sense, inculcated more clearly, and much more efficaciously, the precept, *Be charitable,* than any pretended legislator or prophet, who should insert such a *maxim* in his writings. Of all expressions, those which, together with their other meaning, imply a degree either of blame or approbation, are the least liable to be perverted or mistaken.

It is natural for us to seek a *Standard of Taste;* a rule by which the various sentiments of men may be reconciled; at least a decision afforded confirming one sentiment, and condemning another.

[2] [That is, the Koran.]

There is a species of philosophy, which cuts off all hopes of success in such an attempt, and represents the impossibility of ever attaining any standard of taste. The difference, it is said, is very wide between judgment and sentiment. All sentiment is right; because sentiment has a reference to nothing beyond itself, and is always real, wherever a man is conscious of it. But all determinations of the understanding are not right; because they have a reference to something beyond themselves, to wit, real matter of fact; and are not always conformable to that standard. Among a thousand different opinions which different men may entertain of the same subject, there is one, and but one, that is just and true: and the only difficulty is to fix and ascertain it. On the contrary, a thousand different sentiments, excited by the same object, are all right; because no sentiment represents what is really in the object. It only marks a certain conformity or relation between the object and the organs or faculties of the mind; and if that conformity did not really exist, the sentiment could never possibly have being. Beauty is no quality in things themselves: it exists merely in the mind which contemplates them; and each mind perceives a different beauty. One person may even perceive deformity, where another is sensible of beauty; and every individual ought to acquiesce in his own sentiment, without pretending to regulate those of others. To seek the real beauty, or real deformity, is as fruitless an inquiry, as to pretend to ascertain the real sweet or real bitter. According to the disposition of the organs, the same object may be both sweet and bitter; and the proverb has justly determined it to be fruitless to dispute concerning tastes. It is very natural, and even quite necessary, to extend this axiom to mental, as well as bodily taste; and thus common sense, which is so often at variance with philosophy, especially with the sceptical kind, is found, in one instance at least, to agree in pronouncing the same decision.

But though this axiom, by passing into a proverb, seems to have attained the sanction of common sense; there is certainly a species of common sense, which opposes it, at least serves to modify and restrain it. Whoever would assert an equality of genius and elegance between Ogilby and Milton, or Bunyan and Addison, would be thought to defend no less an extravagance, than if he had maintained a mole-hill to be as high as Teneriffe, or a pond as extensive as the ocean. Though there may be found persons, who give the preference to the former authors; no one pays attention to such a taste; and we pronounce, without scruple, the sentiment of these pretended critics to be absurd and ridiculous. The principle of the natural equality of tastes is then totally forgot, and while we admit it on some occasions, where the objects seem near an equality, it appears an extravagant paradox, or rather a palpable absurdity, where objects so disproportioned are compared together.

It is evident that none of the rules of composition are fixed by reasonings *à priori,* or can be esteemed abstract conclusions of the understanding, from comparing those habitudes and relations of ideas, which are eternal and immutable. Their foundation is the same with that of all the practical sciences, experience; nor are they any thing but general observations, concerning what has been universally found to please in all countries and in all ages. Many of the beauties of poetry, and even of eloquence, are founded on falsehood and fiction, on hyperboles, metaphors, and an abuse or perversion of terms from their natural meaning. To check the sallies of the imagination, and to reduce every expression to geometrical truth and exactness, would be the most contrary to the laws of criticism; because it would produce a work, which, by universal experience, has been found the most insipid and disagreeable. But though poetry can never submit to exact truth, it must be confined by rules of art, discovered to the author either by genius or observation. If some negligent or irregular writers have pleased, they have not pleased by their transgressions of rule or order, but in spite of these transgressions: they have possessed other beauties, which were conformable to just criticism; and the force of these beauties has been able to overpower censure, and give the mind a satisfaction superior to the disgust arising from the blemishes. Ariosto [3] pleases; but not by his monstrous and improbable fictions, by his bizarre mixture of the serious and comic styles, by the want of coherence in his stories, or by the continual interruptions of his narration. He charms by the force and clearness of his expression, by the readiness and variety of his inventions, and by his natural pictures of the passions, especially those of the gay and amorous kind: and, however his faults may diminish our satisfaction, they are not able entirely to destroy it. Did our pleasure really arise from those parts of his poem, which we denominate faults, this would be no objection to criticism in general: it would only be an objection to those particular rules of criticism, which would establish such circumstances to be faults, and would represent them as universally blamable. If they are found to please, they cannot be faults, let the pleasure which they produce be ever so unexpected and unaccountable.

But though all the general rules of art are founded only on experience, and on the observation of the common sentiments of human nature, we must not imagine, that, on every occasion, the feelings of men will be conformable to these rules. Those finer emotions of the mind are of a very tender and delicate nature, and require the concurrence of many favorable circumstances to make them play with facility and exactness, according to their general and established principles. The least exterior hinderance to such small springs, or the least internal disorder, disturbs their motion, and confounds the operations of the whole machine. When we would make an experiment of this nature, and would try the force of any beauty or deformity, we must choose with care a proper time and place, and bring the fancy to a suitable situation and disposition. A perfect serenity of mind, a recollection of thought, a due attention to the object; if any of these circumstances be wanting, our experiment will be fallacious, and we shall be unable to judge of the catholic and universal

3 [Ludovico Ariosto (1474–1533), whose best-known work is the chivalric epic poem *Orlando Furioso* (1516).]

beauty. The relation, which nature has placed between the form and the sentiment, will at least be more obscure; and it will require greater accuracy to trace and discern it. We shall be able to ascertain its influence, not so much from the operation of each particular beauty, as from the durable admiration which attends those works that have survived all the caprices of mode and fashion, all the mistakes of ignorance and envy.

The same Homer who pleased at Athens and Rome two thousand years ago, is still admired at Paris and at London. All the changes of climate, government, religion, and language, have not been able to obscure his glory. Authority or prejudice may give a temporary vogue to a bad poet or orator; but his reputation will never be durable or general. When his compositions are examined by posterity or by foreigners, the enchantment is dissipated, and his faults appear in their true colors. On the contrary, a real genius, the longer his works endure, and the more wide they are spread, the more sincere is the admiration which he meets with. Envy and jealousy have too much place in a narrow circle; and even familiar acquaintance with his person may diminish the applause due to his performances: but when these obstructions are removed, the beauties, which are naturally fitted to excite agreeable sentiments, immediately display their energy; and while the world endures, they maintain their authority over the minds of men.

It appears, then, that amidst all the variety and caprice of taste, there are certain general principles of approbation or blame, whose influence a careful eye may trace in all operations of the mind. Some particular forms or qualities, from the original structure of the internal fabric are calculated to please, and others to displease; and if they fail of their effect in any particular instance, it is from some apparent defect or imperfection in the organ. A man in a fever would not insist on his palate as able to decide concerning flavors; nor would one affected with the jaundice pretend to give a verdict with regard to colors. In each creature there is a sound and a defective state; and the former alone can be

supposed to afford us a true standard of taste and sentiment.
If, in the sound state of the organ, there be an entire or a
considerable uniformity of sentiment among men, we may
thence derive an idea of the perfect beauty; in like manner as
the appearance of objects in daylight, to the eye of a man in
health, is denominated their true and real color, even while
color is allowed to be merely a phantasm of the senses.

Many and frequent are the defects in the internal organs,
which prevent or weaken the influence of those general principles, on which depends our sentiment of beauty or deformity.
Though some objects, by the structure of the mind, be naturally calculated to give pleasure, it is not to be expected
that in every individual the pleasure will be equally felt.
Particular incidents and situations occur, which either throw
a false light on the objects, or hinder the true from convey-
ing to the imagination the proper sentiment and perception.

One obvious cause why many feel not the proper sentiment
of beauty, is the want of that *delicacy* of imagination which
is requisite to convey a sensibility of those finer emotions.
This delicacy every one pretends to: every one talks of it;
and would reduce every kind of taste or sentiment to its standard. But as our intention in this Essay is to mingle some light
of the understanding with the feelings of sentiment, it will
be proper to give a more accurate definition of delicacy than
has hitherto been attempted. And not to draw our philosophy
from too profound a source, we shall have recourse to a noted
story in Don Quixote.[4]

It is with good reason, says Sancho to the squire with the
great nose, that I pretend to have a judgment in wine: this
is a quality hereditary in our family. Two of my kinsmen
were once called to give their opinion of a hogshead, which
was supposed to be excellent, being old and of a good vintage.
One of them tastes it, considers it; and, after mature reflection, pronounces the wine to be good, were it not for a small
taste of leather which he perceived in it. The other, after
using the same precautions, gives also his verdict in favor of

[4] [Cervantes, *Don Quixote*, Part II, chapter 13.]

the wine; but with the reserve of a taste of iron, which he could easily distinguish. You cannot imagine how much they were both ridiculed for their judgment. But who laughed in the end? On emptying the hogshead, there was found at the bottom an old key with a leathern thong tied to it.

The great resemblance between mental and bodily taste will easily teach us to apply this story. Though it be certain that beauty and deformity, more than sweet and bitter, are not qualities in objects, but belong entirely to the sentiment, internal or external, it must be allowed, that there are certain qualities in objects which are fitted by nature to produce those particular feelings. Now, as these qualities may be found in a small degree, or may be mixed and confounded with each other, it often happens that the taste is not affected with such minute qualities, or is not able to distinguish all the particular flavors, amidst the disorder in which they are presented. Where the organs are so fine as to allow nothing to escape them, and at the same time so exact as to perceive every ingredient in the composition, this we call delicacy of taste, whether we employ these terms in the literal or metaphorical sense. Here then the general rules of beauty are of use, being drawn from established models, and from the observation of what pleases or displeases, when presented singly and in a high degree; and if the same qualities, in a continued composition, and in a smaller degree, affect not the organs with a sensible delight or uneasiness, we exclude the person from all pretensions to this delicacy. To produce these general rules or avowed patterns of composition, is like finding the key with the leathern thong, which justified the verdict of Sancho's kinsmen, and confounded those pretended judges who had condemned them. Though the hogshead had never been emptied, the taste of the one was still equally delicate, and that of the other equally dull and languid; but it would have been more difficult to have proved the superiority of the former, to the conviction of every bystander. In like manner, though the beauties of writing had never been methodized, or reduced to general principles; though no excellent models had ever been acknowledged, the different degrees of taste would still have subsisted, and the judgment of one man been preferable to that of another; but it would not have been so easy to silence the bad critic, who might always insist upon his particular sentiment, and refuse to submit to his antagonist. But when we show him an avowed principle of art; when we illustrate this principle by examples, whose operation, from his own particular taste, he acknowledges to be conformable to the principle; when we prove that the same principle may be applied to the present case, where he did not perceive or feel its influence: he must conclude, upon the whole, that the fault lies in himself, and that he wants the delicacy which is requisite to make him sensible of every beauty and every blemish in any composition or discourse.

It is acknowledged to be the perfection of every sense or faculty, to perceive with exactness its most minute objects, and allow nothing to escape its notice and observation. The smaller the objects are which become sensible to the eye, the finer is that organ, and the more elaborate its make and composition. A good palate is not tried by strong flavor, but by a mixture of small ingredients, where we are still sensible of each part, notwithstanding its minuteness and its confusion with the rest. In like manner, a quick and acute perception of beauty and deformity must be the perfection of our mental taste; nor can a man be satisfied with himself while he suspects that any excellence or blemish in a discourse has passed him unobserved. In this case, the perfection of the man, and the perfection of the sense of feeling, are found to be united. A very delicate palate, on many occasions, may be a great inconvenience both to a man himself and to his friends. But a delicate taste of wit or beauty must always be a desirable quality, because it is the source of all the finest and most innocent enjoyments of which human nature is susceptible. In this decision the sentiments of all mankind are agreed. Wherever you can ascertain a delicacy of taste, it is sure to meet with approbation; and the best way of ascertaining it is, to appeal to those models and principles

which have been established by the uniform consent and experience of nations and ages.

But though there be naturally a wide difference, in point of
delicacy, between one person and another, nothing tends further to increase and improve this talent, than *practice* in a
particular art, and frequent survey or contemplation of a particular species of beauty. When objects of any kind are first
presented to the eye or imagination, the sentiment which attends them is obscure and confused; and the mind is, in a
great measure, incapable of pronouncing concerning their
merits or defects. The taste cannot perceive the several excellences of the performance, much less distinguish the particular character of each excellency, and ascertain its quality and
degree. If it pronounce the whole in general to be beautiful
or deformed, it is the utmost that can be expected; and even
this judgment, a person so unpractised will be apt to deliver
with great hesitation and reserve. But allow him to acquire
experience in those objects, his feeling becomes more exact
and nice: he not only perceives the beauties and defects of each
part, but marks the distinguishing species of each quality, and
assigns it suitable praise or blame. A clear and distinct sentiment attends him through the whole survey of the objects;
and he discerns that very degree and kind of approbation or
displeasure which each part is naturally fitted to produce.
The mist dissipates which seemed formerly to hang over the
object; the organ acquires greater perfection in its operations,
and can pronounce, without danger of mistake, concerning
the merits of every performance. In a word, the same address
and dexterity which practice gives to the execution of any
work, is also acquired by the same means in the judging of it.

So advantageous is practice to the discernment of beauty,
that, before we can give judgment on any work of importance,
it will even be requisite that that very individual performance
be more than once perused by us, and be surveyed in different
lights with attention and deliberation. There is a flutter or
hurry of thought which attends the first perusal of any piece,

and which confounds the genuine sentiment of beauty. The relation of the parts is not discerned: the true characters of style are little distinguished. The several perfections and defects seem wrapped up in a species of confusion, and present themselves indistinctly to the imagination. Not to mention, that there is a species of beauty, which, as it is florid and superficial, pleases at first; but being found incompatible with a just expression either of reason or passion, soon palls upon the taste, and is then rejected with disdain, at least rated at a much lower value.

It is impossible to continue in the practice of contemplating any order of beauty, without being frequently obliged to form *comparisons* between the several species and degrees of excellence, and estimating their proportion to each other. A man who has had no opportunity of comparing the different kinds of beauty, is indeed totally unqualified to pronounce an opinion with regard to any object presented to him. By comparison alone we fix the epithets of praise or blame, and learn how to assign the due degree of each. The coarsest daubing contains a certain lustre of colors and exactness of imitation, which are so far beauties, and would affect the mind of a peasant or Indian with the highest admiration. The most vulgar ballads are not entirely destitute of harmony or nature; and none but a person familiarized to superior beauties would pronounce their members harsh, or narration uninteresting. A great inferiority of beauty gives pain to a person conversant in the highest excellence of the kind, and is for that reason pronounced a deformity; as the most finished object with which we are acquainted is naturally supposed to have reached the pinnacle of perfection, and to be entitled to the highest applause. One accustomed to see, and examine, and weigh the several performances, admired in different ages and nations, can alone rate the merits of a work exhibited to his view, and assign its proper rank among the productions of genius.

But to enable a critic the more fully to execute this undertaking, he must preserve his mind free from all *prejudice,* and allow nothing to enter into his consideration, but the very object which is submitted to his examination. We may observe, that every work of art, in order to produce its due effect on the mind, must be surveyed in a certain point of view, and cannot be fully relished by persons whose situation, real or imaginary, is not conformable to that which is required by the performance. An orator addresses himself to a particular audience, and must have a regard to their particular genius, interests, opinions, passions, and prejudices; otherwise he hopes in vain to govern their resolutions, and inflame their affections. Should they even have entertained some prepossessions against him, however unreasonable, he must not overlook this disadvantage; but, before he enters upon the subject, must endeavor to conciliate their affection, and acquire their good graces. A critic of a different age or nation, who should peruse this discourse, must have all these circumstances in his eye, and must place himself in the same situation as the audience, in order to form a true judgment of the oration. In like manner, when any work is addressed to the public, though I should have a friendship or enmity with the author, I must depart from this situation, and, considering myself as a man in general, forget, if possible, my individual being, and my peculiar circumstances. A person influenced by prejudice complies not with this condition, but obstinately maintains his natural position, without placing himself in that point of view which the performance supposes. If the work be addressed to persons of a different age or nation, he makes no allowance for their peculiar views and prejudices; but, full of the manners of his own age and country, rashly condemns what seemed admirable in the eyes of those for whom alone the discourse was calculated. If the work be executed for the public, he never sufficiently enlarges his comprehension, or forgets his interest as a friend or enemy, as a rival or commentator. By this means his sentiments are perverted; nor have the same beauties and blemishes the same influence upon him, as if he had imposed a proper violence on his imagination, and had forgotten himself for a moment. So far his taste evidently departs from the true standard, and of consequence loses all credit and authority.

It is well known, that, in all questions submitted to the understanding, prejudice is destructive of sound judgment, and perverts all operations of the intellectual faculties: it is no less contrary to good taste; nor has it less influence to corrupt our sentiment of beauty. It belongs to *good sense* to check its influence in both cases; and in this respect, as well as in many others, reason, if not an essential part of taste, is at least requisite to the operations of this latter faculty. In all the nobler productions of genius, there is a mutual relation and correspondence of parts; nor can either the beauties or blemishes be perceived by him whose thought is not capacious enough to comprehend all those parts, and compare them with each other, in order to perceive the consistence and uniformity of the whole. Every work of art has also a certain end or purpose for which it is calculated; and is to be deemed more or less perfect, as it is more or less fitted to attain this end. The object of eloquence is to persuade, of history to instruct, of poetry to please, by means of the passions and the imagination. These ends we must carry constantly in our view when we peruse any performance; and we must be able to judge how far the means employed are adapted to their respective purposes. Besides, every kind of composition, even the most poetical, is nothing but a chain of propositions and reasonings; not always, indeed, the justest and most exact, but still plausible and specious, however disguised by the coloring of the imagination. The persons introduced in tragedy and epic poetry must be represented as reasoning, and thinking, and concluding, and acting, suitably to their character and circumstances; and without judgment, as well as taste and invention, a poet can never hope to succeed in so delicate an undertaking. Not to mention, that the same excellence of faculties which contributes to the improvement of reason, the same clearness of conception, the same exactness of distinction, the same vivacity of apprehension, are essential to the operations of true taste, and are its infallible concomitants. It seldom or never happens, that a man of sense, who has experience in any art, cannot judge of its beauty; and it is no less rare to meet with a man who has a just taste without a sound understanding.

Thus, though the principles of taste be universal, and nearly, if not entirely, the same in all men; yet few are qualified to give judgment on any work of art, or establish their own sentiment as the standard of beauty. The organs of internal sensation are seldom so perfect as to allow the general principles their full play, and produce a feeling correspondent to those principles. They either labor under some defect, or are vitiated by some disorder; and by that means excite a sentiment, which may be pronounced erroneous. When the critic has no delicacy, he judges without any distinction, and is only affected by the grosser and more palpable qualities of the object: the finer touches pass unnoticed and disregarded. Where he is not aided by practice, his verdict is attended with confusion and hesitation. Where no comparison has been employed, the most frivolous beauties, such as rather merit the name of defects, are the object of his admiration. Where he lies under the influence of prejudice, all his natural sentiments are perverted. Where good sense is wanting, he is not qualified to discern the beauties of design and reasoning, which are the highest and most excellent. Under some or other of these imperfections, the generality of men labor; and hence a true judge in the finer arts is observed, even during the most polished ages, to be so rare a character: strong sense, united to delicate sentiment, improved by practice, perfected by comparison, and cleared of all prejudice, can alone entitle critics to this valuable character; and the joint verdict of such, wherever they are to be found, is the true standard of taste and beauty.

But where are such critics to be found? By what marks are they to be known? How distinguish them from pretenders? These questions are embarrassing; and seem to throw us back into the same uncertainty from which, during the course of this Essay, we have endeavored to extricate ourselves.

But if we consider the matter aright, these are questions of

fact, not of sentiment. Whether any particular person be endowed with good sense and a delicate imagination, free from
prejudice, may often be the subject of dispute, and be liable
to great discussion and inquiry: but that such a character is
valuable and estimable, will be agreed in by all mankind.
Where these doubts occur, men can do no more than in other
disputable questions which are submitted to the understanding: they must produce the best arguments that their invention suggests to them; they must acknowledge a true and decisive standard to exist somewhere, to wit, real existence and
matter of fact; and they must have indulgence to such as differ
from them in their appeals to this standard. It is sufficient for
our present purpose, if we have proved, that the taste of all
individuals is not upon an equal footing, and that some men
in general, however difficult to be particularly pitched upon,
will be acknowledged by universal sentiment to have a preference above others.

But, in reality, the difficulty of finding, even in particulars,
the standard of taste, is not so great as it is represented.
Though in speculation we may readily avow a certain criterion
in science, and deny it in sentiment, the matter is found in
practice to be much more hard to ascertain in the former case
than in the latter. Theories of abstract philosophy, systems
of profound theology, have prevailed during one age: in a
successsive period these have been universally exploded: their
absurdity has been detected: other theories and systems have
supplied their place, which again gave place to their successors: and nothing has been experienced more liable to the
revolutions of chance and fashion than these pretended decisions of science. The case is not the same with the beauties
of eloquence and poetry. Just expressions of passion and nature are sure, after a little time, to gain public applause, which
they maintain for ever. Aristotle, and Plato, and Epicurus, and
Descartes, may successively yield to each other: but Terence
and Virgil maintain an universal, undisputed empire over the
minds of men. The abstract philosophy of Cicero has lost its

credit: the vehemence of his oratory is still the object of our admiration.

Though men of delicate taste be rare, they are easily to be distinguished in society by the soundness of their understanding, and the superiority of their faculties above the rest of mankind. The ascendant, which they acquire, gives a prevalence to that lively approbation with which they receive any productions of genius, and renders it generally predominant. Many men, when left to themselves, have but a faint and dubious perception of beauty, who yet are capable of relishing any fine stroke which is pointed out to them. Every convert to the admiration of the real poet or orator, is the cause of some new conversion. And though prejudices may prevail for a time, they never unite in celebrating any rival to the true genius, but yield at last to the force of nature and just sentiment. Thus, though a civilized nation may easily be mistaken in the choice of their admired philosopher, they never have been found long to err, in their affection for a favorite epic or tragic author.

But notwithstanding all our endeavors to fix a standard of taste, and reconcile the discordant apprehensions of men, there still remain two sources of variation, which are not sufficient indeed to confound all the boundaries of beauty and deformity, but will often serve to produce a difference in the degrees of our approbation or blame. The one is the different humors of particular men; the other, the particular manners and opinions of our age and country. The general principles of taste are uniform in human nature: where men vary in their judgments, some defect or perversion in the faculties may commonly be remarked; proceeding either from prejudice, from want of practice, or want of delicacy: and there is just reason for approving one taste, and condemning another. But where there is such a diversity in the internal frame or external situation as is entirely blameless on both sides, and leaves no room to give one the preference above the other; in that case a certain degree of diversity in judgment is unavoidable, and we seek in vain for a standard, by which we can reconcile the contrary sentiments.

A young man, whose passions are warm, will be more sensibly touched with amorous and tender images, than a man more advanced in years, who takes pleasure in wise, philosophical reflections, concerning the conduct of life, and moderation of the passions. At twenty, Ovid may be the favorite author, Horace at forty, and perhaps Tacitus at fifty. Vainly would we, in such cases, endeavor to enter into the sentiments of others, and divest ourselves of those propensities which are natural to us. We choose our favorite author as we do our friend, from a conformity of humor and disposition. Mirth or passion, sentiment or reflection; whichever of these most predominates in our temper, it gives us a peculiar sympathy with the writer who resembles us.

One person is more pleased with the sublime, another with the tender, a third with raillery. One has a strong sensibility to blemishes, and is extremely studious of correctness; another has a more lively feeling of beauties, and pardons twenty absurdities and defects for one elevated or pathetic stroke. The ear of this man is entirely turned towards conciseness and energy; that man is delighted with a copious, rich, and harmonious expression. Simplicity is affected by one; ornament by another. Comedy, tragedy, satire, odes, have each its partisans, who prefer that particular species of writing to all others. It is plainly an error in a critic, to confine his approbation to one species or style of writing, and condemn all the rest. But it is almost impossible not to feel a predilection for that which suits our particular turn and disposition. Such performances are innocent and unavoidable, and can never reasonably be the object of dispute, because there is no standard by which they can be decided.

For a like reason, we are more pleased, in the course of our reading, with pictures and characters that resemble objects which are found in our own age and country, than with those which describe a different set of customs. It is not without some effort that we reconcile ourselves to the simplicity of ancient manners, and behold princesses carrying water from the spring, and kings and heroes dressing their own victuals. We may allow in general, that the representation of such manners is no fault in the author, nor deformity in the piece; but we are not so sensibly touched with them. For this reason, comedy is not easily transferred from one age or nation to another. A Frenchman or Englishman is not pleased with the *Andria* of Terence, or *Clitia* of Machiavel; where the fine lady, upon whom all the play turns, never once appears to the spectators, but is always kept behind the scenes, suitably to the reserved humor of the ancient Greeks and modern Italians. A man of learning and reflection can make allowance for these peculiarities of manners; but a common audience can never divest themselves so far of their usual ideas and sentiments, as to relish pictures which nowise resemble them.

But here there occurs a reflection, which may, perhaps, be useful in examining the celebrated controversy concerning ancient and modern learning; where we often find the one side excusing any seeming absurdity in the ancients from the manners of the age, and the other refusing to admit this excuse, or at least admitting it only as an apology for the author, not for the performance. In my opinion, the proper boundaries in this subject have seldom been fixed between the contending parties. Where any innocent peculiarities of manners are represented, such as those above mentioned, they ought certainly to be admitted; and a man who is shocked with them, gives an evident proof of false delicacy and refinement. The poet's *monument more durable than brass,*[5] must fall to the ground like common brick or clay, were men to make no allowance for the continual revolutions of manners and customs, and would admit of nothing but what was suitable to the prevailing fashion. Must we throw aside the pictures of our ancestors, because of their ruffs and farthingales? But where the ideas of morality and decency alter from one age to another, and where vicious manners are described, without being marked with the proper characters of blame and disapproba-

[5] [Horace, *Carmina* III. 30. 1.]

tion, this must be allowed to disfigure the poem, and to be a real deformity. I cannot, nor is it proper I should, enter into such sentiments; and however I may excuse the poet, on account of the manners of his age, I can never relish the composition. The want of humanity and of decency, so conspicuous in the characters drawn by several of the ancient poets, even sometimes by Homer and the Greek tragedians, diminishes considerably the merit of their noble performances, and gives modern authors an advantage over them. We are not interested in the fortunes and sentiments of such rough heroes; we are displeased to find the limits of vice and virtue so much confounded; and whatever indulgence we may give to the writer on account of his prejudices, we cannot prevail on ourselves to enter into his sentiments, or bear an affection to characters which we plainly discover to be blamable.

The case is not the same with moral principles as with speculative opinions of any kind. These are in continual flux and revolution. The son embraces a different system from the father. Nay, there scarcely is any man, who can boast of great constancy and uniformity in this particular. Whatever speculative errors may be found in the polite writings of any age or country, they detract but little from the value of those compositions. There needs but a certain turn of thought or imagination to make us enter into all the opinions which then prevailed, and relish the sentiments or conclusions derived from them. But a very violent effort is requisite to change our judgment of manners, and excite sentiments of approbation or blame, love or hatred, different from those to which the mind, from long custom, has been familiarized. And where a man is confident of the rectitude of that moral standard by which he judges, he is justly jealous of it, and will not pervert the sentiments of his heart for a moment, in complaisance to any writer whatsoever.

Of all speculative errors, those which regard religion are the most excusable in compositions of genius; nor is it ever permitted to judge of the civility or wisdom of any people, or even of single persons, by the grossness or refinement of their theological principles. The same good sense that directs men in the ordinary occurrences of life, is not hearkened to in religious matters, which are supposed to be placed altogether above the cognizance of human reason. On this account, all the absurdities of the Pagan system of theology must be overlooked by every critic, who would pretend to form a just notion of ancient poetry; and our posterity, in their turn, must have the same indulgence to their forefathers. No religious principles can ever be imputed as a fault to any poet, while they remain merely principles, and take not such strong possession of his heart as to lay him under the imputation of *bigotry or superstition*. Where that happens, they confound the sentiments of morality, and alter the natural boundaries of vice and virtue. They are therefore eternal blemishes, according to the principle above mentioned; nor are the prejudices and false opinions of the age sufficient to justify them.

It is essential to the Roman Catholic religion to inspire a violent hatred of every other worship, and to represent all Pagans, Mahometans, and heretics, as the objects of divine wrath and vengeance. Such sentiments, though they are in reality very blamable, are considered as virtues by the zealots of that communion, and are represented in their tragedies and epic poems as a kind of divine heroism. This bigotry has disfigured two very fine tragedies of the French theatre, POLIEUCTE and ATHALIA; [6] where an intemperate zeal for particular modes of worship is set off with all the pomp imaginable, and forms the predominant character of the heroes. "What is this," says the sublime Joad to Josabet, finding her in discourse with Mathan the priest of Baal, "Does the daughter of David speak to this traitor? Are you not afraid lest the earth should open, and pour forth flames to devour you both? Or lest these holy walls should fall and crush you together? What is his purpose? Why comes that enemy of God hither to poison the air, which

[6] [Hume refers here to Pierre Corneille's tragedy *Polyeucte* (1641) and to Jean-Baptiste Racine's religious tragedy *Athalie* (1691). The scene between Joad and Josabet, which Hume goes on to describe, takes place in *Athalie*, Act III, scene 5.]

we breathe, with his horrid presence?" Such sentiments are received with great applause on the theatre of Paris; but at London the spectators would be full as much pleased to hear Achilles tell Agamemnon, that he was a dog in his forehead, and a deer in his heart; or Jupiter threaten Juno with a sound drubbing, if she will not be quiet.

Religious principles are also a blemish in any polite composition, when they rise up to superstition, and intrude themselves into every sentiment, however remote from any connection with religion. It is no excuse for the poet, that the customs of his country had burdened life with so many religious ceremonies and observances, that no part of it was exempt from that yoke. It must for ever be ridiculous in Petrarch to compare his mistress, Laura, to Jesus Christ.[7] Nor is it less ridiculous in that agreeable libertine, Boccace, very seriously to give thanks to God Almighty and the ladies, for their assistance in defending him against his enemies.[8]

7 [Probably Sonnet III. Francesco Petrarch, *Rime* (Naples, 1951).]

8 [Hume probably refers to the *Decameron,* preface to the Fourth Day, where Boccacio says to the ladies: ". . . armed with the help of God and your support, in which I rely, I shall go onward with this work, my back to this wind [of his enemies' criticism], letting it rage as it will." Tr. Frances Winwar (New York: The Modern Library, 1955).]

Of the Delicacy of Taste and Passion

SOME people are subject to a certain *delicacy* of *passion,* which makes them extremely sensible to all the accidents of life, and gives them a lively joy upon every prosperous event, as well as a piercing grief when they meet with misfortune and adversity. Favors and good offices easily engage their friendship, while the smallest injury provokes their resentment. Any honor or mark of distinction elevates them above measure, but they are sensibly touched with contempt. People of this character have, no doubt, more lively enjoyments, as well as more pungent sorrows, than men of cool and sedate tempers. But, I believe, when every thing is balanced, there is no one who would not rather be of the latter character, were he entirely master of his own disposition. Good or ill fortune is very little at our disposal; and when a person that has this sensibility of temper meets with any misfortune, his sorrow or resentment takes entire possession of him, and deprives him of all relish in the common occurrences of life, the right enjoyment of which forms the chief part of our happiness. Great pleasures are much less frequent than great pains, so that a sensible temper must meet with fewer trials in the former way than in the latter. Not to mention, that men of such lively passions are apt to be transported beyond all bounds of prudence and discretion, and to take false steps in the conduct of life, which are often irretrievable.

There is a *delicacy* of *taste* observable in some men, which very much resembles this *delicacy* of *passion,* and produces the same sensibility to beauty and deformity of every kind, as that does to prosperity and adversity, obligations and injuries. When you present a poem or a picture to a man possessed of this talent, the delicacy of his feeling makes him be sensibly touched with every part of it; nor are the masterly strokes perceived with more exquisite relish and satisfaction, than the negligences or absurdities with disgust and uneasiness. A polite and judicious conversation affords him the highest entertainment; rudeness or impertinence is as great punishment to him. In short, delicacy of taste has the same effect as delicacy of passion. It enlarges the sphere both of our happiness and misery, and makes us sensible to pains as well as pleasures which escape the rest of mankind.

I believe, however, every one will agree with me, that notwithstanding this resemblance, delicacy of taste is as much to be desired and cultivated, as delicacy of passion is to be lamented, and to be remedied, if possible. The good or ill accidents of life are very little at our disposal; but we are pretty much masters what books we shall read, what diversions we shall partake of, and what company we shall keep. Philosophers have endeavored to render happiness entirely independent of every thing external. The degree of perfection is impossible to be *attained;* but every wise man will endeavor to place his happiness on such objects chiefly as depend upon himself; and *that* is not to be *attained* so much by any other means as by this delicacy of sentiment. When a man is possessed of that talent, he is more happy by what pleases his taste, than by what gratifies his appetites, and receives more enjoyment from a poem, or a piece of reasoning, than the most expensive luxury can afford.[a]

Whatever connection there may be originally between these two species of delicacy, I am persuaded that nothing is so proper to cure us of this delicacy of passion, as the cultivating of that higher and more refined taste, which enables us to judge of the characters of men, of the compositions of genius, and of the productions of the nobler arts. A greater or less relish for those obvious beauties which strike the senses, depends entirely upon the greater or less sensibility of the temper; but with regard to the sciences and liberal arts, a fine taste is, in some measure, the same with strong sense, or at

[a] All references such as this, indicated by superior italic letters, designate textual notes and variations which have been gathered in the Appendix, pp. 171–183.

least depends so much upon it that they are inseparable. In order to judge aright of a composition of genius, there are so many views to be taken in, so many circumstances to be compared, and such a knowledge of human nature requisite, that no man, who is not possessed of the soundest judgment, will ever make a tolerable critic in such performances. And this is a new reason for cultivating a relish in the liberal arts. Our judgment will strengthen by this exercise. We shall form juster notions of life. Many things which please or afflict others, will appear to us too frivolous to engage our attention; and we shall lose by degrees that sensibility and delicacy of passion which is so incommodious.

But perhaps I have gone too far, in saying that a cultivated taste for the polite arts extinguishes the passions, and renders us indifferent to those objects which are so fondly pursued by the rest of mankind. On further reflection, I find, that it rather improves our sensibility for all the tender and agreeable passions; at the same time that it renders the mind incapable of the rougher and more boisterous emotions.

Ingenuas didicisse fideliter artes,
Emollit mores, nec sinit esse feros.[1]

For this, I think, there may be assigned two very natural reasons. In the *first* place, nothing is so improving to the temper as the study of the beauties either of poetry, eloquence, music, or painting. They give a certain elegance of sentiment to which the rest of mankind are strangers. The emotions which they excite are soft and tender. They draw off the mind from the hurry of business and interest; cherish reflection; dispose to tranquillity; and produce an agreeable melancholy, which, of all dispositions of the mind, is the best suited to love and friendship.

In the *second* place, a delicacy of taste is favorable to love and friendship, by confining our choice to few people, and making us indifferent to the company and conversation of the greater part of men. You will seldom find that mere men of

___
[1] [Ovid, *Epistolae ex Ponto* II. 9. 48.]

the world, whatever strong sense they may be endowed with, are very nice in distinguishing characters, or in marking those insensible differences and gradations, which make one man preferable to another. Any one that has competent sense is sufficient for their entertainment. They talk to him of their pleasures and affairs, with the same frankness that they would to another; and finding many who are fit to supply his place, they never feel any vacancy or want in his absence. But to make use of the allusion of a celebrated French [2] author, the judgment may be compared to a clock or watch, where the most ordinary machine is sufficient to tell the hours; but the most elaborate alone can point out the minutes and seconds, and distinguish the smallest differences of time. One that has well digested his knowledge both of books and men, has little enjoyment but in the company of a few select companions. He feels too sensibly, how much all the rest of mankind fall short of the notions which he has entertained. And, his affections being thus confined within a narrow circle, no wonder he carries them further than if they were more general and undistinguished. The gaiety and frolic of a bottle companion improves with him into a solid friendship; and the ardors of a youthful appetite become an elegant passion.

[2] Mons. Fontenelle, *Pluralité des Mondes*, Soir 6. [Bernard le Bovier de Fontenelle (1657–1757), French academician, essayist, tragedian, and poet.]

Of Tragedy

It seems an unaccountable pleasure which the spectators of a well-written tragedy receive from sorrow, terror, anxiety, and other passions that are in themselves disagreeable and uneasy. The more they are touched and affected, the more are they delighted with the spectacle; and as soon as the uneasy passions cease to operate, the piece is at an end. One scene of full joy and contentment and security is the utmost that any composition of this kind can bear; and it is sure always to be the concluding one. If in the texture of the piece there be interwoven any scenes of satisfaction, they afford only faint gleams of pleasure, which are thrown in by way of variety, and in order to plunge the actors into deeper distress by means of that contrast and disappointment. The whole art of the poet is employed in rousing and supporting the compassion and indignation, the anxiety and resentment, of his audience. They are pleased in proportion as they are afflicted, and never are so happy as when they employ tears, sobs, and cries, to give vent to their sorrow, and relieve their heart, swoln with the tenderest sympathy and compassion.

The few critics who have had some tincture of philosophy have remarked this singular phenomenon, and have endeavored to account for it.

L'Abbé Dubos,[1] in his Reflections on Poetry and Painting, asserts, that nothing is in general so disagreeable to the mind as the languid, listless state of indolence into which it falls upon the removal of all passion and occupation. To get rid of this painful situation, it seeks every amusement and pursuit; business, gaming, shows, executions; whatever will rouse the passions and take its attention from itself. No matter what the

[1] [Jean-Baptiste Dubos (1670–1742), French diplomat, archaeologist, and historian.]

passion is; let it be disagreeable, afflicting, melancholy, disordered; it is still better than that insipid languor which arises from perfect tranquillity and repose.

It is impossible not to admit this account as being, at least in part, satisfactory. You may observe, when there are several tables of gaming, that all the company run to those where the deepest play is, even though they find not there the best players. The view, or, at least, imagination of high passions, arising from great loss or gain, affects the spectator by sympathy, gives him some touches of the same passions, and serves him for a momentary entertainment. It makes the time pass the easier with him, and is some relief to that oppression under which men commonly labor when left entirely to their own thoughts and meditations.

We find that common liars always magnify, in their narrations, all kinds of danger, pain, distress, sickness, deaths, murders, and cruelties, as well as joy, beauty, mirth, and magnificence. It is an absurd secret which they have for pleasing their company, fixing their attention, and attaching them to such marvellous relations by the passions and emotions which they excite.

There is, however, a difficulty in applying to the present subject, in its full extent, this solution, however ingenious and satisfactory it may appear. It is certain that the same object of distress, which pleases in a tragedy, were it really set before us, would give the most unfeigned uneasiness, though it be then the most effectual cure to languor and indolence. Monsieur Fontenelle seems to have been sensible of this difficulty, and accordingly attempts another solution of the phenomenon, at least makes some addition to the theory above mentioned.[2]

"Pleasure and pain," says he, "which are two sentiments so different in themselves, differ not so much in their cause. From the instance of tickling it appears, that the movement of pleasure, pushed a little too far, becomes pain, and that the movement of pain, a little moderate, becomes pleasure. Hence it proceeds, that there is such a thing as a sorrow, soft and agree-

2 *Reflections sur la Poëtique*, § 36. [For Fontenelle, see note 2, p. 28.]

able: it is a pain weakened and diminished. The heart likes naturally to be moved and affected. Melancholy objects suit it, and even disastrous and sorrowful, provided they are softened by some circumstance. It is certain, that, on the theatre, the representation has almost the effect of reality; yet it has not altogether that effect. However we may be hurried away by the spectacle, whatever dominion the senses and imagination may usurp over the reason, there still lurks at the bottom a certain idea of falsehood in the whole of what we see. This idea, though weak and disguised, suffices to diminish the pain which we suffer from the misfortunes of those whom we love, and to reduce that affliction to such a pitch as converts it into a pleasure. We weep for the misfortune of a hero to whom we are attached. In the same instant we comfort ourselves by reflecting, that it is nothing but a fiction: and it is precisely that mixture of sentiments which composes an agreeable sorrow, and tears that delight us. But as that affliction which is caused by exterior and sensible objects is stronger than the consolation which arises from an internal reflection, they are the effects and symptoms of sorrow that ought to predominate in the composition."

This solution seems just and convincing; but perhaps it wants still some new addition, in order to make it answer fully the phenomenon which we here examine. All the passions, excited by eloquence, are agreeable in the highest degree, as well as those which are moved by painting and the theatre. The Epilogues of Cicero are, on this account chiefly, the delight of every reader of taste; and it is difficult to read some of them without the deepest sympathy and sorrow. His merit as an orator, no doubt, depends much on his success in this particular. When he had raised tears in his judges and all his audience, they were then the most highly delighted, and expressed the greatest satisfaction with the pleader. The pathetic description of the butchery made by Verres [3] of the Sicilian captains, is a masterpiece of this kind: but I believe none will affirm, that the being present at a melancholy scene of

[3] [Cicero, *The Second Speech Against Gaius Verres* V. 118–38.]

that nature would afford any entertainment. Neither is the sorrow here softened by fiction; for the audience were convinced of the reality of every circumstance. What is it then which in this case raises a pleasure from the bosom of uneasiness, so to speak, and a pleasure which still retains all the features and outward symptoms of distress and sorrow?

I answer: this extraordinary effect proceeds from that very eloquence with which the melancholy scene is represented. The genius required to paint objects in a lively manner, the art employed in collecting all the pathetic circumstances, the judgment displayed in disposing them; the exercise, I say, of these noble talents, together with the force of expression, and beauty of oratorial numbers, diffuse the highest satisfaction on the audience, and excite the most delightful movements. By this means, the uneasiness of the melancholy passions is not only overpowered and effaced by something stronger of an opposite kind, but the whole impulse of those passions is converted into pleasure, and swells the delight which the eloquence raises in us. The same force of oratory, employed on an uninteresting subject, would not please half so much, or rather would appear altogether ridiculous; and the mind, being left in absolute calmness and indifference, would relish none of those beauties of imagination or expression, which, if joined to passion, give it such exquisite entertainment. The impulse or vehemence arising from sorrow, compassion, indignation, receives a new direction from the sentiments of beauty. The latter, being the predominant emotion, seize the whole mind, and convert the former into themselves, at least tincture them so strongly as totally to alter their nature. And the soul being at the same time roused by passion and charmed by eloquence, feels on the whole a strong movement, which is altogether delightful.

The same principle takes place in tragedy; with this addition, that tragedy is an imitation, and imitation is always of itself agreeable. This circumstance serves still further to smooth the motions of passion, and convert the whole feeling into one uniform and strong enjoyment. Objects of the greatest terror and distress please in painting, and please more than the most beautiful objects that appear calm and indifferent.[4] The affection, rousing the mind, excites a large stock of spirit and vehemence; which is all transformed into pleasure by the force of the prevailing movement. It is thus the fiction of tragedy softens the passion, by an infusion of a new feeling, not merely by weakening or diminishing the sorrow. You may by degrees weaken a real sorrow, till it totally disappears; yet in none of its gradations will it ever give pleasure; except, perhaps, by accident, to a man sunk under lethargic indolence, whom it rouses from that languid state.

To confirm this theory, it will be sufficient to produce other instances, where the subordinate movement is converted into the predominant, and gives force to it, though of a different, and even sometimes though of a contrary nature.

Novelty naturally rouses the mind, and attracts our attention; and the movements which it causes are always converted into any passion belonging to the object, and join their force to it. Whether an event excite joy or sorrow, pride or shame, anger or good-will, it is sure to produce a stronger affection, when new or unusual. And though novelty of itself be agreeable, it fortifies the painful, as well as agreeable passions.

Had you any intention to move a person extremely by the narration of any event, the best method of increasing its effect would be artfully to delay informing him of it, and first to excite his curiosity and impatience before you let him into the secret. This is the artifice practised by Iago in the famous scene of Shakspeare; and every spectator is sensible, that Othello's jealousy acquires additional force from his preceding

---

[4] Painters make no scruple of representing distress and sorrow, as well as any other passion; but they seem not to dwell so much on these melancholy affections as the poets, who, though they copy every motion of the human breast, yet pass quickly over the agreeable sentiments. A painter represents only one instant; and if that be passionate enough, it is sure to affect and delight the spectator; but nothing can furnish to the poet a variety of scenes, and incidents, and sentiments, except distress, terror, or anxiety. Complete joy and satisfaction is attended with security, and leaves no further room for action.

impatience, and that the subordinate passion is here readily transformed into the predominant one.

Difficulties increase passions of every kind; and by rousing our attention, and exciting our active powers, they produce an emotion which nourishes the prevailing affection.

Parents commonly love that child most whose sickly infirm frame of body has occasioned them the greatest pains, trouble, and anxiety, in rearing him. The agreeable sentiment of affection here acquires force from sentiments of uneasiness.

Nothing endears so much a friend as sorrow for his death. The pleasure of his company has not so powerful an influence.

Jealousy is a painful passion; yet without some share of it, the agreeable affection of love has difficulty to subsist in its full force and violence. Absence is also a great source of complaint among lovers, and gives them the greatest uneasiness: yet nothing is more favorable to their mutual passion than short intervals of that kind. And if long intervals often prove fatal, it is only because, through time, men are accustomed to them, and they cease to give uneasiness. Jealousy and absence in love compose the *dolce peccante* [5] of the Italians, which they suppose so essential to all pleasure.

There is a fine observation of the elder Pliny, which illustrates the principle here insisted on. "It is very remarkable," says he, "that the last works of celebrated artists, which they left imperfect, are always the most prized, such as the Iris of Aristides, the Tyndarides of Nicomachus, the Medea of Timomachus, and the Venus of Apelles. These are valued even above their finished productions. The broken lineaments of the piece, and the half-formed idea of the painter, are carefully studied; and our very grief for that curious hand, which had been stopped by death, is an additional increase to our pleasure." [6]

5 ["Sweet failings."]

6 Illud vero perquam rarum ac memoria dignum est suprema opera artificum, imperfectasque tabulas, sicut, Irim Aristidis, Tyndaridas Nicomachi, Mediam Timomachi, et quam diximus Venerem Apellis, in majori admiratione esse quam perfecta. Quippe in iis lineamenta reliqua, ipsaeque cogitationes artificum spectantur, atque in lenocinio commendationis dolor est manus, cum id ageret, extinctae. XXXV. 145.

These instances (and many more might be collected) are sufficient to afford us some insight into the analogy of nature, and to show us, that the pleasure which poets, orators, and musicians give us, by exciting grief, sorrow, indignation, compassion, is not so extraordinary or paradoxical as it may at first sight appear. The force of imagination, the energy of expression, the power of numbers, the charms of imitation; all these are naturally, of themselves, delightful to the mind: and when the object presented lays also hold of some affection, the pleasure still rises upon us, by the conversion of this subordinate movement into that which is predominant. The passion, though perhaps naturally, and when excited by the simple appearance of a real object, it may be painful; yet is so smoothed, and softened, and mollified, when raised by the finer arts, that it affords the highest entertainment.

To confirm this reasoning, we may observe, that if the movements of the imagination be not predominant above those of the passion, a contrary effect follows; and the former, being now subordinate, is converted into the latter, and still further increases the pain and affliction of the sufferer.

Who could ever think of it as a good expedient for comforting an afflicted parent, to exaggerate, with all the force of elocution, the irreparable loss which he has met with by the death of a favorite child? The more power of imagination and expression you here employ, the more you increase his despair and affliction.

The shame, confusion, and terror of Verres, no doubt, rose in proportion to the noble eloquence and vehemence of Cicero: so also did his pain and uneasiness. These former passions were too strong for the pleasure arising from the beauties of elocution; and operated, though from the same principle, yet in a contrary manner, to the sympathy, compassion, and indignation of the audience.

Lord Clarendon,[7] when he approaches towards the catastrophe of the royal party, supposes that his narration must then become infinitely disagreeable; and he hurries over the

[7] [Edward Hyde, First Earl of Clarendon (1609–74), to whose *History of the Rebellion* Hume is probably referring.]

king's death without giving us one circumstance of it. He considers it as too horrid a scene to be contemplated with any satisfaction, or even without the utmost pain and aversion. He himself, as well as the readers of that age, were too deeply concerned in the events, and felt a pain from subjects which an historian and a reader of another age would regard as the most pathetic and most interesting, and, by consequence, the most agreeable.

An action, represented in tragedy, may be too bloody and atrocious. It may excite such movements of horror as will not soften into pleasure; and the greatest energy of expression, bestowed on descriptions of that nature, serves only to augment our uneasiness. Such is that action represented in the *Ambitious Step-mother*,[8] where a venerable old man, raised to the height of fury and despair, rushes against a pillar, and, striking his head upon it, besmears it all over with mingled brains and gore. The English theatre abounds too much with such shocking images.

Even the common sentiments of compassion require to be softened by some agreeable affection, in order to give a thorough satisfaction to the audience. The mere suffering of plaintive virtue, under the triumphant tyranny and oppression of vice, forms a disagreeable spectacle, and is carefully avoided by all masters of the drama. In order to dismiss the audience with entire satisfaction and contentment, the virtue must either convert itself into a noble courageous despair, or the vice receive its proper punishment.

Most painters appear in this light to have been very unhappy in their subjects. As they wrought much for churches and convents, they have chiefly represented such horrible subjects as crucifixions and martyrdoms, where nothing appears but tortures, wounds, executions, and passive suffering, without any action or affection. When they turned their pencil from this ghastly mythology, they had commonly recourse to Ovid, whose fictions, though passionate and agreeable, are scarcely natural or probable enough for painting.

8 [A tragedy by Nicholas Rowe (1674–1718).]

The same inversion of that principle which is here insisted on, displays itself in common life, as in the effects of oratory and poetry. Raise so the subordinate passion that it becomes the predominant, it swallows up that affection which it before nourished and increased. Too much jealousy extinguishes love; too much difficulty renders us indifferent; too much sickness and infirmity disgusts a selfish and unkind parent.

What so disagreeable as the dismal, gloomy, disastrous stories, with which melancholy people entertain their companions? The uneasy passion being there raised alone, unaccompanied with any spirit, genius, or eloquence, conveys a pure uneasiness, and is attended with nothing that can soften it into pleasure or satisfaction.

Of Essay Writing [a]

THE elegant part of mankind, who are not immersed in mere animal life, but employ themselves in the operations of the mind, may be divided into the *learned* and *conversable*. The learned are such as have chosen for their portion the higher and more difficult operations of the mind, which require leisure and solitude, and cannot be brought to perfection, without long preparation and severe labor. The conversable world join to a sociable disposition, and a taste for pleasure, an inclination for the easier and more gentle exercises of the understanding, for obvious reflections on human affairs, and the duties of common life, and for observation of the blemishes or perfections of the particular objects that surround them. Such subjects of thought furnish not sufficient employment in solitude, but require the company and conversation of our fellow-creatures, to render them a proper exercise for the mind; and this brings mankind together in society, where every one displays his thoughts in observations in the best manner he is able, and mutually gives and receives information, as well as pleasure.

The separation of the learned from the conversable world seems to have been the great defect of the last age, and must have had a very bad influence both on books and company: for what possibility is there of finding topics of conversation fit for the entertainment of rational creatures, without having recourse sometimes to history, poetry, politics, and the more obvious principles, at least, of philosophy? Must our whole discourse be a continued series of gossiping stories and idle remarks? Must the mind never rise higher, but be perpetually

> Stunn'd and worn out with endless chat,
> Of Will did this, and Nan did that?

This would be to render the time spent in company the most unentertaining, as well as the most unprofitable, part of our lives.

On the other hand, learning has been as great a loser by being shut up in colleges and cells, and secluded from the world and good company. By that means every part of what we call *belles lettres* became totally barbarous, being cultivated by men without any taste for life or manners, and without that liberty and facility of thought and expression which can only be acquired by conversation. Even philosophy went to wreck by this moping recluse method of study, and became as chimerical in her conclusions, as she was unintelligible in her style and manner of delivery; and, indeed, what could be expected from men who never consulted experience in any of their reasonings, or who never searched for that experience, where alone it is to be found, in common life and conversation?

It is with great pleasure I observe, that men of letters in this age have lost in a great measure that shyness and bashfulness of temper, which kept them at a distance from mankind; and, at the same time, that men of the world are proud of borrowing from books their most agreeable topics of conversation. It is to be hoped that this league between the learned and conversable worlds, which is so happily begun, will be still further improved to their mutual advantage; and to that end, I know nothing more advantageous than such Essays as those with which I endeavor to entertain the public. In this view, I cannot but consider myself as a kind of resident or ambassador from the dominions of learning to those of conversation, and shall think it my constant duty to promote a good correspondence betwixt these two states, which have so great a dependence on each other. I shall give intelligence to the learned of whatever passes in company, and shall endeavor to import into company whatever commodities I find in my native country proper for their use and entertainment. The balance of trade we need not be jealous of, nor will there be any difficulty to preserve it on both sides. The materials of this commerce must chiefly be furnished by conversation and common life: the manufacturing of them alone belongs to learning.

As it would be an unpardonable negligence in an ambassador not to pay his respects to the sovereign of the state where he is commissioned to reside; so it would be altogether inexcusable in me not to address myself with a particular respect to the fair sex, who are the sovereigns of the empire of conversation. I approach them with reverence; and were not my countrymen the learned, a stubborn independent race of mortals, extremely jealous of their liberty, and unaccustomed to subjection, I should resign into their fair hands the sovereign authority over the republic of letters. As the case stands, my commission extends no further than to desire a league, offensive and defensive, against our common enemies, against the enemies of reason and beauty, people of dull heads and cold hearts. From this moment let us pursue them with the severest vengeance: let no quarter be given, but to those of sound understandings and delicate affections; and these characters, it is to be presumed, we shall always find inseparable.

To be serious, and to quit the allusion before it be worn threadbare, I am of opinion that women, that is, women of sense and education (for to such alone I address myself) are much better judges of all polite writing than men of the same degree of understanding; and that it is a vain panic, if they be so far terrified with the common ridicule that is levelled against learned ladies, as utterly to abandon every kind of books and study to our sex. Let the dread of that ridicule have no other effect than to make them conceal their knowledge before fools, who are not worthy of it, nor of them. Such will still presume upon the vain title of the male sex to affect a superiority above them: but my fair readers may be assured, that all men of sense, who know the world, have a great deference for their judgment of such books as lie within the compass of their knowledge, and repose more confidence in the delicacy of their taste, though unguided by rules, than in all the dull labors of pedants and commentators. In a neighboring nation, equally famous for good taste, and for gallantry, the ladies are, in a manner, the sovereigns of the *learned* world, as well as of the *conversable;* and no polite writer pretends to venture before the public, without the approbation of some celebrated judges of that sex. Their verdict is, indeed, sometimes complained of; and, in particular, I find, that the admirers of Corneille, to save that great poet's honor upon the ascendant that Racine began to take over him, always said, that it was not to be expected, that so old a man could dispute the prize, before such judges, with so young a man as his rival. But this observation has been found unjust, since posterity seems to have ratified the verdict of that tribunal: and Racine, though dead, is still the favorite of the fair sex, as well as of the best judges among the men.

There is only one subject of which I am apt to distrust the judgment of females, and that is concerning books of gallantry and devotion, which they commonly affect as high flown as possible; and most of them seem more delighted with the warmth, than with the justness of the passion. I mention gallantry and devotion as the same subject, because, in reality, they become the same when treated in this manner; and we may observe, that they both depend upon the very same complexion. As the fair sex have a great share of the tender and amorous disposition, it perverts their judgment on this occasion, and makes them be easily affected, even by what has no propriety in the expression or nature in the sentiment. Mr. Addison's elegant discourses on religion have no relish with them, in comparison of books of mystic devotion: and Otway's tragedies are rejected for the rakes of Mr. Dryden.[1]

Would the ladies correct their false taste in this particular, let them accustom themselves a little more to books of all kinds; let them give encouragement to men of sense and knowledge to frequent their company; and finally, let them

[1] [Joseph Addison (1672–1719), essayist best known for his contributions to the *Spectator;* Thomas Otway (1652–85), whose works include *Don Carlos, The Orphan,* and *Venice Preserved;* John Dryden (1631–1700), poet, dramatist, and critic who became England's poet laureate in 1668.]

concur heartily in that union I have projected betwixt the learned and conversable worlds. They may, perhaps, meet with more complaisance from their usual followers than from men of learning; but they cannot reasonably expect so sincere an affection: and, I hope, they will never be guilty of so wrong a choice, as to sacrifice the substance for the shadow.

Of Simplicity and Refinement in Writing

FINE writing, according to Mr. Addison, consists of sentiments which are natural, without being obvious. There cannot be a juster and more concise definition of fine writing.

Sentiments, which are merely natural, affect not the mind with any pleasure, and seem not worthy of our attention. The pleasantries of a waterman, the observations of a peasant, the ribaldry of a porter or hackney coachman, all of these are natural and disagreeable. What an insipid comedy should we make of the chit-chat of the tea-table, copied faithfully and at full length? Nothing can please persons of taste, but nature drawn with all her graces and ornaments, *la belle nature;* [1] or if we copy low life, the strokes must be strong and remarkable, and must convey a lively image to the mind. The absurd *naïveté* [a] of *Sancho Panza* is represented in such inimitable colors by Cervantes, that it entertains as much as the picture of the most magnanimous hero or the softest lover.

The case is the same with orators, philosophers, critics, or any author who speaks in his own person, without introducing other speakers or actors. If his language be not elegant, his observations uncommon, his sense strong and masculine, he will in vain boast his nature and simplicity. He may be correct; but he never will be agreeable. It is the unhappiness of such authors, that they are never blamed or censured. The good fortune of a book, and that of a man, are not the same. The secret deceiving path of life, which Horace talks of, *fallentis semita vitæ,* [2] may be the happiest lot of the one; but it is the greatest misfortune which the other can possibly fall into.

1 [That is, nature adorned and perfected by art; not simply imitated, but presented as it might be.]

2 ["Path of the deceitful life." Horace, *Epistles* I. 8. 103.]

On the other hand, productions which are merely surprising, without being natural, can never give any lasting entertainment to the mind. To draw chimeras, is not, properly
speaking, to copy or imitate. The justness of the representation
is lost, and the mind is displeased to find a picture which bears
no resemblance to any original. Nor are such excessive refinements more agreeable in the epistolary or philosophic style,
than in the epic or tragic. Too much ornament is a fault in
every kind of production. Uncommon expressions, strong
flashes of wit, pointed similes, and epigrammatic turns, especially when they recur too frequently, are a disfigurement,
rather than any embellishment of discourse. As the eye, in
surveying a Gothic building, is distracted by the multiplicity
of ornaments, and loses the whole by its minute attention to
the parts; so the mind, in perusing a work overstocked with
wit, is fatigued and disgusted with the constant endeavor to
shine and surprise. This is the case where a writer overabounds
in wit, even though that wit, in itself, should be just and agreeable. But it commonly happens to such writers, that they seek
for their favorite ornaments, even where the subject does not
afford them; and by that means have twenty insipid conceits
for one thought which is really beautiful.

There is no object in critical learning more copious than
this, of the just mixture of simplicity and refinement in writing; and therefore, not to wander in too large a field, I shall
confine myself to a few general observations on that head.

First, I observe, *That though excesses of both kinds are to
be avoided, and though a proper medium ought to be studied
in all productions, yet this medium lies not in a point, but
admits of a considerable latitude.* Consider the wide distance,
in this respect, between Mr. Pope and Lucretius. These seem
to lie in the two greatest extremes of refinement and simplicity
in which a poet can indulge himself, without being guilty of
any blamable excess. All this interval may be filled with poets
who may differ from each other, but may be equally admirable, each in his peculiar style and manner. Corneille and
Congreve, who carry their wit and refinement somewhat fur-

ther than Mr. Pope, (if poets of so different a kind can be compared together,) and Sophocles and Terence, who are more simple than Lucretius, seem to have gone out of that medium in which the most perfect productions are found, and to be guilty of some excess in these opposite characters. Of all the great poets, Virgil and Racine, in my opinion, lie nearest the centre, and are the furthest removed from both the extremities.

My *second* observation on this head is, *That it is very difficult, if not impossible, to explain by words where the just medium lies between the excesses of simplicity and refinement, or to give any rule by which we can know precisely the bounds between the fault and the beauty.* A critic may discourse not only very judiciously on this head without instructing his readers, but even without understanding the matter perfectly himself. There is not a finer piece of criticism than the *Dissertation on Pastorals* by Fontenelle, in which, by a number of reflections and philosophical reasonings, he endeavors to fix the just medium which is suitable to that species of writing. But let any one read the pastorals of that author, and he will be convinced that this judicious critic, notwithstanding his fine reasonings, had a false taste, and fixed the point of perfection much nearer the extreme of refinement than pastoral poetry will admit of. The sentiments of his shepherds are better suited to the toilettes of Paris than to the forests of Arcadia. But this it is impossible to discover from his critical reasonings. He blames all excessive painting and ornament as much as Virgil could have done, had that great poet wrote a dissertation on this species of poetry. However different the tastes of men, their general discourse on these subjects is commonly the same. No criticism can be instructive which descends not to particulars, and is not full of examples and illustrations. It is allowed on all hands, that beauty, as well as virtue, always lies in a medium; but where this medium is placed is a great question, and can never be sufficiently explained by general reasonings.

I shall deliver it as a *third* observation on this subject, *That*

we ought to be more on our guard against the excess of refine-
ment than that of simplicity; and that because the former ex-
cess is both less beautiful, *and more* dangerous *than the latter.*

It is a certain rule, that wit and passion are entirely incompatible. When the affections are moved, there is no place for the imagination. The mind of man being naturally limited, it is impossible that all his faculties can operate at once; and the more any one predominates, the less room is there for the others to exert their vigor. For this reason, a greater degree of simplicity is required in all compositions where men, and actions, and passions are painted, than in such as consist of reflections and observations. And as the former species of writing is the more engaging and beautiful, one may safely, upon this account, give the preference to the extreme of simplicity above that of refinement.

We may also observe, that those compositions which we read the oftenest, and which every man of taste has got by heart, have the recommendation of simplicity, and have nothing surprising in the thought, when divested of that elegance of expression, and harmony of numbers, with which it is clothed. If the merit of the composition lie in a point of wit, it may strike at first; but the mind anticipates the thought in the second perusal, and is no longer affected by it. When I read an epigram of Martial, the first line recalls the whole; and I have no pleasure in repeating to myself what I know already. But each line, each word in Catullus has its merit, and I am never tired with the perusal of him. It is sufficient to run over Cowley [3] once; but Parnell,[4] after the fiftieth reading, is as fresh as at the first. Besides it is with books as with woman, where a certain plainness of manner and of dress is more engaging than that glare of paint, and airs, and apparel, which may dazzle the eye, but reaches not the affections. Terence is a modest and bashful beauty, to whom we grant every

[3] [Abraham Cowley (1618–67), English metaphysical poet.]
[4] [Thomas Parnell (1679–1718), Anglo-Irish poet and contributor to the *Spectator*.]

thing, because he assumes nothing, and whose purity and nature make a durable, though not a violent impression on us.

But refinement, as it is the less *beautiful,* so is it the more *dangerous* extreme, and what we are the aptest to fall into. Simplicity passes for dulness, when it is not accompanied with great elegance and propriety. On the contrary, there is something surprising in a blaze of wit and conceit. Ordinary readers are mightily struck with it, and falsely imagine it to be the most difficult, as well as the most excellent way of writing. Seneca abounds with agreeable faults, says Quintilian, *abundat dulcibus vitiis;* [5] and for that reason is the more dangerous, and the more apt to pervert the taste of the young and inconsiderate.

I shall add, that the excess of refinement is now more to be guarded against than ever; because it is the extreme which men are the most apt to fall into, after learning has made some progress, and after eminent writers have appeared in every species of composition. The endeavor to please by novelty leads men wide of simplicity and nature, and fills their writings with affectation and conceit. It was thus the Asiatic eloquence degenerated so much from the Attic. It was thus the age of Claudius and Nero became so much inferior to that of Augustus in taste and genius. And perhaps there are, at present, some symptoms of a like degeneracy of taste in France, [6] as well as in England.

[5] [Quintilian, *Institutio Oratoria* X. 129.]

[6] [See d'Alembert's *Preliminary Discourse* for the same comparison: "Thus, let us not be astonished that our literary works are generally inferior to those of the preceding century. One can find the reason for this circumstance in the very efforts we make to surpass our predecessors. . . . In this manner did the century of Demetrius of Phalerum immediately follow that of Demosthenes, the century of Lucan and of Seneca that of Cicero and of Virgil, and our century that of Louis XVI." *Preliminary Discourse to the Encyclopedia of Diderot,* tr. Richard N. Schwab and Walter E. Rex, "The Library of Liberal Arts" (New York: Liberal Arts Press, 1963).]

Of Refinement in the Arts^a

LUXURY is a word of an uncertain signification, and may be taken in a good as well as in a bad sense. In general it means great refinement in the gratification of the senses; and any degree of it may be innocent or blamable, according to the age, or country, or condition of the person. The bounds between the virtue and the vice cannot here be exactly fixed, more than in other moral subjects. To imagine, that the gratifying of any sense, or the indulging of any delicacy in meat, drink, or apparel, is of itself a vice, can never enter into a head, that is not disordered by the frenzies of enthusiasm. I have, indeed, heard of a monk abroad, who, because the windows of his cell opened upon a noble prospect, made a *covenant with his eyes* never to turn that way, or receive so sensual a gratification. And such is the crime of drinking Champagne or Burgundy, preferably to small beer or porter. These indulgences are only vices, when they are pursued at the expense of some virtue, as liberality or charity; in like manner as they are follies, when for them a man ruins his fortune, and reduces himself to want and beggary. Where they entrench upon no virtue, but leave ample subject whence to provide for friends, family, and every proper object of generosity or compassion, they are entirely innocent, and have in every age been acknowledged such by almost all moralists. To be entirely occupied with the luxury of the table, for instance, without any relish for the pleasures of ambition, study, or conversation, is a mark of stupidity, and is incompatible with any vigor of temper or genius. To confine one's expense entirely to such a gratification, without regard to friends or family, is an indication of a heart destitute of humanity or benevolence. But if a man reserve time sufficient for all laudable pursuits, and

48

money sufficient for all generous purposes, he is free from every shadow of blame or reproach.

Since luxury may be considered either as innocent or blamable, one may be surprised at those preposterous opinions which have been entertained concerning it; while men of libertine principles bestow praises even on vicious luxury, and represent it as highly advantageous to society; and, on the other hand, men of severe morals blame even the most innocent luxury, and represent it as the source of all the corruptions, disorders, and factions incident to civil government. We shall here endeavor to correct both these extremes, by proving, *first,* that the ages of refinement are both the happiest and most virtuous; *secondly,* that wherever luxury ceases to be innocent, it also ceases to be beneficial; and when carried a degree too far, is a quality pernicious, though perhaps not the most pernicious, to political society.

To prove the first point, we need but consider the effects of refinement both on *private* and on *public* life. Human happiness, according to the most received notions, seems to consist in three ingredients: action, pleasure, and indolence: and though these ingredients ought to be mixed in different proportions, according to the particular disposition of the person; yet no one ingredient can be entirely wanting, without destroying, in some measure, the relish of the whole composition. Indolence or repose, indeed, seems not of itself to contribute much to our enjoyment; but, like sleep, is requisite as an indulgence, to the weakness of human nature, which cannot support an uninterrupted course of business or pleasure. That quick march of the spirits, which takes a man from himself, and chiefly gives satisfaction, does in the end exhaust the mind, and requires some intervals of repose, which, though agreeable for a moment, yet, if prolonged, beget a languor and lethargy, that destroy all enjoyment. Education, custom, and example, have a mighty influence in turning the mind to any of these pursuits; and it must be owned that, where they promote a relish for action and pleasure, they are so favorable to human happiness. In times when industry and the arts flourish, men are kept in perpetual occupation, and enjoy, as their reward, the occupation itself, as well as those pleasures which are the fruit of their labor. The mind acquires new vigor; enlarges its powers and faculties; and, by an assiduity in honest industry, both satisfies its natural appetites, and prevents the growth of unnatural ones, which commonly spring up, when nourished by ease and idleness. Banish those arts from society, you deprive men both of action and of pleasure; and, leaving nothing but indolence in their place, you even destroy the relish of indolence, which never is agreeable, but when it succeeds to labor, and recruits the spirits, exhausted by too much application and fatigue.

Another advantage of industry and of refinements in the mechanical arts, is, that they commonly produce some refinements in the liberal; nor can one be carried to perfection, without being accompanied, in some degree, with the other. The same age which produces great philosophers and politicians, renowned generals and poets, usually abounds with skilful weavers, and ship-carpenters. We cannot reasonably expect, that a piece of woollen cloth will be wrought to perfection in a nation which is ignorant of astronomy, or where ethics are neglected. The spirit of the age affects all the arts, and the minds of men being once roused from their lethargy, and put into a fermentation, turn themselves on all sides, and carry improvements into every art and science. Profound ignorance is totally banished, and men enjoy the privilege of rational creatures, to think as well as to act, to cultivate the pleasures of the mind as well as those of the body.

The more these refined arts advance, the more sociable men become: nor is it possible, that, when enriched with science, and possessed of a fund of conversation, they should be contented to remain in solitude, or live with their fellow-citizens in that distant manner, which is peculiar to ignorant and barbarous nations. They flock into cities; love to receive and communicate knowledge; to show their wit or their breeding; their taste in conversation or living, in clothes or furniture. Curiosity allures the wise; vanity the foolish; and pleasure both. Particular clubs and societies are everywhere formed; both sexes meet in an easy and sociable manner; and the tempers of men, as well as their behavior, refine apace. So that, beside the improvements which they receive from knowledge and the liberal arts, it is impossible but they must feel an increase of humanity, from the very habit of conversing together, and contributing to each other's pleasure and entertainment. Thus *industry, knowledge,* and *humanity,* are linked together, by an indissoluble chain, and are found, from experience as well as reason, to be peculiar to the more polished, and, what are commonly denominated, the more luxurious ages.

Nor are these advantages attended with disadvantages that bear any proportion to them. The more men refine upon pleasure, the less will they indulge in excesses of any kind; because nothing is more destructive to true pleasure than such excesses. One may safely affirm, that the Tartars are oftener guilty of beastly gluttony, when they feast on their dead horses, than European courtiers with all their refinement of cookery. And if libertine love, or even infidelity to the marriage-bed, be more frequent in polite ages, when it is often regarded only as a piece of gallantry; drunkenness, on the other hand, is much less common; a vice more odious, and more pernicious, both to mind and body. And in this matter I would appeal, not only to an Ovid or a Petronius, but to a Seneca or a Cato. We know that Cæsar, during Catiline's conspiracy, being necessitated to put into Cato's hands a *billet-doux,* which discovered an intrigue with Servilla, Cato's own sister, that stern philosopher threw it back to him with indignation; and, in the bitterness of his wrath, gave him the appellation of drunkard, as a term more opprobrious than that with which he could more justly have reproached him.

But industry, knowledge, and humanity, are not advantageous in private life alone; they diffuse their beneficial influence on the *public,* and render the government as great and flourishing as they make individuals happy and prosperous. The increase and consumption of all the commodities, which serve to the ornament and pleasure of life, are advantages to society; because, at the same time that they multiply those innocent gratifications to individuals, they are a kind of *storehouse* of labor, which, in the exigencies of state, may be turned to the public service. In a nation where there is no demand for such superfluities, men sink into indolence, lose all enjoyment of life, and are useless to the public, which cannot maintain or support its fleets and armies from the industry of such slothful members.

The bounds of all the European kingdoms are, at present, nearly the same they were two hundred years ago. But what a difference is there in the power and grandeur of those kingdoms? which can be ascribed to nothing but the increase of art and industry. When Charles VIII. of France invaded Italy, he carried with him about 20,000 men; yet this armament so exhausted the nation, as we learn from Guicciardin,[1] that for some years it was not able to make so great an effort. The late king of France, in time of war, kept in pay above 400,000 men;[2] though from Mazarine's death to his own, he was engaged in a course of wars that lasted near thirty years.

This industry is much promoted by the knowledge inseparable from ages of art and refinement; as, on the other hand, this knowledge enables the public to make the best advantage of the industry of its subjects. Laws, order, police, discipline; these can never be carried to any degree of perfection, before human reason has refined itself by exercise, and by an application to the more vulgar arts, at least of commerce and manufacture. Can we expect that a government will be well modelled by a people, who know not how to make a spinning wheel, or to employ a loom to advantage? Not to mention, that all ignorant ages are infested with superstition, which throws the government off its bias, and disturbs men in the pursuit of their interest and happiness. Knowledge in the arts of government begets mildness and moderation, by instructing men in the advantages of human maxims above

1 [Francesco Guicciardini (1483–1540), Florentine historian.]
2 The inscription on the Place-Vendome says 440,000.

rigor and severity, which drive subjects into rebellion, and make the return to submission impracticable, by cutting off all hopes of pardon. When the tempers of men are softened as well as their knowledge improved, this humanity appears still more conspicuous, and is the chief characteristic which distinguishes a civilized age from times of barbarity and ignorance. Factions are then less inveterate, revolutions less tragical, authority less severe, and seditions less frequent. Even foreign wars abate of their cruelty; and after the field of battle, where honor and interest steel men against compassion, as well as fear, the combatants divest themselves of the brute, and resume the man.

Nor need we fear, that men, by losing their ferocity, will lose their martial spirit, or become less undaunted and vigorous in defence of their country or their liberty. The arts have no such effect in enervating either the mind or body. On the contrary, industry, their inseparable attendant, adds new force to both. And if anger, which is said to be the whetstone of courage, loses somewhat of its asperity, by politeness and refinement; a sense of honor, which is a stronger, more constant, and more governable principle, acquires fresh vigor by that elevation of genius which arises from knowledge and a good education. Add to this, that courage can neither have any duration, nor be of any use, when not accompanied with discipline and martial skill, which are seldom found among a barbarous people. The ancients remarked, that Datames was the only barbarian that ever knew the art of war. And Pyrrhus, seeing the Romans marshal their army with some art and skill, said with surprise, *These barbarians have nothing barbarous in their discipline!* [3] It is observable, that, as the old Romans, by applying themselves solely to war, were almost the only uncivilized people that ever possessed military discipline; so the modern Italians are the only civilized people, among Europeans, that ever wanted courage and a martial spirit. Those who would ascribe this effeminacy of the Italians to their luxury, or politeness, or application to the arts, need

[3] Plutarch, *Pyrrhus*, XVI. 5.

but consider the French and English, whose bravery is as incontestable as their love for the arts, and their assiduity in commerce. The Italian historians give us a more satisfactory reason for the degeneracy of their countrymen. They show us how the sword was dropped at once by all the Italian sovereigns; while the Venetian aristocracy was jealous of its subjects, the Florentine democracy applied itself entirely to commerce; Rome was governed by priests, and Naples by women. War then became the business of soldiers of fortune, who spared one another, and, to the astonishment of the world, could engage a whole day in what they called a battle, and return at night to their camp without the least bloodshed.

What has chiefly induced severe moralists to declaim against refinement in the arts, is the example of ancient Rome, which joining to its poverty and rusticity virtue and public spirit, rose to such a surprising height of grandeur and liberty; but, having learned from its conquered provinces the Asiatic luxury, fell into every kind of corruption; whence arose sedition and civil wars, attended at last with the total loss of liberty. All the Latin classics, whom we peruse in our infancy, are full of these sentiments, and universally ascribe the ruin of their state to the arts and riches imported from the East; insomuch, that Sallust [4] represents a taste for painting as a vice, no less than lewdness and drinking. And so popular were these sentiments, during the latter ages of the republic, that this author abounds in praises of the old rigid Roman virtue, though himself the most egregious instance of modern luxury and corruption; speaks contemptuously of the Grecian eloquence,[5] though the most elegant writer in the world; nay, employs preposterous digressions and declamations to this purpose, though a model of taste and correctness.

But it would be easy to prove, that these writers mistook the cause of the disorders in the Roman state, and ascribed to luxury and the arts, what really proceeded from an ill-modelled government, and the unlimited extent of conquests. Re-

4 *The War With Catiline* XI. 6.

5 *Ibid.*, LIII. 3.

finement on the pleasures and conveniences of life has no natural tendency to beget venality and corruption. The value which all men put upon any particular pleasure, depends on comparison and experience; nor is a porter less greedy of money, which he spends on bacon and brandy, than a courtier, who purchases champagne and ortolans. Riches are valuable at all times, and to all men; because they always purchase pleasures, such as men are accustomed to and desire: nor can anything restrain or regulate the love of money, but a sense of honor and virtue; which, if it be not nearly equal at all times, will naturally abound most in ages of knowledge and refinement.

Of all European kingdoms Poland seems the most defective in the arts of war as well as peace, mechanical as well as liberal; yet it is there that venality and corruption do most prevail. The nobles seem to have preserved their crown elective for no other purpose, than regularly to sell it to the highest bidder. This is almost the only species of commerce with which that people are acquainted.

The liberties of England, so far from decaying since the improvements in the arts, have never flourished so much as during that period. And though corruption may seem to increase of late years; this is chiefly to be ascribed to our established liberty, when our princes have found the impossibility of governing without parliaments, or of terrifying parliaments by the phantom of prerogative. Not to mention, that this corruption or venality prevails much more among the electors than the elected; and therefore cannot justly be ascribed to any refinements in luxury.

If we consider the matter in a proper light, we shall find, that a progress in the arts is rather favorable to liberty, and has a natural tendency to preserve, if not produce a free government. In rude unpolished nations, where the arts are neglected, all labor is bestowed on the cultivation of the ground; and the whole society is divided into two classes, proprietors of land, and their vassals or tenants. The latter are necessarily dependent, and fitted for slavery and subjection; especially where they possess no riches, and are not valued for their knowledge in agriculture; as must always be the case where the arts are neglected. The former naturally erect themselves into petty tyrants; and must either submit to an absolute master, for the sake of peace and order; or, if they will preserve their independency, like the ancient barons, they must fall into feuds and contests among themselves, and throw the whole society into such confusion, as is perhaps worse than the most despotic government. But where luxury nourishes commerce and industry, the peasants, by a proper cultivation of the land, become rich and independent: while the tradesmen and merchants acquire a share of the property, and draw authority and consideration to that middling rank of men, who are the best and firmest basis of public liberty. These submit not to slavery, like the peasants, from poverty and meanness of spirit; and, having no hopes of tyrannizing over others, like the barons, they are not tempted, for the sake of that gratification, to submit to the tyranny of their sovereign. They covet equal laws, which may secure their property, and preserve them from monarchical, as well as aristocratical tyranny.

The lower house is the support of our popular government; and all the world acknowledges, that it owed its chief influence and consideration to the increase of commerce, which threw such a balance of property into the hands of the Commons. How inconsistent, then, is it to blame so violently a refinement in the arts, and to represent it as the bane of liberty and public spirit!

To declaim against present times, and magnify the virtue of remote ancestors, is a propensity almost inherent in human nature: and as the sentiments and opinions of civilized ages alone are transmitted to posterity, hence it is that we meet with so many severe judgments pronounced against luxury, and even science; and hence it is that at present we give so ready an assent to them. But the fallacy is easily perceived, by comparing different nations that are contemporaries; where we both judge more impartially, and can better set in opposition those manners, with which we are sufficiently acquainted. Treachery and cruelty, the most pernicious and most odious of all vices, seem peculiar to uncivilized ages; and, by the refined Greeks and Romans, were ascribed to all the barbarous nations which surrounded them. They might justly, therefore, have presumed, that their own ancestors, so highly celebrated, possessed no greater virtue, and were as much inferior to their posterity in honor and humanity, as in taste and science. An ancient Frank or Saxon may be highly extolled: but I believe every man would think his life or fortune much less secure in the hands of a Moor or Tartar, than in those of a French or English gentleman, the rank of men the most civilized in the most civilized nations.

We come now to the *second* position which we proposed to illustrate, to wit, that, as innocent luxury, or a refinement in the arts and conveniences of life, is advantageous to the public; so, wherever luxury ceases to be innocent, it also ceases to be beneficial; and when carried a degree further, begins to be a quality pernicious, though perhaps not the most pernicious, to political society.

Let us consider what we call vicious luxury. No gratification, however sensual, can of itself be esteemed vicious. A gratification is only vicious when it engrosses all a man's expense, and leaves no ability for such acts of duty and generosity as are required by his situation and fortune. Suppose that he correct the vice, and employ part of his expense in the education of his children, in the support of his friends, and in relieving the poor; would any prejudice result to society? On the contrary, the same consumption would arise; and that labor, which at present is employed only in producing a slender gratification to one man, would relieve the necessitous, and bestow satisfaction on hundreds. The same care and toil that raise a dish of peas at Christmas, would give bread to a whole family, during six months. To say that, without a vicious luxury, the labor would not have been employed at all, is only to say, that there is some other defect in human nature, such as indolence, selfishness, inattention to others, for which luxury, in some measure, provides a remedy; as one poison may be an antidote to another. But virtue, like wholesome food, is better than poisons, however corrected.

Suppose the same number of men that are at present in Great Britain, with the same soil and climate; I ask, is it not possible for them to be happier, by the most perfect way of life that can be imagined, and by the greatest reformation that Omnipotence itself could work in their temper and disposition? To assert that they cannot, appears evidently ridiculous. As the land is able to maintain more than all its present inhabitants, they could never in such a Utopian state, feel any other ills than those which arise from bodily sickness: and these are not the half of human miseries. All other ills spring from some vice, either in ourselves or others; and even many of our diseases proceed from the same origin. Remove the vices, and the ills follow. You must only take care to remove all the vices. If you remove part, you may render the matter worse. By banishing *vicious* luxury, without curing sloth and an indifference to others, you only diminish industry in the state, and add nothing to men's charity or their generosity. Let us, therefore, rest contented with asserting, that two opposite vices in a state may be more advantageous than either of them alone; but let us never pronounce vice in itself advantageous. It is not very inconsistent for an author to assert in one page, that moral distinctions are inventions of politicians for public interest, and in the next page maintain, that vice is advantageous to the public. And indeed it seems, upon any system of morality, little less than a contradiction in terms, to talk of a vice, which is in general beneficial to society.[b]

I thought this reasoning necessary, in order to give some light to a philosophical question, which has been much disputed in England. I call it a *philosophical* question, not a *political* one. For whatever may be the consequence of such a miraculous transformation of mankind, as would endow them with every species of virtue, and free them from every species of vice, this concerns not the magistrate, who aims only at possibilities. He cannot cure every vice by substituting a virtue in its place. Very often he can only cure one vice by another; and in that case he ought to prefer what is least pernicious to society. Luxury, when excessive, is the source of many ills, but is in general preferable to sloth and idleness, which would commonly succeed in its place, and are more hurtful both to private persons and to the public. When sloth reigns, a mean uncultivated way of life prevails amongst individuals, without society, without enjoyment. And if the sovereign, in such a situation, demands the service of his subjects, the labor of the state suffices only to furnish the necessaries of life to the laborers, and can afford nothing to those who are employed in the public service.

Of Eloquence

THOSE who consider the periods and revolutions of human kind, as represented in history, are entertained with a spectacle full of pleasure and variety, and see with surprise the manners, customs, and opinions of the same species susceptible of such prodigious changes in different periods of time. It may, however, be observed, that, in *civil* history, there is found a much greater uniformity than in the history of learning and science, and that the wars, negotiations, and politics of one age, resemble more those of another than the taste, wit, and speculative principles. Interest and ambition, honor and shame, friendship and enmity, gratitude and revenge, are the prime movers in all public transactions; and these passions are of a very stubborn and untractable nature, in comparison of the sentiments and understanding, which are easily varied by education and example. The Goths were much more inferior to the Romans in taste and science than in courage and virtue.

But not to compare together nations so widely different, it may be observed, that even this latter period of human learning is, in many respects, of an opposite character to the ancient; and that, if we be superior in philosophy, we are still, notwithstanding all our refinements, much inferior in eloquence.

In ancient times, no work of genius was thought to require so great parts and capacity as the speaking in public; and some eminent writers have pronounced the talents even of a great poet or philosopher to be of an inferior nature to those which are requisite for such an undertaking. Greece and Rome produced, each of them, but one accomplished orator; and, whatever praises the other celebrated speakers might merit, they were still esteemed much inferior to those great models of eloquence. It is observable, that the ancient critics could scarcely find two orators in any age who deserved to be placed precisely in the same rank, and possessed the same degree of merit. Calvus, Caelius, Curio, Hortensius, Caesar, rose one above another: but the greatest of that age was inferior to Cicero, the most eloquent speaker that had ever appeared in Rome. Those of fine taste, however, pronounced this judgment of the Roman orator, as well as of the Grecian, that both of them surpassed in eloquence all that had ever appeared, but that they were far from reaching the perfection of their art, which was infinite, and not only exceeded human force to attain, but human imagination to conceive. Cicero declares himself dissatisfied with his own performances, nay, even with those of Demosthenes. *Ita sunt avidae et capaces meae aures,* says he, *et semper aliquid immensum, infinitumque desiderant.*[1]

Of all the polite and learned nations, England alone possesses a popular government, or admits into the legislature such numerous assemblies as can be supposed to lie under the dominion of eloquence. But what has England to boast of in this particular? In enumerating the great men who have done honor to our country, we exult in our poets and philosophers; but what orators are ever mentioned? or where are the monuments of their genius to be met with? There are found, indeed, in our histories, the names of several, who directed the resolutions of our parliament: but neither themselves nor others have taken the pains to preserve their speeches: and the authority, which they possessed, seems to have been owing to their experience, wisdom, or power, more than to their talents for oratory. At present there are above half a dozen speakers in the two Houses, who, in the judgment of the public, have reached very near the same pitch of eloquence; and no man pretends to give any one the preference above the rest. This seems to me a certain proof, that none of them have attained much beyond a mediocrity in their art, and that the species of eloquence, which they aspire to, gives no exercise to the

[1] ["So greedy and insatiate are [my ears] and so often yearn for something vast and boundless." *Orator* XXIX. 104, tr. H. M. Hubbell "Loeb Classical Library" (Cambridge, Mass.: Cambridge University Press, 1952).]

sublimer faculties of the mind, but may be reached by ordinary talents and a slight application. A hundred cabinet-makers
in London can work a table or a chair equally well; but no
one poet can write verses with such spirit and elegance as Mr.
Pope.

We are told, that, when Demosthenes was to plead, all ingenious men flocked to Athens from the most remote parts
of Greece, as to the most celebrated spectacle of the world.[2]
At London, you may see men sauntering in the court of re-
quests, while the most important debate is carrying on in the
two Houses; and many do not think themselves sufficiently
compensated for the losing of their dinners, by all the eloquence of our most celebrated speakers. When old Cibber[3]
is to act, the curiosity of several is more excited, than when our
prime minister is to defend himself from a motion for his removal or impeachment.

Even a person, unacquainted with the noble remains of
ancient orators, may judge, from a few strokes, that the style
or species of their eloquence was infinitely more sublime than
that which modern orators aspire to. How absurd would it
appear, in our temperate and calm speakers, to make use of
an *Apostrophe,* like that noble one of Demosthenes,[4] so much
celebrated by Quintilian and Longinus, when, justifying the
unsuccessful battle of Chæronea, he breaks out, "No, my fel-

[2] Ne illud quidem intelligunt, non modo ita memoriae proditum esse,
sed ita necesse fuisse, cum Demosthenes dicturus esset, ut concursus,
audiendi causa, ex tota Graecia fierent. At cum isti Attici dicunt, non
modo a corona (quod est ipsum miserabile) sed etiam ab advocatis re-
linquuntur. ["They don't even see, not only that history records it, but
it must have been so, that when Demosthenes was to speak all Greece
flocked to hear him. But when these Atticists of ours speak they are deserted not only by the curious crowd, which is humiliating enough, but
even by the friends and supporters of their client." *Brutus* LXXIV. 289,
tr. G. L. Hendrickson "Loeb Classical Library" (Cambridge, Mass.: Cambridge University Press, 1952).]

[3] [Colley Cibber (1671–1757), English actor, dramatist, and poet, appointed poet laureate in 1730.]

[4] [In *De Corona* 208; mentioned by Quintilian (IX. 2, 62) and Longinus
(*On the Sublime* III. 16).]

low-citizens, No: you have not erred. I swear by the *manes* of those heroes, who fought for the same cause in the plains of Marathon and Platæa." Who could now endure such a bold and poetical figure as that which Cicero employs, after describing, in the most tragical terms, the crucifixion of a Roman citizen? "Should I paint the horrors of this scene, not to Roman citizens, not to the allies of our state, not to those who have ever heard of the Roman name, not even to men, but to brute creatures; or, to go further, should I lift up my voice in the most desolate solitude, to the rocks and mountains, yet should I surely see those rude and inanimate parts of nature moved with horror and indignation at the recital of so enormous an action." [5] With what a blaze of eloquence must such a sentence be surrounded to give it grace, or cause it to make any impression on the hearers! And what noble art and sublime talents are requisite to arrive, by just degrees, at a sentiment so bold and excessive! To inflame the audience, so as to make them accompany the speaker in such violent passions, and such elevated conceptions; and to conceal, under a torrent of eloquence, the artifice by which all this is effectuated! Should this sentiment even appear to us excessive, as perhaps justly it may, it will at least serve to give an idea of the style of ancient eloquence, where such swelling expressions were not rejected as wholly monstrous and gigantic.

Suitable to this vehemence of thought and expression, was the vehemence of action, observed in the ancient orators. The *supplosio pedis,* or stamping with the foot, was one of the most usual and moderate gestures which they made use of; [6]

[5] The original is "Quod si haec non ad cives Romanos, non ad aliquos amicos nostrae civitatis, non ad eos qui populi Romani nomen audissent; denique si non ad homines, verum ad bestias; aut etiam, ut longius progrediar, si in aliqua desertissima solitudine, ad saxa et ad scopulos haec conqueri et deplorare vellem, tamen omnia muta atque inanima, tanta et tam indigna rerum acerbitate commoverentur." [*The Second Speech Against Gaius Verres* V. 171.]

[6] Ubi dolor? Ubi ardor animi, qui etiam ex infantium ingeniis elicere voces et querelas solet? nulla perturbatio animi, nulla corporis; frons non percussa, non femur; pedis (*quod minimum est*) nulla supplosio. Itaque

though that is now esteemed too violent, either for the senate, bar, or pulpit, and is only admitted into the theatre to accompany the most violent passions which are there represented.

One is somewhat at a loss to what cause we may ascribe so sensible a decline of eloquence in latter ages. The genius of mankind, at all times, is perhaps equal: the moderns have applied themselves, with great industry and success, to all the other arts and sciences: and a learned nation possesses a popular government; a circumstance which seems requisite for the full display of these noble talents: but notwithstanding all these advantages, our progress in eloquence is very inconsiderable, in comparison of the advances which we have made in all other parts of learning.

Shall we assert, that the strains of ancient eloquence are unsuitable to our age, and ought not to be imitated by modern orators? Whatever reasons may be made use of to prove this, I am persuaded they will be found, upon examination, to be unsound and unsatisfactory.

First, It may be said, that, in ancient times, during the flourishing period of Greek and Roman learning, the municipal laws, in every state, were but few and simple, and the decision of causes was, in a great measure, left to the equity and common sense of the judges. The study of the laws was not then a laborious occupation, requiring the drudgery of a whole life to finish it, and incompatible with every other study or profession. The great statesmen and generals among the Romans were all lawyers; and Cicero, to show the facility of acquiring this science, declares, that in the midst of all his occupations, he would undertake, in a few days, to make himself a complete

---

tantum abfuit ut inflammares nostros animos; somnum isto loco vix tenebamus.—*Cicero de Claris Oratoribus.* ["What trace of anger, of that burning indignation, which stirs even men quite incapable of eloquence to loud outbursts of complaint against wrongs? But no hint of indignation in you, neither of mind nor of body! Did you smite your brow, slap your thigh, or at least stamp your foot? No. So far from touching my feelings, I could scarcely refrain from going to sleep then and there." *Brutus* LXXX. 278, tr. G. L. Hendrickson, "Loeb Classical Library" (Cambridge, Mass.: Cambridge University Press, 1952).]

civilian. Now, where a pleader addresses himself to the equity of his judges, he has much more room to display his eloquence, than where he must draw his arguments from strict laws, statutes, and precedents. In the former case many circumstances must be taken in, many personal considerations regarded, and even favor and inclination, which it belongs to the orator, by his art and eloquence, to conciliate, may be disguised under the appearance of equity. But how shall a modern lawyer have leisure to quit his toilsome occupations, in order to gather the flowers of Parnassus? Or what opportunity shall he have of displaying them, amidst the rigid and subtile arguments, objections, and replies, which he is obliged to make use of? The greatest genius, and greatest orator, who should pretend to plead before the *Chancellor,* after a month's study of the laws, would only labor to make himself ridiculous.

I am ready to own, that this circumstance, of the multiplicity and intricacy of laws, is a discouragement to eloquence in modern times: but I assert, that it will not entirely account for the decline of that noble art. It may banish oratory from Westminster Hall, but not from either house of Parliament. Among the Athenians, the Areopagites [7] expressly forbade all allurements of eloquence; and some have pretended, that in the Greek orations, written in the *judiciary* form, there is not so bold and rhetorical a style as appears in the Roman. But to what a pitch did the Athenians carry their eloquence in the *deliberative* kind, when affairs of state were canvassed, and the liberty, happiness, and honor of the republic, were the subject of debate! Disputes of this nature elevate the genius above all others, and give the fullest scope to eloquence; and such disputes are very frequent in this nation.

Secondly, It may be pretended, that the decline of eloquence is owing to the superior good sense of the moderns, who reject with disdain all those rhetorical tricks employed to seduce the judges, and will admit of nothing but solid argument in

[7] [The Areopagites were members of the court which held its sittings on the Areopagus ("Hill of Ares") in Athens.]

any debate of deliberation. If a man be accused of murder, the fact must be proved by witnesses and evidence, and the laws will afterwards determine the punishment of the criminal. It would be ridiculous to describe, in strong colors, the horror and cruelty of the action; to introduce the relations of the dead, and, at a signal, make them throw themselves at the feet of the judges, imploring justice, with tears and lamentations: and still more ridiculous would it be, to employ a picture representing the bloody deed, in order to move the judges by the display of so tragical a spectacle, though we know that this artifice was sometimes practised by the pleaders of old.[8] Now, banish the pathetic from public discourses, and you reduce the speakers merely to modern eloquence; that is, to good sense, delivered in proper expressions.

Perhaps it may be acknowledged, that our modern customs, or our superior good sense, if you will, should make our orators more cautious and reserved than the ancient, in attempting to inflame the passions, or elevate the imagination of their audience: but I see no reason why it should make them despair absolutely of succeeding in that attempt. It should make them redouble their art, not abandon it entirely. The ancient orators seem also to have been on their guard against this jealousy of their audience; but they took a different way of eluding it.[9] They hurried away with such a torrent of sublime and pathetic, that they left their hearers no leisure to perceive the artifice by which they were deceived. Nay, to consider the matter aright, they were not deceived by any artifice. The orator, by the force of his own genius and eloquence, first inflamed himself with anger, indignation, pity, sorrow; and then communicated those impetuous movements to his audience.

Does any man pretend to have more good sense than Julius Caesar? yet that haughty conqueror, we know, was so subdued by the charms of Cicero's eloquence, that he was, in a manner, constrained to change his settled purpose and resolution, and

8 Quintilian, VI. 1.
9 Longinus, II. 15.

to absolve a criminal, whom, before that orator pleaded, he was determined to condemn.

Some objections, I own, notwithstanding his vast success, may lie against some passages of the Roman orator. He is too florid and rhetorical: his figures are too striking and palpable: the divisions of his discourse are drawn chiefly from the rules of the schools: and his wit disdains not always the artifice even of a pun, rhyme, or jingle of words. The Grecian addressed himself to an audience much less refined than the Roman senate or judges. The lowest vulgar of Athens were his sovereigns, and the arbiters of his eloquence.[10] Yet is his manner more chaste and austere than that of the other. Could it be copied, its success would be infallible over a modern assembly. It is rapid harmony, exactly adjusted to the sense: it is vehement reasoning, without any appearance of art: it is disdain, anger, boldness, freedom, involved in a continued stream of argument: and, of all human productions, the orations of Demosthenes present to us the models which approach the nearest to perfection.[a]

Thirdly, It may be pretended, that the disorders of the ancient governments, and the enormous crimes of which the citizens were often guilty, afforded much ampler matter for eloquence than can be met with among the moderns. Were there no Verres or Catiline, there would be no Cicero. But that this reason can have no great influence, is evident. It would be easy to find a Philip in modern times, but where shall we find a Demosthenes?

[10] The orators formed the taste of the Athenian people, not the people of the orators. Gorgias Leontinus was very taking with them, till they became acquainted with a better manner. His figures of speech, says Diodorus Siculus, his antithesis, his ἰσόκηλος, his ὁμοιτελεύτον [sentences with equal members or balanced clauses], which are now despised, had a great effect upon the audience. [XII. 53. 2–5.] It is in vain, therefore, for modern orators to plead the taste of their hearers as an apology for their lame performances. It would be strange prejudice in favor of antiquity, not to allow a British Parliament to be naturally superior in judgment and delicacy to an Athenian mob.

What remains, then, but that we lay the blame on the want of genius, or of judgment, in our speakers, who either found themselves incapable of reaching the heights of ancient eloquence, or rejected all such endeavors, as unsuitable to the spirit of modern assemblies? A few successful attempts of this nature might rouse the genius of the nation, excite the emulation of the youth, and accustom our ears to a more sublime and more pathetic elocution, than what we have been hitherto entertained with. There is certainly something accidental in the first rise and progress of the arts in any nation. I doubt whether a very satisfactory reason can be given why ancient Rome, though it received all its refinements from Greece, could attain only to a relish for statuary, painting, and architecture, without reaching the practice of these arts. While modern Rome has been excited by a few remains found among the ruins of antiquity, and has produced artists of the greatest eminence and distinction. Had such a cultivated genius for oratory, as Waller's [11] for poetry,[b] arisen during the civil wars, when liberty began to be fully established, and popular assemblies to enter into all the most material points of government, I am persuaded so illustrious an example would have given a quite different turn to British eloquence, and made us reach the perfection of the ancient model. Our orators would then have done honor to their country, as well as our poets, geometers, and philosophers; and British Ciceros have appeared, as well as British Archimedeses and Virgils.[c]

It is seldom or never found, when a false taste in poetry or eloquence prevails among any people, that it has been preferred to a true, upon comparison and reflection. It commonly prevails merely from ignorance of the true, and from the want of perfect models to lead men into a juster apprehension, and more refined relish of those productions of genius. When *these* appear, they soon unite all suffrages in their favor, and, by

11 [Edmund Waller (1606–87), English poet known for the harmonious smoothness of his verse. He participated in a Royalist plot during the civil war, and for a time was banished from England; during the Commonwealth he wrote a panegyric on Cromwell, and in the Restoration wrote verse in praise of Charles II.]

their natural and powerful charms, gain over even the most prejudiced to the love and admiration of them. The principles of every passion, and of every sentiment, is in every man; and, when touched properly, they rise to life, and warm the heart, and convey that satisfaction, by which a work of genius is distinguished from the adulterate beauties of a capricious wit and fancy. And, if this observation be true, with regard to all the liberal arts, it must be peculiarly so with regard to eloquence; which, being merely calculated for the public, and for men of the world, cannot, with any pretence of reason, appeal from the people to more refined judges, but must submit to the public verdict without reserve or limitation. Whoever, upon comparison, is deemed by a common audience the greatest orator, ought most certainly to be pronounced such by men of science and erudition. And though an indifferent speaker may triumph for a long time, and be esteemed altogether perfect by the vulgar, who are satisfied with his accomplishments, and know not in what he is defective; yet, whenever the true genius arises, *he* draws to him the attention of every one, and immediately appears superior to his rival.

Now, to judge by this rule, ancient eloquence, that is, the sublime and passionate, is of a much juster taste than the modern, or the argumentative and rational, and, if properly executed, will always have more command and authority over mankind. We are satisfied with our mediocrity, because we have had no experience of any thing better: but the ancients had experience of both; and upon comparison, gave the preference to that kind of which they have left us such applauded models. For, if I mistake not, our modern eloquence is of the same style or species with that which ancient critics denominated Attic eloquence, that is, calm, elegant, and subtile, which instructed the reason more than affected the passions, and never raised its tone above argument or common discourse. Such was the eloquence of Lysias among the Athenians, and of Calvus among the Romans. These were esteemed in their time; but, when compared with Demosthenes and Cicero, were eclipsed like a taper when set in the rays of a merid-

ian sun. Those latter orators possessed the same elegance, and
subtilty, and force of argument with the former; but, what
rendered them chiefly admirable, was that pathetic and sublime, which, on proper occasions, they threw into their discourse, and by which they commanded the resolution of their
audience.

Of this species of eloquence we have scarcely had any instance in England, at least in our public speakers. In our
writers, we have had some instances which have met with great
applause, and might assure our ambitious youth of equal or
superior glory in attempts for the revival of ancient eloquence.
Lord Bolingbroke's [12] productions, with all their defects in
argument, method, and precision, contain a force and energy
which our orators scarcely ever aim at; though it is evident
that such an elevated style has much better grace in a speaker
than in a writer, and is assured of more prompt and more
astonishing success. It is there seconded by the graces of voice
and action: the movements are mutually communicated between the orator and the audience: and the very aspect of a
large assembly, attentive to the discourse of one man, must
inspire him with a peculiar elevation, sufficient to give a propriety to the strongest figures and expressions. It is true, there
is a great prejudice against *set speeches;* and a man cannot
escape ridicule, who repeats a discourse as a school-boy does
his lesson, and takes no notice of any thing that has been advanced in the course of the debate. But where is the necessity
of falling into this absurdity? A public speaker must know
beforehand the question under debate. He may compose all
the arguments, objections, and answers, such as he thinks will
be most proper for his discourse.[13] If any thing new occur, he
may supply it from his own invention; nor will the difference

12 [Bolingbroke, Henry St. John, 1st Viscount, English statesman and
political writer, 1678–1751. Hume apparently refers to his writings.]

13 The first of the Athenians, who composed and wrote his speeches,
was Pericles, a man of business and a man of sense, if ever there was one.
Πρῶτος γραπτὸν λόγον ἐν δικαστηρίῳ εἶπε, τῶν πρὸ αὐτῷ σχεδιαζόντων.
Suidas in Περικλῆς.

be very apparent between his elaborate and his extemporary compositions. The mind naturally continues with the same *impetus* or *force,* which it has acquired by its motion, as a vessel, once impelled by the oars, carries on its course for some time when the original impulse is suspended.

I shall conclude this subject with observing, that, even though our modern orators should not elevate their style, or aspire to a rivalship with the ancient; yet there is, in most of their speeches, a material defect which they might correct, without departing from that composed air of argument and reasoning to which they limit their ambition. Their great affectation of extemporary discourses has made them reject all order and method, which seems so requisite to argument, and without which it is scarcely possible to produce an entire conviction on the mind. It is not that one would recommend many divisions in a public discourse, unless the subject very evidently offer them: but it is easy, without this formality, to observe a method, and make that method conspicuous to the hearers, who will be infinitely pleased to see the arguments rise naturally from one another, and will retain a more thorough persuasion than can arise from the strongest reasons which are thrown together in confusion.

Of the Rise and Progress of the Arts and Sciences

NOTHING requires greater nicety, in our inquiries concerning human affairs, than to distinguish exactly what is owing to *chance,* and what proceeds from *causes;* nor is there any subject in which an author is more liable to deceive himself by false subtilties and refinements. To say that any event is derived from chance, cuts short all further inquiry concerning it, and leaves the writer in the same state of ignorance with the rest of mankind. But when the event is supposed to proceed from certain and stable causes, he may then display his ingenuity in assigning these causes; and as a man of any subtilty can never be at a loss in this particular, he has thereby an opportunity of swelling his volumes, and discovering his profound knowledge in observing what escapes the vulgar and ignorant.

The distinguishing between chance and causes must depend upon every particular man's sagacity in considering every particular incident. But if I were to assign any general rule to help us in applying this distinction, it would be the following: *What depends upon a few persons is, in a great measure, to be ascribed to chance, or secret and unknown causes: what arises from a great number, may often be accounted for by determinate and known causes.*

Two natural reasons may be assigned for this rule. *First,* If you suppose a die to have any bias, however small, to a particular side, this bias, though perhaps it may not appear in a few throws, will certainly prevail in a great number, and will cast the balance entirely to that side. In like manner, when any *causes* beget a particular inclination or passion, at a certain time, and among a certain people, though many individuals may escape the contagion, and be ruled by passions peculiar to themselves, yet the multitude will certainly be seized by the common affection, and be governed by it in all their actions.

Secondly, Those principles or causes which are fitted to operate on a multitude, are always of a grosser and more stubborn nature, less subject to accidents, and less influenced by whim and private fancy, than those which operate on a few only. The latter are commonly so delicate and refined, that the smallest incident in the health, education, or fortune of a particular person, is sufficient to divert their course and retard their operation; nor is it possible to reduce them to any general maxims or observations. Their influence at one time will never assure us concerning their influence at another, even though all the general circumstances should be the same in both cases.

To judge by this rule, the domestic and the gradual revolutions of a state must be a more proper subject of reasoning and observation than the foreign and the violent, which are commonly produced by single persons, and are more influenced by whim, folly, or caprice, than by general passions and interests. The depression of the Lords, and rise of the Commons in England, after the statutes of alienation, and the increase of trade and industry, are more easily accounted for by general principles, than the depression of the Spanish, and rise of the French monarchy, after the death of Charles Quint. Had Harry IV., Cardinal Richelieu, and Louis XIV. been Spaniards, and Philip II., III., and IV., and Charles II. been Frenchmen, the history of these two nations had been entirely reversed.

For the same reason, it is more easy to account for the rise and progress of commerce in any kingdom than for that of learning; and a state, which should apply itself to the encouragement of one, would be more assured of success than one which should cultivate the other. Avarice, or the desire of gain, is an universal passion, which operates at all times, in all places, and upon all persons: but curiosity, or the love of knowledge, has a very limited influence, and requires youth, leisure, education, genius, and example, to make it govern any person. You will never want booksellers while there are buyers of books: but there may frequently be readers where there are no authors. Multitudes of people, necessity and liberty, have begotten commerce in Holland: but study and application have scarcely produced any eminent writers.

We may therefore conclude, that there is no subject in which we must proceed with more caution than in tracing the history of the arts and sciences, lest we assign causes which never existed, and reduce what is merely contingent to stable and universal principles. Those who cultivate the sciences in any state are always few in number; the passion which governs them limited; their taste and judgment delicate and easily perverted; and their application disturbed with the smallest accident. Chance, therefore, or secret and unknown causes, must have a great influence on the rise and progress of all the refined arts.

But there is a reason which induces me not to ascribe the matter altogether to chance. Though the persons who cultivate the sciences with such astonishing success as to attract the admiration of posterity, be always few in all nations and all ages, it is impossible but a share of the same spirit and genius must be antecedently diffused throughout the people among whom they arise, in order to produce, form, and cultivate, from their earliest infancy, the taste and judgment of those eminent writers. The mass cannot be altogether insipid from which such refined spirits are extracted. *There is a God within us,* says Ovid, *who breathes that divine fire by which we are animated.*[1] Poets in all ages have advanced this claim to inspiration. There is not, however, any thing supernatural in the case. Their fire is not kindled from heaven. It only runs along the earth, is caught from one breast to another, and burns brightest where the materials are best prepared and most happily disposed. The question, therefore, concerning the rise and progress of the arts and sciences is not altogether a question

---

[1] Est Deus in nobis; agitante calescimus illo:
Impetus hic, sacrae semina mentis habet. Ovid, *Fasti* [VI. 5–6].

concerning the taste, genius, and spirit of a few, but concerning those of a whole people, and may therefore be accounted for, in some measure, by general causes and principles. I grant that a man, who should inquire why such a particular poet, as Homer, for instance, existed at such a place, in such a time, would throw himself headlong into chimera, and could never treat of such a subject without a multitude of false subtilties and refinements. He might as well pretend to give a reason why such particular generals as Fabius and Scipio lived in Rome at such a time, and why Fabius came into the world before Scipio. For such incidents as these no other reason can be given than that of Horace:—

Scit genius, natale comes, qui temperat astrum,
Naturae Deus humanae, mortalis in unum——
——Quodque caput, vultu mutabilis, albus et ater.[2]

But I am persuaded that in many cases good reasons might be given why such a nation is more polite and learned, at a particular time, than any of its neighbors. At least this is so curious a subject, that it were a pity to abandon it entirely before we have found whether it be susceptible of reasoning, and can be reduced to any general principles.

My first observation on this head is, *That it is impossible for the arts and sciences to arise, at first, among any people, unless that people enjoy the blessing of a free government.*

In the first ages of the world, when men are as yet barbarous and ignorant, they seek no further security against mutual violence and injustice than the choice of some rulers, few or many, in whom they place an implicit confidence, without providing any security, by laws or political institutions, against the violence and injustice of these rulers. If the authority be centred in a single person, and if the people, either by conquest or by the ordinary course of propagation, increase to a great multitude, the monarch, finding it impossible, in his own person, to execute every office of sovereignty, in every place, must delegate his authority to inferior magistrates, who pre-

2 [Horace, *Epistles* II. 2. 187.]

serve peace and order in their respective districts. As experience and education have not yet refined the judgments of men to any considerable degree, the prince, who is himself unrestrained, never dreams of restraining his ministers, but delegates his full authority to every one whom he sets over any portion of the people. All general laws are attended with inconveniences, when applied to particular cases; and it requires great penetration and experience, both to perceive that these inconveniences are fewer than what result from full discretionary powers in every magistrate, and also to discern what general laws are, upon the whole, attended with fewest inconveniences. This is a matter of so great difficulty, that men may have made some advances, even in the sublime arts of poetry and eloquence, where a rapidity of genius and imagination assists their progress, before they have arrived at any great refinement in their municipal laws, where frequent trials and diligent observation can alone direct their improvements. It is not, therefore, to be supposed, that a barbarous monarch, unrestrained and uninstructed, will ever become a legislator, or think of restraining his *Bashaws* in every province, or even his *Cadis* in every village. We are told, that the late *Czar*, though actuated with a noble genius, and smit with the love and admiration of European arts; yet professed an esteem for the Turkish policy in this particular, and approved of such summary decisions of causes, as are practised in that barbarous monarchy, where the judges are not restrained by any methods, forms, or laws. He did not perceive, how contrary such a practice would have been to all his other endeavors for refining his people. Arbitrary power, in all cases, is somewhat oppressive and debasing; but it is altogether ruinous and intolerable, when contracted into a small compass; and becomes still worse, when the person, who possesses it, knows that the time of his authority is limited and uncertain. *Habet subjectos tanquam suos; viles ut alienos.*[3] He governs the subjects with full authority, as if they were his own; and with negligence or tyranny, as belonging to another. A people, governed after

[3] Tacitus, *The Histories*, I.

such a manner, are slaves in the full and proper sense of the word; and it is impossible they can ever aspire to any refinements of taste or reason. They dare not so much as pretend to enjoy the necessaries of life in plenty or security.

To expect, therefore, that the arts and sciences should take their first rise in a monarchy, is to expect a contradiction. Before these refinements have taken place, the monarch is ignorant and uninstructed; and not having knowledge sufficient to make him sensible of the necessity of balancing his government upon general laws, he delegates his full power to all inferior magistrates. This barbarous policy debases the people, and for ever prevents all improvements. Were it possible, that, before science were known in the world, a monarch could possess so much wisdom as to become a legislator, and govern his people by law, not by the arbitrary will of their fellow-subjects, it might be possible for that species of government to be the first nursery of arts and sciences. But that supposition seems scarcely to be consistent or rational.

It may happen, that a republic, in its infant state, may be supported by as few laws as a barbarous monarchy, and may intrust as unlimited an authority to its magistrates or judges. But, besides that the frequent elections by the people are a considerable check upon authority; it is impossible, but in time, the necessity of restraining the magistrates, in order to preserve liberty, must at last appear, and give rise to general laws and statutes. The Roman Consuls, for some time, decided all causes, without being confined by any positive statutes, till the people, bearing this yoke with impatience, created the *decemvirs,* who promulgated the *Twelve Tables;* a body of laws which, though perhaps they were not equal in bulk to one English act of Parliament, were almost the only written rules, which regulated property and punishment, for some ages, in that famous republic. They were, however, sufficient, together with the forms of a free government, to secure the lives and properties of the citizens; to exempt one man from the dominion of another; and to protect every one against the violence or tyranny of his fellow-citizens. In such a situation, the sciences may raise their heads and flourish; but never can have being amidst such a scene of oppression and slavery, as always results from barbarous monarchies, where the people alone are restrained by the authority of the magistrates, and the magistrates are not restrained by any law or statute. An unlimited despotism of this nature, while it exists, effectually puts a stop to all improvements, and keeps men from attaining that knowledge, which is requisite to instruct them in the advantages arising from a better police, and more moderate authority.

Here then are the advantages of free states. Though a republic should be barbarous, it necessarily, by an infallible operation, gives rise to Law, even before mankind have made any considerable advances in the other sciences. From law arises security; from security curiosity; and from curiosity knowledge. The latter steps of this progress may be more accidental; but the former are altogether necessary. A republic without laws can never have any duration. On the contrary, in a monarchical government, law arises not necessarily from the forms of government. Monarchy, when absolute, contains even something repugnant to law. Great wisdom and reflection can alone reconcile them. But such a degree of wisdom can never be expected, before the greater refinements and improvements of human reason. These refinements require curiosity, security, and law. The *first* growth, therefore, of the arts and sciences, can never be expected in despotic governments.[a]

There are other causes, which discourage the rise of the refined arts in despotic governments; though I take the want of laws, and the delegation of full powers to every petty magistrate, to be the principal. Eloquence certainly springs up more naturally in popular governments. Emulation, too, in every accomplishment, must there be more animated and enlivened; and genius and capacity have a fuller scope and career. All these causes render free governments the only proper *nursery* for the arts and sciences.

The next observation which I shall make on this head is, *That nothing is more favorable to the rise of politeness and learning, than a number of neighboring and independent states, connected together by commerce and policy.* The emulation which naturally arises among those neighboring states is an obvious source of improvement. But what I would chiefly insist on is the stop which such limited territories give both to *power* and to *authority.*

Extended governments, where a single person has great influence, soon become absolute; but small ones change naturally into commonwealths. A large government is accustomed by degrees to tyranny, because each act of violence is at first performed upon a part, which, being distant from the majority, is not taken notice of, nor excites any violent ferment. Besides, a large government, though the whole be discontented, may, by a little art, be kept in obedience; while each part, ignorant of the resolutions of the rest, is afraid to begin any commotion or insurrection: not to mention that there is a superstitious reverence for princes, which mankind naturally contract when they do not often see the sovereign, and when many of them become not acquainted with him so as to perceive his weaknesses. And as large states can afford a great expense in order to support the pomp of majesty, this is a kind of fascination on men, and naturally contributes to the enslaving of them.

In a small government any act of oppression is immediately known throughout the whole; the murmurs and discontents proceeding from it are easily communicated; and the indignation arises the higher, because the subjects are not to apprehend, in such states, that the distance is very wide between themselves and their sovereign. "No man," said the Prince of Condé, "is a hero to his *valet de chambre.*" It is certain that admiration and acquaintance are altogether incompatible towards any mortal creature. Sleep and love convinced even Alexander himself that he was not a God. But I suppose that such as daily attended him could easily, from the numberless weaknesses to which he was subject, have given him many still more convincing proofs of his humanity.

But the divisions into small states are favorable to learning, by stopping the progress of *authority* as well as that of *power*. Reputation is often as great a fascination upon men as sovereignty, and is equally destructive to the freedom of thought and examination. But where a number of neighboring states have a great intercourse of arts and commerce, their mutual jealousy keeps them from receiving too lightly the law from each other, in matters of taste and of reasoning, and makes them examine every work of art with the greatest care and accuracy. The contagion of popular opinion spreads not so easily from one place to another. It readily receives a check in some state or other, where it concurs not with the prevailing prejudices. And nothing but nature and reason, or at least what bears them a strong resemblance, can force its way through all obstacles, and unite the most rival nations into an esteem and admiration of it.

Greece was a cluster of little principalities, which soon became republics; and being united both by their near neighborhood, and by the ties of the same language and interest, they entered into the closest intercourse of commerce and learning. There concurred a happy climate, a soil not unfertile, and a most harmonious and comprehensive language; so that every circumstance among that people seemed to favor the rise of the arts and sciences. Each city produced its several artists and philosophers, who refused to yield the preference to those of the neighboring republics; their contention and debates sharpened the wits of men; a variety of objects was presented to the judgment, while each challenged the preference to the rest; and the sciences, not being dwarfed by the restraint of authority, were enabled to make such considerable shoots as are even at this time the objects of our admiration. After the Roman *Christian* or *Catholic* church had spread itself over the civilized world, and had engrossed all the learning of the times, being really one large state within itself, and united under one head, this variety of sects immediately disappeared, and the Peripatetic philosophy was alone admitted into all the schools, to the utter depravation of every kind of learning. But mankind having at length thrown off this yoke, affairs are now returned nearly to the same situation as before, and Europe is at present a copy, at large, of what Greece was formerly a pattern in miniature. We have seen the advantage of this situation in several instances. What checked the progress of the Cartesian philosophy, to which the French nation showed such a strong propensity towards the end of the last century, but the opposition made to it by the other nations of Europe, who soon discovered the weak sides of that philosophy? The severest scrutiny which Newton's theory has undergone proceeded not from his own countrymen, but from foreigners; and if it can overcome the obstacles which it meets with at present in all parts of Europe, it will probably go down triumphant to the latest posterity. The English are become sensible of the scandalous licentiousness of their stage, from the example of the French decency and morals. The French are convinced that their theatre has become somewhat effeminate by too much love and gallantry, and begin to approve of the more masculine taste of some neighboring nations.

In China, there seems to be a pretty considerable stock of politeness and science, which, in the course of so many centuries, might naturally be expected to ripen into something more perfect and finished than what has yet arisen from them. But China is one vast empire, speaking one language, governed by one law, and sympathizing in the same manners. The authority of any teacher, such as Confucius, was propagated easily from one corner of the empire to the other. None had courage to resist the torrent of popular opinion: and posterity was not bold enough to dispute what had been universally received by their ancestors. This seems to be one natural reason why the sciences have made so slow a progress in that mighty empire.[4]

[4] If it be asked how we can reconcile to the foregoing principles the happiness, riches, and good police of the Chinese, who have always been governed by a monarch, and can scarcely form an idea of a free government; I would answer, that though the Chinese government be a pure monarchy, it is not, properly speaking, absolute. This proceeds from a peculiarity in the situation of that country: they have no neighbors, except the Tartars, from whom they were, in some measure, secured, at least

If we consider the face of the globe, Europe, of all the four parts of the world, is the most broken by seas, rivers, and mountains, and Greece of all countries of Europe. Hence these regions were naturally divided into several distinct govern- ments; and hence the sciences arose in Greece, and Europe has been hitherto the most constant habitation of them.

I have sometimes been inclined to think, that interruptions in the periods of learning, were they not attended with such a destruction of ancient books, and the records of history, would be rather favorable to the arts and sciences, by break- ing the progress of authority, and dethroning the tyrannical usurpers over human reason. In this particular, they have the same influence as interruptions in political governments and societies. Consider the blind submission of the ancient philoso- phers to the several masters in each school, and you will be convinced, that little good could be expected from a hundred centuries of such a servile philosophy. Even the Eclectics, who arose about the age of Augustus, notwithstanding their pro- fessing to choose freely what pleased them from every different sect, were yet, in the main, as slavish and dependent as any of their brethren; since they sought for truth, not in Nature, but in the several schools; where they supposed she must neces- sarily be found, though not united in a body, yet dispersed in parts. Upon the revival of learning, those sects of Stoics and Epicureans, Platonists and Pythagoreans, could never regain any credit or authority; and, at the same time, by the example

---

seemed to be secured, by their famous wall, and by the great superiority of their numbers. By this means, military discipline has always been much neglected amongst them: and their standing forces are mere militia of the worst kind, and unfit to suppress any general insurrection in countries so extremely populous. The sword, therefore, may properly be said to be always in the hands of the people; which is a sufficient restraint upon the monarch, and obliges him to lay his *mandarins,* or governors of provinces, under the restraint of general laws, in order to prevent those rebellions which we learn from history to have been so frequent and dangerous in that government. Perhaps a pure monarchy of this kind, were it fitted for defence against foreign enemies, would be the best of all governments, as having both the tranquillity attending kingly power, and the moderation and liberty of popular assemblies.

of their fall, kept men from submitting, with such blind deference, to those new sects, which have attempted to gain an ascendant over them.

The *third* observation, which I shall form on this head, of the rise and progress of the arts and sciences, is, *That, though the only proper nursery of these noble plants be a free state, yet may they be transplanted into any government; and that a republic is most favorable to the growth of the sciences, and a civilized monarchy to that of the polite arts.*

To balance a large state or society, whether monarchical or republican, on general laws, is a work of so great difficulty, that no human genius, however comprehensive, is able, by the mere dint of reason and reflection, to effect it. The judgments of many must unite in this work: experience must guide their labor: time must bring it to perfection: and the feeling of inconveniences must correct the mistakes, which they inevitably fall into, in their first trials and experiments. Hence appears the impossibility that this undertaking should be begun and carried on in any monarchy; since such a form of government, ere civilized, knows no other secret or policy, than that of intrusting unlimited powers to every governor or magistrate, and subdividing the people into so many classes and orders of slavery. From such a situation, no improvement can ever be expected in the sciences, in the liberal arts, in laws, and scarcely in the manual arts and manufactures. The same barbarism and ignorance, with which the government commences, is propagated to all posterity, and can never come to a period by the efforts or ingenuity of such unhappy slaves.

But though law, the source of all security and happiness, arises late in any government, and is the slow product of order and of liberty, it is not preserved with the same difficulty with which it is produced; but when it has once taken root, is a hardy plant, which will scarcely ever perish through the ill culture of men, or the rigor of the seasons. The arts of luxury, and much more the liberal arts, which depend on a refined taste or sentiment, are easily lost; because they are always relished by a few only, whose leisure, fortune, and genius, fit them for such amusements. But what is profitable to every mortal, and in common life, when once discovered, can scarcely fall into oblivion, but by the total subversion of society, and by such furious inundations of barbarous invaders, as obliterate all memory of former arts and civility. Imitation also is apt to transport these coarser and more useful arts from one climate to another, and to make them precede the refined arts in their progress; though, perhaps, they sprang after them in their first rise and propagation. From these causes proceed civilized monarchies, where the arts of government, first invented in free states, are preserved to the mutual advantage and security of sovereign and subject.

However perfect, therefore, the monarchical form may appear to some politicians, it owes all its perfection to the republican; nor is it possible that a pure despotism, established among a barbarous people, can ever, by its native force and energy, refine and polish itself. It must borrow its laws, and methods, and institutions, and consequently its stability and order, from free governments. These advantages are the sole growth of republics. The extensive despotism of a barbarous monarchy, by entering into the detail of the government, as well as into the principal points of administration, for ever prevents all such improvements.

In a civilized monarchy, the prince alone is unrestrained in the exercise of his authority, and possesses alone a power, which is not bounded by any thing but custom, example, and the sense of his own interest. Every minister or magistrate, however eminent, must submit to the general laws which govern the whole society, and must exert the authority delegated to him after the manner which is prescribed. The people depend on none but their sovereign for the security of their property. He is so far removed from them, and is so much exempt from private jealousies or interests, that this dependence is scarcely felt. And thus a species of government arises, to which, in a high political rant, we may give the name of *Tyranny*, but which, by a just and prudent administration, may afford tolerable security to the people, and may answer most of the ends of political society.

But though in a civilized monarchy, as well as in a republic, the people have security for the enjoyment of their property, yet in both these forms of government, those who possess the supreme authority have the disposal of many honors and advantages, which excite the ambition and avarice of mankind. The only difference is, that, in a republic, the candidates for office must look downwards to gain the suffrages of the people; in a monarchy, they must turn their attention upwards, to court the good graces and favor of the great. To be successful in the former way, it is necessary for a man to make himself *useful* by his industry, capacity, or knowledge: to be prosperous in the latter way, it is requisite for him to render himself *agreeable* by his wit, complaisance, or civility. A strong genius succeeds best in republics; a refined taste in monarchies. And, consequently, the sciences are the more natural growth of the one, and the polite arts of the other.

Not to mention, that monarchies, receiving their chief stability from a superstitious reverence to priests and princes, have commonly abridged the liberty of reasoning, with regard to religion and politics, and consequently metaphysics and morals. All these form the most considerable branches of science. Mathematics and natural philosophy, which only remain, are not half so valuable.[b]

Among the arts of conversation, no one pleases more than mutual deference or civility, which leads us to resign our own inclinations to those of our companion, and to curb and conceal that presumption and arrogance so natural to the human mind. A good-natured man, who is well educated, practises this civility to every mortal, without premeditation or interest. But in order to render that valuable quality general among any people, it seems necessary to assist the natural disposition by some general motive. Where power rises upwards from the people to the great, as in all republics, such refinements of civility are apt to be little practised, since the whole state is, by that means, brought near to a level, and every member of it is rendered, in a great measure, independent of another. The people have the advantage, by the authority of their suffrages; the great by the superiority of their station. But in a civilized monarchy, there is a long train of dependence from the prince to the peasant, which is not great enough to render property precarious; or depress the minds of the people; but is sufficient to beget in every one an inclination to please his superiors, and to form himself upon those models which are most acceptable to people of condition and education. Politeness of manners, therefore, arises most naturally in monarchies and courts; and where that flourishes, none of the liberal arts will be altogether neglected or despised.

The republics in Europe are at present noted for want of politeness. *The good manners of a Swiss civilized in Holland,*[5] is an expression for rusticity among the French. The English, in some degree, fall under the same censure, notwithstanding their learning and genius. And if the Venetians be an exception to the rule, they owe it, perhaps, to their communication with the other Italians, most of whose governments beget a dependence more than sufficient for civilizing their manners.

It is difficult to pronounce any judgment concerning the refinements of the ancient republics in this particular: but I am apt to suspect, that the arts of conversation were not brought so near to perfection among them as the arts of writing and composition. The scurrility of the ancient orators, in many instances, is quite shocking, and exceeds all belief. Vanity, too, is often not a little offensive in authors of those ages; [6] as well as the common licentiousness and immodesty of their style. *Quicunque impudicus, aduller, ganeo, manu, ventre, pene, bona patria laceraverat,* says Sallust,[7] in one of the gravest and most moral passages of his history. *Nam fuit ante Helenam*

---

[5] C'est la politesse d'un Suisse

En Hollande civilisé.   —Rousseau.

[6] It is needless to cite Cicero or Pliny on this head: they are too much noted. But one is a little surprised to find Arrian, a very grave, judicious writer, interrupt the thread of his narration all of a sudden, to tell his readers that he himself is as eminent among the Greeks for eloquence, as Alexander was for arms. [*Anabasis* I. 12. 5.]

[7] ["Whatever wanton, glutton, or gamester had wasted his patrimony in play, feasting, or debauchery. . . ." *The War With Catiline* XIV. 2, tr. J. C. Rolfe, "Loeb Classical Library" (Cambridge, Mass.: Cambridge University Press, 1960.]

Cunnus, teterrima belli causa, is an expression of Horace,[8] in tracing the origin of moral good and evil. Ovid and Lucretius [9] are almost as licentious in their style as Lord Rochester; though the former were fine gentlemen and delicate writers, and the latter, from the corruptions of that court in which he lived, seems to have thrown off all regard to shame and decency. Juvenal inculcates modesty with great zeal; but sets a very bad example of it, if we consider the impudence of his expressions.

I shall also be bold to affirm, that among the ancients, there was not much delicacy of breeding, or that polite deference and respect, which civility obliges us either to express or counterfeit towards the persons with whom we converse. Cicero was certainly one of the finest gentlemen of his age; yet, I must confess, I have frequently been shocked with the poor figure under which he represents his friend Atticus, in those dialogues where he himself is introduced as a speaker. That learned and virtuous Roman, whose dignity, though he was only a private gentleman, was inferior to that of no one in Rome, is there shown in rather a more pitiful light than Philalethes's friend in our modern dialogues. He is a humble admirer of the orator, pays him frequent compliments, and receives his instructions, with all the deference which a scholar owes to his master.[10] Even Cato is treated in somewhat of a cavalier manner in the dialogues *De Finibus.*[c]

[8] ["For before Helen's day a wench was the most dreadful cause of war." *Satires* I. 3. 107, tr. H. R. Fairclough (Cambridge, Mass.: "Loeb Classical Library," 1961).]

[9] This poet (see IV. 1175) recommends a very extraordinary cure for love, and what one expects not to meet with in so elegant and philosophical a poem. It seems to have been the original of some of Dr. Swift's images. The elegant Catullus and Phaedrus fall under the same censure.

[10] ATT. Non mihi videtur ad beate vivendum satis esse virtutem. MAR. At hercule Bruto meo videtur; enjus ego judicium, pace tua dixerim, longe antepono tuo. ["*A.* It does not seem to me that virtue can be sufficient for leading a happy life. *M.* But, I can asure you, my friend Brutus thinks it sufficient and with your permission I put his judgment far above yours." *Tusculan Disputations* V. 4, 12, tr. J. E. King, "Loeb Classical Library" (Cambridge, Mass.: Cambridge University Press, 1960).]

One of the most particular details of a real dialogue, which we meet with in antiquity, is related by Polybius; [11] when Philip king of Macedon, a prince of wit and parts, met with Titus Flamininus, one of the politest of the Romans, as we learn from Plutarch, accompanied with ambassadors from almost all the Greek cities. The Ætolian ambassador very abruptly tells the king, that he talked like a fool or madman (λῃρεῖν). "That's evident (says his Majesty), even to a blind man;" which was a raillery on the blindness of his excellency. Yet all this did not pass the usual bounds: for the conference was not disturbed; and Flamininus was very well diverted with these strokes of humor. At the end, when Philip craved a little time to consult with his friends, of whom he had none present, the Roman general, being desirous also to show his wit, as the historian says, tells him, "That perhaps the reason why he had none of his friends with him, was because he had murdered them all;" which was actually the case. This unprovoked piece of rusticity is not condemned by the historian; caused no further resentment in Philip than to excite a Sardonian smile, or what we call a grin; and hindered him not from renewing the conference next day. Plutarch,[12] too, mentions this raillery amongst the witty and agreeable sayings of Flamininus.

Cardinal Wolsey apologized for his famous piece of insolence, in saying, EGO ET REX MEUS, *I and my king,* by observing, that this expression was conformable to the *Latin* idiom, and that a Roman always named himself before the person to whom, or of whom, he spake. Yet this seems to have been an instance of want of civility among that people. The ancients made it a rule, that the person of the greatest dignity should be mentioned first in the discourse; insomuch, that we find the spring of a quarrel and jealousy between the Romans and Ætolians, to have been a poet's naming the Ætolians before the Romans in celebrating a victory gained by their united

11 [XVIII. 7.]
12 [*Titus Flamininus* XVII. 2.]

arms over the Macedonians.[13] Thus Livia disgusted Tiberius by placing her own name before his in an inscription.[14]

No advantages in this world are pure and unmixed. In like manner, as modern politeness, which is naturally so ornamental, runs often into affectation and foppery, disguise and insincerity; so the ancient simplicity, which is naturally so amiable and affecting, often degenerates into rusticity and abuse, scurrility and obscenity.

If the superiority in politeness should be allowed to modern times, the modern notions of *gallantry*, the natural produce of courts and monarchies, will probably be assigned as the causes of this refinement. No one denies this invention to be modern: [15] but some of the more zealous partisans of the ancients have asserted it to be foppish and ridiculous, and a reproach, rather than a credit, to the present age.[16] It may here be proper to examine this question.

Nature has implanted in all living creatures an affection between the sexes, which, even in the fiercest and most rapacious animals, is not merely confined to the satisfaction of the bodily appetite, but begets a friendship and mutual sympathy, which runs through the whole tenor of their lives. Nay, even in those species, where nature limits the indulgence of this appetite to one season and to one object, and forms a kind of marriage or association between a single male and female, there is yet a visible complacency and benevolence, which extends further, and mutually softens the affections of the sexes towards each other. How much more must this have place in man, where the confinement of the appetite is not natural, but either is derived accidentally from some strong charm of love, or arises from reflections on duty and convenience! Nothing, therefore, can proceed less from affectation than the passion of

13 [Plutarch, *Titus Flamininus* IX. 1–2.]

14 Tacitus, *The Annals* III. 64.

15 In the *Self-Tormentor* of Terence, Clinias, whenever he comes to town, instead of waiting on his mistress, sends for her to come to him.

16 Lord Shaftesbury. See his *Moralists*. [Anthony Ashley Cooper, Earl of Shaftesbury, author of *An Inquiry concerning Virtue or Merit*.]

gallantry. It is *natural* in the highest degree. Art and education, in the most elegant courts, make no more alteration on
it than on all the other laudable passions. They only turn the
mind more towards it; they refine it; they polish it; and give
it a proper grace and expression.

But gallantry is as *generous* as it is *natural*. To correct such
gross vices as lead us to commit real injury on others, is the
part of morals, and the object of the most ordinary education.
Where *that* is not attended to in some degree, no human society can subsist. But, in order to render conversation, and
the intercourse of minds more easy and agreeable, good manners have been invented, and have carried the matter somewhat further. Wherever nature has given the mind a propensity to any vice, or to any passion disagreeable to others, refined breeding has taught men to throw the bias on the opposite side, and to preserve, in all their behavior, the appearance
of sentiments different from those to which they naturally incline. Thus, as we are commonly proud and selfish, and apt
to assume the preference above others, a polite man learns to
behave with deference towards his companions, and to yield
the superiority to them in all the common incidents of society.
In like manner, wherever a person's situation may naturally
beget any disagreeable suspicion in him, it is the part of good
manners to prevent it, by a studied display of sentiments, directly contrary to those of which he is apt to be jealous. Thus,
old men know their infirmities, and naturally dread contempt
from the youth: hence well-educated youth redouble the instances of respect and deference to their elders. Strangers and
foreigners are without protection: hence, in all polite countries, they receive the highest civilities, and are entitled to the
first place in every company. A man is lord in his own family;
and his guests are, in a manner, subject to his authority: hence,
he is always the lowest person in the company, attentive to
the wants of every one, and giving himself all the trouble in
order to please, which may not betray too visible an affecta-

tion, or impose too much constraint on his guests.[17] Gallantry is nothing but an instance of the same generous attention. As nature has given *man* the superiority above *woman*, by endowing him with greater strength both of mind and body, it is his part to alleviate that superiority, as much as possible, by the generosity of his behavior, and by a studied deference and complaisance for all her inclinations and opinions. Barbarous nations display this superiority, by reducing their females to the most abject slavery; by confining them, by beating them, by selling them, by killing them. But the male sex, among a polite people, discover their authority in a more generous, though not a less evident manner; by civility, by respect, by complaisance, and, in a word, by gallantry. In good company, you need not ask, who is the master of the feast? The man who sits in the lowest place, and who is always industrious in helping every one, is certainly the person. We must either condemn all such instances of generosity as foppish and affected, or admit of gallantry among the rest. The ancient Muscovites wedded their wives with a whip, instead of a ring. The same people, in their own houses, took always the precedency above foreigners, even foreign ambassadors.[18] These two instances of their generosity and politeness are much of a piece.

Gallantry is not less compatible with *wisdom* and *prudence*, than with *nature* and *generosity*; and, when under proper regulations, contributes more than any other invention to the *entertainment* and *improvement* of the youth of both sexes. Among every species of animals, nature has founded on the love between the sexes their sweetest and best enjoyment. But the satisfaction of the bodily appetite is not alone sufficient to gratify the mind; and, even among brute creatures, we find

[17] The frequent mention in ancient authors of that illbred custom of the master of the family's eating better bread, or drinking better wine at table, than he afforded his guests, is but an indifferent mark of the civility of those ages. See Juvenal, Satire V; Pliny, XIV. 13; also Pliny's *Letters*, Lucian's *De Mercede conductis, Saturnalia*, etc. There is scarcely any part of Europe at present so uncivilized as to admit of such a custom.
[18] See *Relation of Three Embassies*, by the Earl of Carlisle.

that their play and dalliance, and other expressions of fond-
ness, form the greatest part of the entertainment. In rational
beings, we must certainly admit the mind for a considerable
share. Were we to rob the feast of all its garniture of reason,
discourse, sympathy, friendship, and gaiety, what remains
would scarcely be worth acceptance, in the judgment of the
truly elegant and luxurious.

What better school for manners than the company of virtuous women, where the mutual endeavor to please must insensibly polish the mind, where the example of the female softness and modesty must communicate itself to their admirers,
and where the delicacy of that sex puts every one on his guard,
lest he give offence by any breach of decency? [d]

Among the ancients, the character of the fair sex was considered as altogether domestic; nor were they regarded as part of
the polite world, or of good company. This, perhaps, is the
true reason why the ancients have not left us one piece of
pleasantry that is excellent (unless one may except the Banquet of Xenophon, and the Dialogues of Lucian), though
many of their serious compositions are altogether inimitable.
Horace condemns the coarse railleries and cold jests of
Plautus: but, though the most easy, agreeable, and judicious
writer in the world, is his own talent for ridicule very striking
or refined? This, therefore, is one considerable improvement
which the polite arts have received from gallantry, and from
courts where it first arose. [e]

But to return from this digression, I shall advance it as a
fourth observation on this subject, of the rise and progress of
the arts and sciences, *That when the arts and sciences come to
perfection in any state, from that moment they naturally, or
rather necessarily, decline, and seldom or never revive in that
nation where they formerly flourished.*

It must be confessed, that this maxim, though conformable
to experience, may at first sight be esteemed contrary to reason. If the natural genius of mankind be the same in all ages,
and in almost all countries (as seems to be the truth), it must
very much forward and cultivate this genius, to be possessed

of patterns in every art, which may regulate the taste, and fix the objects of imitation. The models left us by the ancients gave birth to all the arts about two hundred years ago, and have mightily advanced their progress in every country of Europe. Why had they not a like effect during the reign of Trajan and his successors, when they were much more entire, and were still admired and studied by the whole world? So late as the emperor Justinian, the Poet, by way of distinction, was understood, among the Greeks, to be Homer; among the Romans, Virgil. Such admirations still remained for these divine geniuses; though no poet had appeared for many centuries, who could justly pretend to have imitated them.

A man's genius is always, in the beginning of life, as much unknown to himself as to others; and it is only after frequent trials, attended with success, that he dares think himself equal to those undertakings, in which those who have succeeded have fixed the admiration of mankind. If his own nation be already possessed of many models of eloquence, he naturally compares his own juvenile exercises with these; and, being sensible of the great disproportion, is discouraged from any further attempts, and never aims at a rivalship with those authors whom he so much admires. A noble emulation is the source of every excellence. Admiration and modesty naturally extinguish this emulation; and no one is so liable to an excess of admiration and modesty as a truly great genius.

Next to emulation, the greatest encourager of the noble arts is praise and glory. A writer is animated with new force when he hears the applauses of the world for his former productions; and, being roused by such a motive, he often reaches a pitch of perfection, which is equally surprising to himself and to his readers. But when the posts of honor are all occupied, his first attempts are but coldly received by the public; being compared to productions which are both in themselves more excellent, and have already the advantage of an established reputation. Were Moliere and Corneille to bring upon the stage at present their early productions, which were formerly so well received, it would discourage the young poets to see

the indifference and disdain of the public. The ignorance of
the age alone could have given admission to the *Prince of Tyre;*
but it is to that we owe the *Moor.*[19] Had *Every Man in his
Humor* been rejected, we had never seen *Volpone.*[20]

Perhaps it may not be for the advantage of any nation to
have the arts imported from their neighbors in too great perfection. This extinguishes emulation, and sinks the ardor of
the generous youth. So many models of Italian painting
brought to England, instead of exciting our artists, is the cause
of their small progress in that noble art. The same, perhaps,
was the case of Rome when it received the arts from Greece.
That multitude of polite productions in the French language,
dispersed all over Germany and the North, hinder these nations from cultivating their own language, and keep them still
dependent on their neighbors for those elegant entertainments.

It is true, the ancients had left us models in every kind of
writing, which are highly worthy of admiration. But besides
that they were written in languages known only to the learned;
besides this, I say, the comparison is not so perfect or entire between modern wits, and those who lived in so remote an age.
Had Waller been born in Rome, during the reign of Tiberius,
his first productions had been despised, when compared to
the finished odes of Horace. But in this Island, the superiority
of the Roman poet diminished nothing from the fame of the
English. We esteemed ourselves sufficiently happy that our
climate and language could produce but a faint copy of so
excellent an original.

In short, the arts and sciences, like some plants, require a
fresh soil; and however rich the land may be, and however you
may recruit it by art or care, it will never, when once exhausted, produce any thing that is perfect or finished in the
kind.

19 [Hume refers to Shakespeare's *Pericles, Prince of Tyre* and his
Othello.]

20 [*Every Man in His Humor* (1598) was Ben Jonson's first play; *Volpone or the Fox* (1606), one of his most famous.]

Of the Study of History [a]

THERE is nothing which I would recommend more earnestly to my female readers than the study of history, as an occupation, of all others, the best suited both to their sex and education, much more instructive than their ordinary books of amusement, and more entertaining than those serious compositions, which are usually to be found in their closets. Among other important truths, which they may learn from history, they may be informed of two particulars, the knowledge of which may contribute very much to their quiet and repose. That our sex, as well as theirs, are far from being such perfect creatures as they are apt to imagine, and that Love is not the only passion which governs the male world, but is often overcome by avarice, ambition, vanity, and a thousand other passions. Whether they be the false representations of mankind in those two particulars, which endear novels and romances so much to the fair sex, I know not; but must confess, that I am sorry to see them have such an aversion to matter of fact, and such an appetite for falsehood. I remember I was once desired by a young beauty, for whom I had some passion, to send her some novels and romances for her amusement to the country; but was not so ungenerous as to take the advantage, which such a course of reading might have given me, being resolved not to make use of poisoned arms against her. I therefore sent her Plutarch's Lives, assuring her, at the same time, that there was not a word of truth in them from beginning to end. She perused them very attentively, till she came to the lives of Alexander and Caesar, whose names she had heard of by accident, and then returned me the book, with many reproaches for deceiving her.

I may, indeed, be told, that the fair sex have no such aversion to history as I have represented, provided it be *secret* history, and contain some memorable transaction proper to excite their curiosity. But as I do not find that truth, which is the basis of history, is at all regarded in these anecdotes, I cannot admit of this as a proof of their passion for that study. However this may be, I see not why the same curiosity might not receive a more proper direction, and lead them to desire accounts of those who lived in past ages, as well as of their contemporaries. What is it to Cleora, whether Fulvia entertains a secret commerce of love with Philander, or not? Has she not equal reason to be pleased, when she is informed (what is whispered about among historians) that Cato's sister had an intrigue with Caesar, and palmed her son, Marcus Brutus, upon her husband for his own, though in reality he was her gallant's? And are not the loves of Messalina or Julia as proper subjects of discourse as any intrigue that this city has produced of late years?

But I know not whence it comes that I have been thus seduced into a kind of raillery against the ladies; unless, perhaps, it proceed from the same cause, which makes the person, who is the favorite of the company, be often the object of their good-natured jests and pleasantries. We are pleased to address ourselves after any manner to one who is agreeable to us, and at the same time presume, that nothing will be taken amiss by a person, who is secure of the good opinion and affections of every one present. I shall now proceed to handle my subject more seriously, and shall point out the many advantages, which flow from the study of history, and show how well suited it is to every one, but particularly to those who are debarred the severer studies, by the tenderness of their complexion, and the weakness of their education. The advantages found in history seem to be of three kinds, as it amuses the fancy, as it improves the understanding, and as it strengthens virtue.

In reality, what more agreeable entertainment to the mind, than to be transported into the remotest ages of the world, and to observe human society, in its infancy, making the first faint essays towards the arts and sciences; to see the policy of government, and the civility of conversation refining by degrees, and every thing which is ornamental to human life advancing toward its perfection? To remark the rise, progress, declension, and final extinction of the most flourishing empires; the virtues which contributed to their greatness, and the vices which drew on their ruin? In short, to see all the human race, from the beginning of time, pass, as it were, in review before us, appearing in their true colors, without any of those disguises which, during their lifetime, so much perplexed the judgment of the beholders. What spectacle can be imagined so magnificent, so various, so interesting? What amusement, either of the senses or imagination, can be compared with it? Shall those trifling pastimes, which engross so much of our time, be preferred as more satisfactory, and more fit to engage our attention? How perverse must that taste be which is capable of so wrong a choice of pleasures?

But history is a most improving part of knowledge, as well as an agreeable amusement; and a great part of what we commonly call erudition, and value so highly, is nothing but an acquaintance with historical facts. An extensive knowledge of this kind belongs to men of letters; but I must think it an unpardonable ignorance in persons, of whatever sex or condition, not to be acquainted with the history of their own country, together with the histories of ancient Greece and Rome. A woman may behave herself with good manners, and have even some vivacity in her turn of wit; but where her mind is so unfurnished, it is impossible her conversation can afford any entertainment to men of sense and reflection.

I must add, that history is not only a valuable part of knowledge, but opens the door to many other parts, and affords materials to most of the sciences. And, indeed, if we consider the shortness of human life, and our limited knowledge, even of what passes in our own time, we must be sensible that we should be for ever children in understanding, were it not for this invention, which extends our experience to all past ages, and to the most distant nations; making them contribute as much to our improvement in wisdom, as if they had actually lain under our observation. A man acquainted with history may, in some respect, be said to have lived from the beginning of the world, and to have been making continual additions to his stock of knowledge in every century.

There is also an advantage in that experience, which is acquired by history, above what is learned by the practice of the world, that it brings us acquainted with human affairs, without diminishing in the least from the most delicate sentiments of virtue. And to tell the truth, I know not any study or occupation so unexceptionable as history in this particular. Poets can paint virtue in the most charming colors; but as they address themselves entirely to the passions, they often become advocates for vice. Even philosophers are apt to bewilder themselves in the subtilty of their speculations; and we have seen some go so far as to deny the reality of all moral distinctions. But I think it a remark worthy the attention of the speculative, that the historians have been, almost without exception, the true friends of virtue, and have always represented it in its proper colors, however they may have erred in their judgments of particular persons. Machiavel himself discovers a true sentiment of virtue in his history of Florence. When he talks as a politician, in his general reasonings, he considers poisoning, assassination, and perjury, as lawful arts of power; but when he speaks as an historian, in his particular narrations, he shows so keen an indignation against vice, and so warm an approbation of virtue in many passages, that I could not forbear applying to him that remark of Horace, that if you chase away Nature, though with ever so great indignity, she will always return upon you. Nor is this combination of historians in favor of virtue, at all difficult to be accounted for. When a man of business enters into life and action, he is more apt to consider the characters of men, as they have relation to his interest, than as they stand in themselves; and has his judgment warped on every occasion by the violence of his passion. When a philosopher contemplates characters and manners in his closet, the general abstract view of the objects leaves the mind so cold and unmoved, that the sentiments of nature have no room to play, and he scarce feels the difference between vice and virtue. History keeps in a just medium between these extremes, and places the objects in their true point of view. The writers of history, as well as the readers, are sufficiently interested in the characters and events, to have a lively sentiment of blame or praise: and, at the same time, have no particular interest or concern to pervert their judgment.

> Vero voces tum demum pectore ab imo
> Eliciuntur.
>
> Lucretius [1]

---

1 ["For only then true words are drawn from his inmost heart." Lucretius, *On Nature,* tr. Russel M. Geer, "The Library of Liberal Arts" (New York: Liberal Arts Press, 1965).]

The Epicurean[1]

IT is a great mortification to the vanity of man, that his utmost art and industry can never equal the meanest of Nature's productions, either for beauty or value. Art is only the under-workman, and is employed to give a few strokes of embellishment to those pieces which come from the hand of the master. Some of the drapery may be of his drawing, but he is not allowed to touch the principal figure. Art may make a suit of clothes, but Nature must produce a man.

Even in those productions commonly denominated works of art, we find that the noblest of the kind are beholden for their chief beauty to the force and happy influence of nature. To the native enthusiasm of the poets we owe whatever is admirable in their productions. The greatest genius, where nature at any time fails him (for she is not equal), throws aside the lyre, and hopes not, from the rules of art, to reach that divine harmony which must proceed from her inspiration alone. How poor are those songs where a happy flow of fancy has not furnished materials for art to embellish and refine!

But of all the fruitless attempts of art, no one is so ridiculous as that which the severe philosophers have undertaken, the producing of an *artificial happiness,* and making us be pleased by rules of reason and by reflection. Why did none of them claim the reward which Xerxes promised to him who should invent a new pleasure? Unless, perhaps, they invented so many pleasures for their own use, that they despised riches, and stood in no need of any enjoyments which the rewards of

[1] Or, *The man of elegance and pleasure*. The intention of this and the three following Essays, is not so much to explain accurately the sentiments of the ancient sects of philosophy, as to deliver the sentiments of sects that naturally form themselves in the world, and entertain different ideas of human life and happiness. I have given each of them the name of the philosophical sect to which it bears the greatest affinity.

that monarch could produce them. I am apt, indeed, to think, that they were not willing to furnish the Persian court with a new pleasure, by presenting it with so new and unusual an object of ridicule. Their speculations, when confined to theory, and gravely delivered in the schools of Greece, might excite admiration in their ignorant pupils; but the attempting to reduce such principles to practice would soon have betrayed their absurdity.

You pretend to make me happy, by reason and by rules of art. You must then create me anew by rules of art, for on my original frame and structure does my happiness depend. But you want power to effect this, and skill too, I am afraid; nor can I entertain a less opinion of Nature's wisdom than yours; and let her conduct the machine which she has so wisely framed; I find that I should only spoil it by tampering.

To what purpose should I pretend to regulate, refine, or invigorate any of those springs or principles which nature has implanted in me? Is this the road by which I must reach happiness? But happiness implies ease, contentment, repose, and pleasure; not watchfulness, care, and fatigue. The health of my body consists in the facilty with which all its operations are performed. The stomach digests the aliments; the heart circulates the blood; the brain separates and refines the spirits: and all this without my concerning myself in the matter. When by my will alone I can stop the blood, as it runs with impetuosity along its canals, then may I hope to change the course of my sentiments and passions. In vain should I strain my faculties, and endeavor to receive pleasure from an object which is not fitted by nature to affect my organs with delight. I may give myself pain by my fruitless endeavors, but shall never reach any pleasure.

Away then with all those vain pretences of making ourselves happy within ourselves, of feasting on our own thoughts, of being satisfied with the consciousness of well-doing, and of despising all assistance and all supplies from external objects. This is the voice of pride, not of nature. And it were well if even this pride could support itself, and communicate a real *inward* pleasure, however melancholy or severe. But this impotent pride can do no more than regulate the *outside,* and, with infinite pains and attention, compose the language and countenance to a philosophical dignity, in order to deceive the ignorant vulgar. The heart, meanwhile, is empty of all enjoyment, and the mind, unsupported by its proper objects, sinks into the deepest sorrow and dejection. Miserable, but vain mortal! Thy mind be happy within itself! With what resources is it endowed to fill so immense a void, and supply the place of all thy bodily senses and faculties? Can thy head subsist without thy other members? In such a situation,

> What foolish figure must it make?
> Do nothing else but sleep and ake.

In such a lethargy, or such a melancholy, must thy mind be plunged, when deprived of foreign occupations and enjoyments.

Keep me, therefore, no longer in this violent constraint. Confine me not within myself, but point out to me those objects and pleasures which afford the chief enjoyment. But why do I apply to you, proud and ignorant sages, to show me the road to happiness? Let me consult my own passions and inclinations. In them must I read the dictates of nature, not in your frivolous discourses.

But see, propitious to my wishes, the divine, the amiable PLEASURE,[2] the supreme love of GODS and men, advances towards me. At her approach my heart beats with genial heat, and every sense and every faculty is dissolved in joy, while she pours around me all the embellishments of the spring, and all the treasures of the autumn. The melody of her voice charms my ears with the softest music, as she invites me to partake of those delicious fruits, which, with a smile that diffuses a glory on the heavens and the earth, she presents to me. The sportive cupids who attend her, or fan me with their odoriferous wings, or pour on my head the most fragrant oils, or offer me their sparkling nectar in golden goblets; O! for ever let me spread

---

2 Dia Voluptas. [Lucretius, *On Nature,* II. 172.]

my limbs on this bed of roses, and thus, thus feel the delicious moments, with soft and downy steps, glide along. But cruel chance! Whither do you fly so fast? Why do my ardent wishes, and that load of pleasures under which you labor, rather hasten than retard your unrelenting pace? Suffer me to enjoy this soft repose, after all my fatigues in search of happiness. Suffer me to satiate myself with these delicacies, after the pains of so long and so foolish an abstinence.

But it will not do. The roses have lost their hue, the fruit its flavor, and that delicious wine, whose fumes so late intoxicated all my senses with such delight, now solicits in vain the sated palate. *Pleasure* smiles at my languor. She beckons her sister, *Virtue,* to come to her assistance. The gay, the frolic *Virtue,* observes the call, and brings along the whole troop of my jovial friends. Welcome, thrice welcome, my ever dear companions, to these shady bowers, and to this luxurious repast. Your presence has restored to the rose its hue, and to the fruit its flavor. The vapors of this sprightly nectar now again ply round my heart; while you partake of my delights, and discover, in your cheerful looks, the pleasure which you receive from my happiness and satisfaction. The like do I receive from yours; and, encouraged by your joyous presence, shall again renew the feast, with which, from too much enjoyment, my senses are wellnigh sated, while the mind kept not pace with the body, nor afforded relief to her overburdened partner.

In our cheerful discourses, better than in the formal reasoning of the schools, is true wisdom to be found. In our friendly endearments, better than in the hollow debates of statesmen and pretended patriots, does true virtue display itself. Forgetful of the past, secure of the future, let us here enjoy the present; and while we yet possess a being, let us fix some good, beyond the power of fate or fortune. To-morrow will bring its own pleasures along with it: or, should it disappoint our fond wishes, we shall at least enjoy the pleasure of reflecting on the pleasures of today.

Fear not, my friends, that the barbarous dissonance of Bacchus, and of his revellers should break in upon this entertainment, and confound us with their turbulent and clamorous pleasures. The sprightly Muses wait around, and, with their charming symphony, sufficient to soften the wolves and tigers of the savage desert, inspire a soft joy into every bosom. Peace, harmony, and concord, reign in this retreat; nor is the silence ever broken but by the music of our songs, or the cheerful accents of our friendly voices.

But hark! the favorite of the Muses, the gentle Damon [3] strikes the lyre; and, while he accompanies its harmonious notes with his more harmonious song, he inspires us with the same happy debauch of fancy by which he is himself transported. "Ye happy youth!" he sings, "Ye favored of Heaven! [4] while the wanton spring pours upon you all her blooming honors, let not *glory* seduce you with her delusive blaze, to pass in perils and dangers this delicious season, this prime of life. Wisdom points out to you the road to pleasure: Nature, too, beckons you to follow her in that smooth and flowery path. Will you shut your ears to their commanding voice? Will you harden your heart to their soft allurements? Oh, deluded mortals! thus to lose your youth, thus to throw away so invaluable a present, to trifle with so perishing a blessing. Contemplate well your recompense. Consider that glory, which so allures your proud hearts, and seduces you with your own praises. It is an echo, a dream, nay the shadow of a dream, dissipated by every wind, and lost by every contrary breath of the ignorant and ill-judging multitude. You fear not that even death itself shall ravish it from you. But behold! while you are yet alive, calumny bereaves you of it; ignorance neglects it; nature enjoys it not; fancy alone, renouncing every pleasure, receives this airy recompense, empty and unstable as herself."

[3] [The name of a goatherd in Virgil's *Eclogues*, hence used by pastoral poets for country youths.]

[4] An imitation of the Syren's song in Tasso:—

"O Giovenetti, mentre Aprile et Maggio
V'ammantan di fiorite et verde spoglie," etc.

Gerusalemme Liberata, XIV, 489–90.

Thus the hours pass unperceived along, and lead in their
wanton train all the pleasures of sense, and all the joys of harmony and friendship. Smiling *Innocence* closes the procession;
and, while she presents herself to our ravished eyes, she embellishes the whole scene, and renders the view of these pleasures as transporting after they have passed us, as when, with
laughing countenances, they were yet advancing towards us.

But the sun has sunk below the horizon; and darkness, steal-
ing silently upon us, has now buried all nature in an universal
shade. "Rejoice, my friends, continue your repast, or change
it for soft repose. Though absent, your joy or your tranquillity
shall still be mine." *But whither do you go? Or what new
pleasures call you from our society? Is there aught agreeable
without your friends? And can aught please in which we partake not?* "Yes, my friends, the joy which I now seek admits
not of your participation. Here alone I wish your absence:
and here alone can I find a sufficient compensation for the
loss of your society."

But I have not advanced far through the shades of the thick
wood, which spreads a double night around me, ere, methinks,
I perceive through the gloom the charming Cælia, the mistress
of my wishes, who wanders impatient through the grove, and,
preventing the appointed hour, silently chides my tardy steps.
But the joy which she receives from my presence best pleads
my excuse, and, dissipating every anxious and every angry
thought, leaves room for nought but mutual joy and rapture.
With what words, my fair one, shall I express my tenderness,
or describe the emotions which now warm my transported
bosom! Words are too faint to describe my love; and if, alas!
you feel not the same flame within you, in vain shall I endeavor to convey to you a just conception of it. But your every
word and every motion suffice to remove this doubt; and while
they express your passion, serve also to inflame mine. How
amiable this solitude, this silence, this darkness! No objects
now importune the ravished soul. The thought, the sense, all
full of nothing but our mutual happiness, wholly possess the

mind, and convey a pleasure which deluded mortals vainly seek for in every other enjoyment.————

But why does your bosom heave with these sighs, while tears bathe your glowing cheeks? Why distract your heart with such vain anxieties? Why so often ask me, *How long my love shall yet endure?* Alas! my Cælia, can I resolve this question? *Do I know how long my life shall yet endure?* But does this also disturb your tender breast? And is the image of our frail mortality for ever present with you, to throw a damp on your gayest hours, and poison even those joys which love inspires? Consider rather, that if life be frail, if youth be transitory, we should well employ the present moment, and lose no part of so perishable an existence. Yet a little moment, and *these* shall be no more. We shall be as if we had never been. Not a memory of us be left upon earth; and even the fabulous shades below will not afford us a habitation. Our fruitless anxieties, our vain projects, our uncertain speculations, shall all be swallowed up and lost. Our present doubts, concerning the original cause of all things, must never, alas! be resolved. This alone we may be certain of, that if any governing mind preside, he must be pleased to see us fulfil the ends of our being, and enjoy that pleasure for which alone we were created. Let this reflection give ease to your anxious thoughts; but render not your joys too serious, by dwelling for ever upon it. It is sufficient once to be acquainted with this philosophy, in order to give an unbounded loose to love and jollity, and remove all the scruples of a vain superstition: but while youth and passion, my fair one, prompt our eager desires, we must find gayer subjects of discourse to intermix with these amorous caresses.

The Stoic[1]

THERE is this obvious and material difference in the conduct of nature, with regard to man and other animals, that, having endowed the former with a sublime celestial spirit, and having given him an affinity with superior beings, she allows not such noble faculties to lie lethargic or idle, but urges him by necessity to employ, on every emergence, his utmost *art* and *industry*. Brute creatures have many of their necessities supplied by nature, being clothed and armed by this beneficent parent of all things: and where their own *industry* is requisite on any occasion, nature, by implanting instincts, still supplies them with the *art*, and guides them to their good by her unerring precepts. But man, exposed naked and indigent to the rude elements, rises slowly from that helpless state by the care and vigilance of his parents; and, having attained his utmost growth and perfection, reaches only a capacity of subsisting by his own care and vigilance. Every thing is sold to skill and labor; and where nature furnishes the materials, they are still rude and unfinished, till industry, ever active and intelligent, refines them from their brute state, and fits them for human use and convenience.

Acknowledge, therefore, O man! the beneficence of nature; for she has given thee that intelligence which supplies all thy necessities. But let not indolence, under the false appearance of gratitude, persuade thee to rest contented with her presents. Wouldst thou return to the raw herbage for thy food, to the open sky for thy covering, and to stones and clubs for thy defence against the ravenous animals of the desert? Then return also to thy savage manners, to thy timorous superstition, to thy brutal ignorance, and sink thyself below those animals whose condition thou admirest and wouldst so fondly imitate.

1 Or the man of action and virtue.

Thy kind parent, Nature, having given thee art and intelligence, has filled the whole globe with materials to employ these talents. Hearken to her voice, which so plainly tells thee that thou thyself shouldst also be the object of thy industry, and that by art and attention alone thou canst acquire that ability which will raise thee to thy proper station in the universe. Behold this artisan who converts a rude and shapeless stone into a noble metal; and, moulding that metal by his cunning hands, creates, as it were, by magic, every weapon for his defence, and every utensil for his convenience. He has not this skill from nature: use and practice have taught it him; and if thou wouldst emulate his success, thou must follow his laborious footsteps.

But while thou *ambitiously* aspirest to perfecting thy bodily powers and faculties, wouldst thou *meanly* neglect thy mind, and, from a preposterous sloth, leave it still rude and uncultivated, as it came from the hands of nature? Far be such folly and negligence from every rational being. If nature has been frugal in her gifts and endowments, there is the more need of art to supply her defects. If she has been generous and liberal, know that she still expects industry and application on our part, and revenges herself in proportion to our negligent ingratitude. The richest genius, like the most fertile soil, when uncultivated, shoots up into the rankest weeds; and instead of vines and olives for the pleasure and use of man, produces, to its slothful owner, the most abundant crop of poisons.

The great end of all human industry, is the attainment of happiness. For this were arts invented, sciences cultivated, laws ordained, and societies modelled, by the most profound wisdom of patriots and legislators. Even the lonely savage, who lies exposed to the inclemency of the elements and the fury of wild beasts, forgets not, for a moment, this grand object of his being. Ignorant as he is of every art of life, he still keeps in view the end of all those arts, and eagerly seeks for felicity amidst that darkness with which he is environed. But as much as the wildest savage is inferior to the polished citizen, who, under the protection of laws, enjoys every convenience which industry has invented, so much is this citizen himself inferior to the man of virtue, and the true philosopher, who governs his appetites, subdues his passions, and has learned, from reason, to set a just value on every pursuit and enjoyment. For is there an art and apprenticeship necessary for every other attainment? And is there no art of life, no rule, no precepts, to direct us in this principal concern? Can no particular pleasure be attained without skill; and can the whole be regulated, without reflection or intelligence, by the blind guidance of appetite and instinct? Sure then no mistakes are ever committed in this affair; but every man, however dissolute and negligent, proceeds in the pursuit of happiness with as unerring a motion as that which the celestial bodies observe, when, conducted by the hand of the Almighty, they roll along the ethereal plains. But if mistakes be often, be inevitably committed, let us register these mistakes; let us consider their causes; let us weigh their importance; let us inquire for their remedies. When from this we have fixed all the rules of conduct, we are *philosophers*. When we have reduced these rules to practice, we are *sages*.

Like many subordinate artists, employed to form the several wheels and springs of a machine, such are those who excel in all the particular arts of life. *He* is the master workman who puts those several parts together, moves them according to just harmony and proportion, and produces true felicity as the result of their conspiring order.

While thou hast such an alluring object in view, shall that labor and attention, requisite to the attainment of thy end, ever seem burdensome and intolerable? Know, that this labor itself is the chief ingredient of the felicity to which thou aspirest, and that every enjoyment soon becomes insipid and distasteful, when not acquired by fatigue and industry. See the hardy hunters rise from their downy couches, shake off the slumbers which still weigh down their heavy eyelids, and, ere *Aurora* has yet covered the heavens with her flaming mantle, hasten to the forest. They leave behind, in their own houses, and in the neighboring plains, animals of every kind, whose flesh furnishes the most delicious fare, and which offer themselves to the fatal stroke. Laborious man disdains so easy a purchase. He seeks for a prey, which hides itself from his search, or flies from his pursuit, or defends itself from his violence. Having exerted in the chase every passion of the mind, and every member of the body, he then finds the charms of repose, and with joy compares his pleasures to those of his engaging labors.

And can vigorous industry give pleasure to the pursuit even of the most worthless prey, which frequently escapes our toils? And cannot the same industry render the cultivating of our mind, the moderating of our passions, the enlightening of our reason, an agreeable occupation; while we are every day sensible of our progress, and behold our inward features and countenance brightening incessantly with new charms? Begin by curing yourself of this lethargic indolence; the task is not difficult: you need but taste the sweets of honest labor. Proceed to learn the just value of every pursuit; long study is not requisite. Compare, though but for once, the mind to the body, virtue to fortune, and glory to pleasure. You will then perceive the advantages of industry; you will then be sensible what are the proper objects of your industry.

In vain do you seek repose from beds of roses: in vain do you hope for enjoyment from the most delicious wines and fruits. Your indolence itself becomes a fatigue; your pleasure itself creates disgust. The mind, unexercised, finds every delight insipid and loathsome; and ere yet the body, full of noxious humors, feels the torment of its multiplied diseases, your nobler part is sensible of the invading poison, and seeks in vain to relieve its anxiety by new pleasures, which still augment the fatal malady.

I need not tell you, that, by this eager pursuit of pleasure, you more and more expose yourself to fortune and accidents, and rivet your affections on external objects, which chance may, in a moment, ravish from you. I shall suppose that your indulgent stars favor you still with the enjoyment of your

riches and possessions. I prove to you, that, even in the midst
of your luxurious pleasures, you are unhappy; and that, by
too much indulgence, you are incapable of enjoying what prosperous fortune still allows you to possess.

But surely the instability of fortune is a consideration not
to be overlooked or neglected. Happiness cannot possibly exist where there is no security; and security can have no place
where fortune has any dominion. Though that unstable deity
should not exert her rage against you, the dread of it would
still torment you; would disturb your slumbers, haunt your
dreams, and throw a damp on the jollity of your most delicious
banquets.

The temple of wisdom is seated on a rock, above the rage of
the fighting elements, and inaccessible to all the malice of
man. The rolling thunder breaks below; and those more ter-
rible instruments of human fury reach not to so sublime a
height. The sage, while he breathes that serene air, looks
down with pleasure, mixed with compassion, on the errors of
mistaken mortals, who blindly seek for the true path of life,
and pursue riches, nobility, honor, or power, for genuine
felicity. The greater part he beholds disappointed of their
fond wishes: some lament, that having once possessed the
object of their desires, it is ravished from them by envious fortune; and all complain, that even their own vows, though
granted, cannot give them happiness, or relieve the anxiety of
their distracted minds.

But does the sage always preserve himself in this philosophical indifference, and rest contented with lamenting the miseries of mankind, without ever employing himself for their relief? Does he constantly indulge this severe wisdom, which,
by pretending to elevate him above human accidents, does in
reality harden his heart, and render him careless of the interests of mankind, and of society? No; he knows that in this
sullen *Apathy* neither true wisdom nor true happiness can be
found. He feels too strongly the charm of the social affections,
ever to counteract so sweet, so natural, so virtuous a propensity. Even when, bathed in tears, he laments the miseries of

the human race, of his country, of his friends, and, unable to
give succor, can only relieve them by compassion; he yet re-
joices in the generous disposition, and feels a satisfaction superior to that of the most indulged sense. So engaging are the
sentiments of humanity, that they brighten up the very face
of sorrow, and operate like the sun, which, shining on a dusky
cloud or falling rain, paints on them the most glorious colors
which are to be found in the whole circle of nature.

But it is not here alone that the social virtues display their
energy. With whatever ingredients you mix them, they are
still predominant. As sorrow cannot overcome them, so neither
can sensual pleasure obscure them. The joys of love, however
tumultuous, banish not the tender sentiments of sympathy
and affection. They even derive their chief influence from that
generous passion: and when presented alone, afford nothing
to the unhappy mind but lassitude and disgust. Behold this
sprightly debauchee, who professes a contempt of all other
pleasures but those of wine and jollity: separate him from his
companions, like a spark from a fire, where before it contributed to the general blaze: his alacrity suddenly extinguishes; and, though surrounded with every other means of
delight, he loathes the sumptuous banquet, and prefers even
the most abstracted study and speculation, as more agreeable
and entertaining.

But the social passions never afford such transporting pleasures, or make so glorious an appearance in the eyes both of
GOD and man, as when, shaking off every earthly mixture, they
associate themselves with the sentiments of virtue, and prompt
us to laudable and worthy actions. As harmonious colors mutually give and receive a lustre by their friendly union, so do
these ennobling sentiments of the human mind. See the triumph of nature in parental affection! What selfish passion,
what sensual delight is a match for it, whether a man exults
in the prosperity and virtue of his offspring, or flies to their
succor through the most threatening and tremendous dangers?

Proceed still in purifying the generous passions, you will
still the more admire its shining glories. What charms are

there in the harmony of minds, and in a friendship founded on mutual esteem and gratitude! What satisfaction in relieving the distressed, in comforting the afflicted, in raising the fallen, and in stopping the career of cruel fortune, or of more cruel man, in their insults over the good and virtuous! But what supreme joy in the victories over vice as well as misery, when, by virtuous example or wise exhortation, our fellow-creatures are taught to govern their passions, reform their vices, and subdue their worst enemies, which inhabit within their own bosoms!

But these objects are still too limited for the human mind, which, being of celestial origin, swells with the divinest and most enlarged affections, and, carrying its attention beyond kindred and acquaintance, extends its benevolent wishes to the most distant posterity. It views liberty and laws as the source of human happiness, and devotes itself, with the utmost alacrity, to their guardianship and protection. Toils, dangers, death itself, carry their charms, when we brave them for the public good, and ennoble that being which we generously sacrifice for the interests of our country. Happy the man whom indulgent fortune allows to pay to virtue what he owes to nature, and to make a generous gift of what must otherwise be ravished from him by cruel necessity.

In the true sage and patriot are united whatever can distinguish human nature, or elevate mortal man to a resemblance with the Divinity. The softest benevolence, the most undaunted resolution, the tenderest sentiments, the most sublime love of virtue, all these animate successively his transported bosom. What satisfaction, when he looks within, to find the most turbulent passions tuned to just harmony and concord, and every jarring sound banished from this enchanting music! If the contemplation, even of inanimate beauty, is so delightful; if it ravishes the senses, even when the fair form is foreign to us; what must be the effects of moral beauty? and what influence must it have, when it embellishes our own mind, and is the result of our own reflection and industry?

*But where is the reward of virtue? And what recompense
has Nature provided for such important sacrifices as those of
life and fortune, which we must often make to it?* Oh, sons of
earth! Are ye ignorant of the value of this celestial mistress?
And do ye meanly inquire for her portion, when ye observe
her genuine charms? But know, that Nature has been indulgent to human weakness, and has not left this favorite
child naked and unendowed. She has provided virtue with the
richest dowry; but being careful lest the allurements of interest
should engage such suitors as were insensible of the native
worth of so divine a beauty, she has wisely provided, that this
dowry can have no charms but in the eyes of those who are
already transported with the love of virtue. Glory is the
portion of virtue, the sweet reward of honorable toils, the triumphant crown which covers the thoughtful head of the disinterested patriot, or the dusty brow of the victorious war-
rior. Elevated by so sublime a prize, the man of virtue looks
down with contempt on all the allurements of pleasure, and
all the menaces of danger. Death itself loses its terrors, when
he considers, that its dominion extends only over a part of
him, and that, in spite of death and time, the rage of the
elements, and the endless vicissitude of human affairs, he is
assured of an immortal fame among all the sons of men.

There surely is a Being who presides over the universe, and
who, with infinite wisdom and power, has reduced the jarring
elements into just order and proportion. Let the speculative
reasoners dispute, how far this beneficent Being extends his
care, and whether he prolongs our existence beyond the grave,
in order to bestow on virtue its just reward, and render it fully
triumphant. The man of morals, without deciding any thing
on so dubious a subject, is satisfied with the portion marked
out to him by the Supreme Disposer of all things. Gratefully
he accepts of that further reward prepared for him; but if disappointed, he thinks not virtue an empty name; but, justly
esteeming it his own reward, he gratefully acknowledges the
bounty of his Creator, who, by calling him into existence, has
thereby afforded him an opportunity of once acquiring so
invaluable a possession.

The Platonist[1]

To some philosophers it appears matter of surprise, that all mankind, possessing the same nature, and being endowed with the same faculties, should yet differ so widely in their pursuits and inclinations, and that one should utterly condemn what is fondly sought after by another. To some it appears matter of still more surprise, that a man should differ so widely from himself at different times; and, after possession, reject with disdain what before was the object of all his vows and wishes. To me this feverish uncertainty and irresolution, in human conduct, seems altogether unavoidable; nor can a rational soul, made for the contemplation of the Supreme Being, and of his works, ever enjoy tranquillity or satisfaction, while detained in the ignoble pursuits of sensual pleasure or popular applause. The Divinity is a boundless ocean of bliss and glory: human minds are smaller streams, which, arising at first from this ocean, seek still, amid all their wanderings, to return to it, and to lose themselves in that immensity of perfection. When checked in this natural course by vice or folly, they become furious and enraged; and, swelling to a torrent, do then spread horror and devastation on the neighboring plains.

In vain, by pompous phrase and passionate expression, each recommends his own pursuit, and invites the credulous hearers to an imitation of his life and manners. The heart belies the countenance, and sensibly feels, even amid the highest success, the unsatisfactory nature of all those pleasures which detain it from its true object. I examine the voluptuous man before enjoyment; I measure the vehemence of his desire, and the importance of his object; I find that all his happiness proceeds only from that hurry of thought, which takes him from himself, and turns his view from his guilt and misery. I consider him a moment after; he has now enjoyed the pleasure which

[1] Or the man of contemplation and *philosophical* devotion.

he fondly sought after. The sense of his guilt and misery returns upon him with double anguish: his mind tormented with fear and remorse; his body depressed with disgust and satiety.

But a more august, at least a more haughty personage, presents himself boldly to our censure; and, assuming the title of a philosopher and man of morals, offers to submit to the most rigid examination. He challenges with a visible, though concealed impatience, our approbation and applause; and seems offended, that we should hesitate a moment before we break out into admiration of his virtue. Seeing this impatience, I hesitate still more; I begin to examine the motives of his seeming virtue: but, behold! ere I can enter upon this inquiry, he flings himself from me; and, addressing his discourse to that crowd of heedless auditors, fondly amuses them by his magnificent pretensions.

O philosopher! thy wisdom is vain, and thy virtue unprofitable. Thou seekest the ignorant applauses of men, not the solid reflections of thy own conscience, or the more solid approbation of that Being, who, with one regard of his all-seeing eye, penetrates the universe. Thou surely art conscious of the hollowness of thy pretended probity; whilst calling thyself a citizen, a son, a friend, thou forgettest thy higher sovereign, thy true father, thy greatest benefactor. Where is the adoration due to infinite perfection, whence every thing good and valuable is derived! Where is the gratitude owing to thy Creator, who called thee forth from nothing, who placed thee in all these relations to thy fellow-creatures, and, requiring thee to fulfil the duty of each relation, forbids thee to neglect what thou owest to himself, the most perfect being, to whom thou art connected by the closest tie?

But thou art thyself thy own idol. Thou worshippest thy *imaginary* perfections; or rather, sensible of thy *real* imperfections, thou seekest only to deceive the world, and to please thy fancy, by multiplying thy ignorant admirers. Thus, not content with neglecting what is most excellent in the universe, thou desirest to substitute in his place what is most vile and contemptible.

Consider all the works of men's hands, all the inventions of human wit, in which thou affectest so nice a discernment. Thou wilt find, that the most perfect production still proceeds from the most perfect thought, and that it is MIND alone which we admire, while we bestow our applause on the graces of a well-proportioned statue, or the symmetry of a noble pile. The statuary, the architect, come still in view, and makes us reflect on the beauty of his art and contrivance, which, from a heap of unformed matter, could extract such expressions and proportions. This superior beauty of thought and intelligence thou thyself acknowledgest, while thou invitest us to contemplate, in thy conduct, the harmony of affections, the dignity of sentiments, and all those graces of a mind which chiefly merit our attention. But why stoppest thou short? Seest thou nothing further that is valuable? Amid thy rapturous applauses of beauty and order, art thou still ignorant where is to be found the most consummate beauty, the most perfect order? Compare the works of art with those of nature. The one are but imitations of the other. The nearer art approaches to nature, the more perfect is it esteemed. But still how wide are its nearest approaches, and what an immense interval may be observed between them! Art copies only the outside of nature, leaving the inward and more admirable springs and principles as exceeding her imitation, as beyond her comprehension. Art copies only the minute productions of nature, despairing to reach that grandeur and magnificence which are so astonishing in the masterly works of her original. Can we then be so blind as not to discover an intelligence and a design in the exquisite and most stupendous contrivance of the universe? Can we be so stupid as not to feel the warmest raptures of worship and adoration upon the contemplation of that intelligent Being, so infinitely good and wise?

The most perfect happiness surely must arise from the contemplation of the most perfect object. But what more perfect than beauty and virtue? And where is beauty to be found equal to that of the universe, or virtue which can be compared to the benevolence and justice of the Deity? If aught can diminish the pleasure of this contemplation, it must be either

the narrowness of our faculties, which conceals from us the
greatest part of these beauties and perfections, or the shortness
of our lives, which allows not time sufficient to instruct us in
them. But it is our comfort, that if we employ worthily the
faculties here assigned us, they will be enlarged in another
state of existence, so as to render us more suitable worshippers
of our Maker; and that the task, which can never be finished
in time, will be the business of an eternity.

The Sceptic

I HAVE long entertained a suspicion with regard to the decisions of philosophers upon all subjects, and found in myself a greater inclination to dispute than assent to their conclusions. There is one mistake to which they seem liable, almost without exception; they confine too much their principles, and make no account of that vast variety which nature has so much affected in all her operations. When a philosopher has once laid hold of a favorite principle, which perhaps accounts for many natural effects, he extends the same principle over the whole creation, and reduces to it every phenomenon, though by the most violent and absurd reasoning. Our own mind being narrow and contracted, we cannot extend our conception to the variety and extent of nature, but imagine that she is as much bounded in her operations as we are in our speculation.

But if ever this infirmity of philosophers is to be suspected on any occasion, it is in their reasonings concerning human life, and the methods of attaining happiness. In that case they are led astray, not only by the narrowness of their understandings, but by that also of their passions. Almost every one has a predominant inclination, to which his other desires and affections submit, and which governs him, though perhaps with some intervals, through the whole course of his life. It is difficult for him to apprehend, that any thing which appears totally indifferent to him can ever give enjoyment to any person, or can possess charms which altogether escape his observation. His own pursuits are always, in his account, the most engaging, the objects of his passion the most valuable, and the road which he pursues the only one that leads to happiness.

But would these prejudiced reasoners reflect a moment, there are many obvious instances and arguments sufficient to undeceive them, and make them enlarge their maxims and principles. Do they not see the vast variety of inclinations and

pursuits among our species, where each man seems fully satisfied with his own course of life, and would esteem it the greatest unhappiness to be confined to that of his neighbor? Do
they not feel in themselves, that what pleases at one time, displeases at another, by the change of inclination, and that it
is not in their power, by their utmost efforts, to recall that
taste or appetite which formerly bestowed charms on what
now appears indifferent or disagreeable? What is the meaning,
therefore, of those general preferences of the town or country
life, of a life of action or one of pleasure, of retirement or
society; when, besides the different inclinations of different
men, every one's experience may convince him that each of
these kinds of life is agreeable in its turn, and that their variety or their judicious mixture chiefly contributes to the rendering all of them agreeable?

But shall this business be allowed to go altogether at ad-
ventures? and must a man only consult his humor and inclination, in order to determine his course of life, without
employing his reason to inform him what road is preferable,
and leads most surely to happiness? Is there no difference,
then, between one man's conduct and another?

I answer, there is a great difference. One man, following his
inclination, in choosing his course of life, may employ much
surer means for succeeding than another, who is led by his
inclination into the same course of life, and pursues the same
object. *Are riches the chief object of your desires?* Acquire
skill in your profession; be diligent in the exercise of it; enlarge the circle of your friends and acquaintance; avoid pleasure and expense; and never be generous, but with a view of
gaining more than you could save by frugality. *Would you
acquire the public esteem?* Guard equally against the extremes
of arrogance and fawning. Let it appear that you set a value
upon yourself, but without despising others. If you fall into
either of the extremes, you either provoke men's pride by your
insolence, or teach them to despise you by your timorous submission, and by the mean opinion which you seem to entertain
of yourself.

These, you say, are the maxims of common prudence and discretion; what every parent inculcates on his child, and what every man of sense pursues in the course of life which he has chosen. What is it then you desire more? Do you come to a philosopher as to a *cunning man,* to learn something by magic or witchcraft, beyond what can be known by common prudence and discretion?—Yes; we come to a philosopher to be instructed, how we shall choose our ends, more than the means for attaining these ends: we want to know what desire we shall gratify, what passion we shall comply with, what appetite we shall indulge. As to the rest, we trust to common sense, and the general maxims of the world, for our instruction.

I am sorry, then, I have pretended to be a philosopher; for I find your questions very perplexing, and am in danger, if my answer be too rigid and severe, of passing for a pedant and scholastic; if it be too easy and free, of being taken for a preacher of vice and immorality. However, to satisfy you, I shall deliver my opinion upon the matter, and shall only desire you to esteem it of as little consequence as I do myself. By that means you will neither think it worthy of your ridicule nor your anger.

If we can depend upon any principle which we learn from philosophy, this, I think, may be considered as certain and undoubted, that there is nothing, in itself, valuable or despicable, desirable or hateful, beautiful or deformed; but that these attributes arise from the particular constitution and fabric of human sentiment and affection. What seems the most delicious food to one animal, appears loathsome to another; what affects the feeling of one with delight, produces uneasiness in another. This is confessedly the case with regard to all the bodily senses. But, if we examine the matter more accurately, we shall find that the same observation holds even where the mind concurs with the body, and mingles its sentiment with the exterior appetite.

Desire this passionate lover to give you a character of his mistress: he will tell you, that he is at a loss for words to describe her charms, and will ask you very seriously, if ever you were acquainted with a goddess or an angel? If you answer that you never were, he will then say that it is impossible for you to form a conception of such divine beauties as those which his charmer possesses; so complete a shape; such well-proportioned features; so engaging an air; such sweetness of disposition; such gaiety of humor. You can infer nothing, however, from all this discourse, but that the poor man is in love; and that the general appetite between the sexes, which nature has infused into all animals, is in him determined to a particular object by some qualities which give him pleasure. The same divine creature, not only to a different animal, but also to a different man, appears a mere mortal being, and is beheld with the utmost indifference.

Nature has given all animals a like prejudice in favor of their offspring. As soon as the helpless infant sees the light, though in every other eye it appears a despicable and a miserable creature, it is regarded by its fond parent with the utmost affection, and is preferred to every other object, however perfect and accomplished. The passion alone, arising from the original structure and formation of human nature, bestows a value on the most insignificant object.

We may push the same observation further, and may conclude that, even when the mind operates alone, and feeling the sentiment of blame or approbation, pronounces one object deformed and odious, another beautiful and amiable; I say that, even in this case, those qualities are not really in the objects, but belong entirely to the sentiment of that mind which blames or praises. I grant, that it will be more difficult to make this proposition evident, and, as it were, palpable, to negligent thinkers; because nature is more uniform in the sentiments of the mind than in most feelings of the body, and produces a nearer resemblance in the inward than in the outward part of human kind. There is something approaching to principles in mental taste; and critics can reason and dispute more plausibly than cooks or perfumers. We may observe, however, that this uniformity among human kind hinders not, but that there is a considerable diversity in the sentiments of beauty and worth, and that education, custom, prejudice, caprice, and humor, frequently vary our taste of this kind. You will never convince a man, who is not accustomed to Italian music, and has not an ear to follow its intricacies, that a Scots tune is not preferable. You have not even any single argument beyond your own taste, which you can employ in your behalf: and to your antagonist his particular taste will always appear a more convincing argument to the contrary. If you be wise, each of you will allow that the other may be in the right; and having many other instances of this diversity of taste, you will both confess, that beauty and worth are merely of a relative nature, and consist in an agreeable sentiment, produced by an object in a particular mind, according to the peculiar structure and constitution of that mind.

By this diversity of sentiment, observable in human kind, nature has, perhaps, intended to make us sensible of her authority, and let us see what surprising changes she could produce on the passions and desires of mankind, merely by the change of their inward fabric, without any alteration on the objects. The vulgar may even be convinced by this argument. But men, accustomed to thinking, may draw a more convincing, at least a more general argument, from the very nature of the subject.

In the operation of reasoning, the mind does nothing but run over its objects, as they are supposed to stand in reality, without adding any thing to them, or diminishing any thing from them. If I examine the Ptolomaic and Copernican systems, I endeavor only, by my inquiries, to know the real situation of the planets; that is, in other words, I endeavor to give them, in my conception, the same relations that they bear towards each other in the heavens. To this operation of the mind, therefore, there seems to be always a real, though often an unknown standard, in the nature of things; nor is truth or falsehood variable by the various apprehensions of mankind. Though all human race should for ever conclude that the sun moves, and the earth remains at rest, the sun stirs not an inch from his place for all these reasonings; and such conclusions are eternally false and erroneous.

But the case is not the same with the qualities of *beautiful and deformed, desirable and odious,* as with truth and falsehood. In the former case, the mind is not content with merely surveying its objects, as they stand in themselves: it also feels a sentiment of delight or uneasiness, approbation or blame, consequent to that survey; and this sentiment determines it to affix the epithet *beautiful or deformed, desirable or odious.* Now, it is evident, that this sentiment must depend upon the particular fabric or structure of the mind, which enables such particular forms to operate in such a particular manner, and produces a sympathy or conformity between the mind and its objects. Vary the structure of the mind or inward organs, the sentiment no longer follows, though the form remains the same. The sentiment being different from the object, and arising from its operation upon the organs of the mind, an alteration upon the latter must vary the effect; nor can the same object, presented to a mind totally different, produce the same sentiment.

This conclusion every one is apt to draw of himself, without much philosophy, where the sentiment is evidently distinguishable from the object. Who is not sensible that power, and glory, and vengeance, are not desirable of themselves, but derive all their value from the structure of human passions, which begets a desire towards such particular pursuits? But with regard to beauty, either natural or moral, the case is commonly supposed to be different. The agreeable quality is thought to lie in the object, not in the sentiment; and that merely because the sentiment is not so turbulent and violent as to distinguish itself, in an evident manner, from the perception of the object.

But a little reflection suffices to distinguish them. A man may know exactly all the circles and ellipses of the Copernican system, and all the irregular spirals of the Ptolomaic, without perceiving that the former is more beautiful than the latter.

Euclid has fully explained every quality of the circle, but has not, in any proposition, said a word of its beauty. The reason is evident. Beauty is not a quality of the circle. It lies not in any part of the line *whose* parts are all equally distant from a common centre. It is only the effect, which that figure produces upon a mind, whose particular fabric or structure renders it susceptible of such sentiments. In vain would you look for it in the circle, or seek it, either by your senses, or by mathematical reasonings, in all the properties of that figure.

The mathematician, who took no other pleasure in reading Virgil, but that of examining Æneas's voyage by the map, might perfectly understand the meaning of every Latin word employed by that divine author; and, consequently, might have a distinct idea of the whole narration. He would even have a more distinct idea of it, than they could attain who had not studied so exactly the geography of the poem. He knew, therefore, every thing in the poem: but he was ignorant of its beauty, because the beauty, properly speaking, lies not in the poem, but in the sentiment or taste of the reader. And where a man has no such delicacy of temper as to make him feel this sentiment, he must be ignorant of the beauty, though possessed of the science and understanding of an angel.[1]

The inference upon the whole is, that it is not from the value or worth of the object which any person pursues, that we can determine his enjoyment, but merely from the passion

[1] Were I not afraid of appearing too philosophical, I should remind my reader of that famous doctrine, supposed to be fully proved in modern times, "That tastes and colors, and all other sensible qualities, lie not in the bodies, but merely in the senses." The case is the same with beauty and deformity, virtue and vice. This doctrine, however, takes off no more from the reality of the latter qualities, than from that of the former; nor need it give any umbrage either to critics or moralists. Though colors were allowed to lie only in the eye, would dyers or painters ever be less regarded or esteemed? There is a sufficient uniformity in the senses and feelings of mankind, to make all these qualities the objects of art and reasoning, and to have the greatest influence on life and manners. And as it is certain, that the discovery above mentioned in natural philosophy, makes no alteration on action and conduct, why should a like discovery in moral philosophy make any alteration?

with which he pursues it, and the success which he meets with in his pursuit. Objects have absolutely no worth or value in themselves. They derive their worth merely from the passion. If that be strong and steady, and successful, the person is happy. It cannot reasonably be doubted, but a little miss, dressed in a new gown for a dancing-school ball, receives as complete enjoyment as the greatest orator, who triumphs in the splendor of his eloquence, while he governs the passions and resolutions of a numerous assembly.

All the difference, therefore, between one man and another, with regard to life, consists either in the *passion,* or in the *enjoyment:* and these differences are sufficient to produce the wide extremes of happiness and misery.

To be happy, the *passion* must neither be too violent, nor too remiss. In the first case, the mind is in a perpetual hurry and tumult; in the second, it sinks into a disagreeable indolence and lethargy.

To be happy, the passion must be benign and social, not rough or fierce. The affections of the latter kind are not near so agreeable to the feeling as those of the former. Who will compare rancor and animosity, envy and revenge, to friendship, benignity, clemency, and gratitude?

To be happy, the passion must be cheerful and gay, not gloomy and melancholy. A propensity to hope and joy is real riches; one to fear and sorrow, real poverty.

Some passions or inclinations, in the *enjoyment* of their object, are not so steady or constant as others, nor convey such durable pleasure and satisfaction. *Philosophical devotion,* for instance, like the enthusiasm of a poet, is the transitory effect of high spirits, great leisure, a fine genius, and a habit of study and contemplation: but notwithstanding all these circumstances, an abstract, invisible object, like that which *natural* religion [2] alone presents to us, cannot long actuate the

---

[2] [Religious beliefs rationally obtained, as contrasted with those based on revelation. Hume holds, furthermore, that while such rational beliefs in God are problematic, man nonetheless is, because of his nature, inclined to have them.]

mind, or be of any moment in life. To render the passion of continuance, we must find some method of affecting the senses and imagination, and must embrace some *historical* as well as *philosophical* account of the Divinity. Popular superstitions and observances are even found to be of use in this particular.

Though the tempers of men be very different, yet we may safely pronounce in general, that a life of pleasure cannot support itself so long as one of business, but is much more subject to satiety and disgust. The amusements which are the most durable, have all a mixture of application and attention in them; such as gaming and hunting. And in general, business and action fill up all the great vacancies in human life.

But where the temper is the best disposed for any *enjoyment*, the object is often wanting: and in this respect, the passions, which pursue external objects, contribute not so much to happiness as those which rest in ourselves; since we are neither so certain of attaining such objects, nor so secure in possessing them. A passion for learning is preferable, with regard to happiness, to one for riches.

Some men are possessed of great strength of mind; and even when they pursue *external* objects, are not much affected by a disappointment, but renew their application and industry with the greatest cheerfulness. Nothing contributes more to happiness than such a turn of mind.

According to this short and imperfect sketch of human life, the happiest disposition of mind is the *virtuous;* or, in other words, that which leads to action and employment, renders us sensible to the social passions, steels the heart against the assaults of fortune, reduces the affections to a just moderation, makes our own thoughts an entertainment to us, and inclines us rather to the pleasures of society and conversation than to those of the senses. This, in the mean time, must be obvious to the most careless reasoner, that all dispositions of mind are not alike favorable to happiness, and that one passion or humor may be extremely desirable, while another is equally disagreeable. And, indeed, all the difference between the conditions of life depends upon the mind; nor is there any one situation of affairs, in itself, preferable to another. Good and ill, both natural and moral, are entirely relative to human sentiment and affection. No man would ever be unhappy, could he alter his feelings. Proteus-like, he would elude all attacks, by the continual alterations of his shape and form.

But of this resource nature has, in a great measure, deprived us. The fabric and constitution of our mind no more depends on our choice, than that of our body. The generality of men have not even the smallest notion that any alteration in this respect can ever be desirable. As a stream necessarily follows the several inclinations of the ground on which it runs, so are the ignorant and thoughtless part of mankind actuated by their natural propensities. Such are effectually excluded from all pretensions to philosophy, and the *medicine of the mind,* so much boasted. But even upon the wise and thoughtful, nature has a prodigious influence; nor is it always in a man's power, by the utmost art and industry, to correct his temper, and attain that virtuous character to which he aspires. The empire of philosophy extends over a few; and with regard to these, too, her authority is very weak and limited. Men may well be sensible of the value of virtue, and may desire to attain it; but it is not always certain that they will be successful in their wishes.

Whoever considers, without prejudice, the course of human actions, will find, that mankind are almost entirely guided by constitution and temper, and that general maxims have little influence, but so far as they affect our taste or sentiment. If a man have a lively sense of honor and virtue, with moderate passions, his conduct will always be conformable to the rules of morality: or if he depart from them, his return will be easy and expeditious. On the other hand, where one is born of so perverse a frame of mind, of so callous and insensible a disposition, as to have no relish for virtue and humanity, no sympathy with his fellow-creatures, no desire of esteem and applause, such a one must be allowed entirely incurable; nor is there any remedy in philosophy. He reaps no satisfaction but from low and sensual objects, or from the indulgence of malignant passions: he feels no remorse to control his vicious inclinations: he has not even that sense or taste, which is requisite to make him desire a better character. For my part, I know not how I should address myself to such a one, or by what arguments I should endeavor to reform him. Should I tell him of the inward satisfaction which results from laudable and humane actions, and delicate pleasure of disinterested love and friendship, the lasting enjoyments of a good name and an established character, he might still reply, that these were, perhaps, pleasures to such as were susceptible of them; but that, for his part, he finds himself of a quite different turn and disposition. I must repeat it, my philosophy affords no remedy in such a case; nor could I do any thing but lament this person's unhappy condition. But then I ask, If any other philosophy can afford a remedy; or if it be possible, by any system, to render all mankind virtuous, however perverse may be their natural frame of mind? Experience will soon convince us of the contrary; and I will venture to affirm, that, perhaps, the chief benefit which results from philosophy, arises in an indirect manner, and proceeds more from its secret insensible influence, than from its immediate application.

It is certain, that a serious attention to the sciences and liberal arts softens and humanizes the temper, and cherishes those fine emotions, in which true virtue and honor consists. It rarely, very rarely happens, that a man of taste and learning is not, at least, an honest man, whatever frailties may attend him. The bent of his mind to speculative studies must mortify in him the passions of interest and ambition, and must, at the same time, give him a greater sensibility of all the decencies and duties of life. He feels more fully a moral distinction in characters and manners; nor is his sense of this kind diminished, but, on the contrary, it is much increased, by speculation.

Besides such insensible changes upon the temper and disposition, it is highly probable, that others may be produced by study and application. The prodigious effects of education may convince us, that the mind is not altogether stubborn and inflexible, but will admit of many alterations from its original make and structure. Let a man propose to himself the model of a character which he approves: let him be well acquainted with those particulars in which his own character deviates from this model: let him keep a constant watch over himself, and bend his mind, by a continual effort, from the vices, towards the virtues; and I doubt not but, in time, he will find, in his temper, an alteration for the better.

Habit is another powerful means of reforming the mind, and implanting in it good dispositions and inclinations. A man, who continues in a course of sobriety and temperance, will hate riot and disorder: if he engage in business or study, indolence will seem a punishment to him: if he constrain himself to practise beneficence and affability, he will soon abhor all instances of pride and violence. Where one is thoroughly convinced that the virtuous course of life is preferable; if he have but resolution enough, for some time, to impose a violence on himself; his reformation needs not be despaired of. The misfortune is, that this conviction and this resolution never can have place, unless a man be, beforehand, tolerably virtuous.

Here then is the chief triumph of art and philosophy: it insensibly refines the temper, and it points out to us those dispositions which we should endeavor to attain, by a constant *bent* of mind, and by repeated *habit*. Beyond this I cannot acknowledge it to have great influence; and I must entertain doubts concerning all those exhortations and consolations, which are in such vogue among speculative reasoners.

We have already observed, that no objects are, in themselves, desirable or odious, valuable or despicable; but that objects acquire these qualities from the particular character and constitution of the mind which surveys them. To diminish, therefore, or augment any person's value for an object, to excite or moderate his passions, there are no direct arguments or reasons, which can be employed with any force or influence. The catching of flies, like Domitian, if it give more pleasure, is preferable to the hunting of wild beasts, like William Rufus, or conquering of kingdoms, like Alexander.

But though the value of every object can be determined only

by the sentiment or passion of every individual, we may observe, that the passion, in pronouncing its verdict, considers not the object simply, as it is in itself, but surveys it with all the circumstances which attend it. A man, transported with joy on account of his possessing a diamond, confines not his view to the glittering stone before him. He also considers its rarity; and thence chiefly arises his pleasure and exultation. Here, therefore, a philosopher may step in, and suggest particular views, and considerations, and circumstances, which otherwise would have escaped us, and by that means he may either moderate or excite any particular passion.

It may seem unreasonable absolutely to deny the authority of philosophy in this respect: but it must be confessed, that there lies this strong presumption against it, that, if these views be natural and obvious, they would have occurred of themselves without the assistance of philosophy: if they be not natural, they never can have any influence on the affections. *These* are of a very delicate nature, and cannot be forced or constrained by the utmost art or industry. A consideration which we seek for on purpose, which we enter into with difficulty, which we cannot retain without care and attention, will never produce those genuine and durable movements of passion which are the result of nature, and the constitution of the mind. A man may as well pretend to cure himself of love, by viewing his mistress through the *artificial* medium of a microscope or prospect, and beholding there the coarseness of her skin, and monstrous disproportion of her features, as hope to excite or moderate any passion by the *artificial* arguments of a Seneca or an Epictetus. The remembrance of the natural aspect and situation of the object will, in both cases, still recur upon him. The reflections of philosophy are too subtile and distant to take place in common life, or eradicate any affection. The air is too fine to breathe in, where it is above the winds and clouds of the atmosphere.

Another defect of those refined reflections which philosophy suggests to us, is, that commonly they cannot diminish or extinguish our vicious passions, without diminishing or extinguishing such as are virtuous, and rendering the mind totally indifferent and inactive. They are, for the most part, general, and are applicable to all our affections. In vain do we hope to direct their influence only to one side. If by incessant study and meditation we have rendered them intimate and present to us, they will operate throughout, and spread an universal insensibility over the mind. When we destroy the nerves, we extinguish the sense of pleasure, together with that of pain, in the human body.

It will be easy, by one glance of the eye, to find one or other of these defects in most of those philosophical reflections, so much celebrated both in ancient and modern times. *Let not the injuries or violence of men,* say the philosophers,[3] *ever discompose you by anger or hatred. Would you be angry at the ape for its malice, or the tiger for its ferocity?* This reflection leads us into a bad opinion of human nature, and must extinguish the social affections. It tends also to prevent all remorse for a man's own crimes, when he considers that vice is as natural to mankind as the particular instincts to brute creatures.

All ills arise from the order of the universe, which is absolutely perfect. Would you wish to disturb so divine an order for the sake of your own particular interest? What if the ills I suffer arise from malice or oppression? *But the vices and imperfections of men are also comprehended in the order of the universe.*

> If plagues and earthquakes break not heaven's design,
> Why then a BORGIA or a CATILINE?[4]

Let this be allowed, and my own vices will also be a part of the same order.

To one who said that none were happy who were not above opinion, a Spartan replied, *Then none are happy but knaves and robbers.*[5]

---

3 Plutarch, *De cohibenda Ira.*
4 [Pope, *Essay on Man,* I, 155–56.]
5 Plutarch, *Lacaenarum Apophegmata.*

Man is born to be miserable; and is he surprised at any particular misfortune? And can he give way to sorrow and lamentation upon account of any disaster? Yes: he very reasonably laments that he should be born to be miserable. Your consolation presents a hundred ills for one, of which you pretend to ease him.

You should always have before your eyes death, disease, poverty, blindness, exile, calumny, and infamy, as ills which are incident to human nature. If any one of these ills fall to your lot, you will bear it the better when you have reckoned upon it. I answer, if we confine ourselves to a general and distant reflection on the ills of human life, *that* can have no effect to prepare us for them. If by close and intense meditation we render them present and intimate to us, *that* is the true secret for poisoning all our pleasures, and rendering us perpetually miserable.

Your sorrow is fruitless, and will not change the course of destiny. Very true; and for that very reason I am sorry.

Cicero's consolation for deafness is somewhat curious. *How many languages are there,* says he, *which you do not understand? The Punic, Spanish, Gallic, Egyptian, etc. With regard to all these, you are as if you were deaf, yet you are indifferent about the matter. Is it then so great a misfortune to be deaf to one language more?* [6]

I like better the repartee of Antipater the Cyrenaic, when some women were condoling with him for his blindness: *What!* says he, *Do you think there are no pleasures in the dark?* [7]

Nothing can be more destructive, says Fontenelle,[8] *to ambition, and the passion for conquest, than the true system of astronomy. What a poor thing is even the whole globe in comparison of the infinite extent of nature!* This consideration is evidently too distant ever to have any effect; or, if it had any, would it not destroy patriotism as well as ambition? The

6 [*Tusculan Disputations* V. 40.]
7 [*Ibid.,* V. 38.]
8 [In *Entretiens sur la Pluralité des Mondes.*]

same gallant author adds, with some reason, that the bright
eyes of the ladies are the only objects which lose nothing of
their lustre or value from the most extensive views of astronomy, but stand proof against every system. Would philosophers
advise us to limit our affection to them?

Exile, says Plutarch to a friend in banishment, *is no evil:
Mathematicians tell us that the whole earth is but a point,
compared to the heavens. To change one's country, then, is
little more than to remove from one street to another. Man is
not a plant, rooted to a certain spot of earth: all soils and all
climates are alike suited to him.*[9] These topics are admirable,
could they fall only into the hands of banished persons. But
what if they come also to the knowledge of those who are employed in public affairs, and destroy all their attachment to
their native country? Or will they operate like the quack's
medicine, which is equally good for a diabetes and a dropsy?

It is certain, were a superior being thrust into a human
body, that the whole of life would to him appear so mean,
contemptible, and puerile, that he never could be induced to
take part in any thing, and would scarcely give attention to
what passes around him. To engage him to such a condescen-
sion as to play even the part of a Philip with zeal and alacrity,
would be much more difficult than to constrain the same
Philip, after having been a king and a conqueror during fifty
years, to mend old shoes with proper care and attention, the
occupation which Lucian assigns him in the infernal regions.
Now, all the same topics of disdain towards human affairs,
which could operate on this supposed being, occur also to a
philosopher; but being, in some measure, disproportioned to
human capacity, and not being fortified by the experience of
any thing better, they make not a full impression on him. He
sees, but he feels not sufficiently their truth; and is always a
sublime philosopher when he needs not; that is, as long as
nothing disturbs him, or rouses his affections. While others
play, he wonders at their keenness and ardor; but he no
sooner puts in his own stake, than he is commonly transported

9 *De Exilio* [600–601].

with the same passions that he had so much condemned while
he remained a simple spectator.

There are two considerations chiefly to be met with in books
of philosophy, from which any important effect is to be expected, and that because these considerations are drawn from
common life, and occur upon the most superficial view of human affairs. When we reflect on the shortness and uncertainty
of life, how despicable seem all our pursuits of happiness! And
even if we would extend our concern beyond our own life,
how frivolous appear our most enlarged and most generous
projects, when we consider the incessant changes and revolutions of human affairs, by which laws and learning, books and
governments, are hurried away by time, as by a rapid stream,
and are lost in the immense ocean of matter! Such a reflection
certainly tends to mortify all our passions: but does it not
thereby counterwork the artifice of nature, who has happily
deceived us into an opinion, that human life is of some importance? And may not such a reflection be employed with
success by voluptuous reasoners, in order to lead us from the
paths of action and virtue, into the flowery fields of indolence
and pleasure?

We are informed by Thucydides,[10] that, during the famous
plague of Athens, when death seemed present to every one, a
dissolute mirth and gaiety prevailed among the people, who
exhorted one another to make the most of life as long as it
endured. The same observation is made by Boccace,[11] with regard to the plague of Florence. A like principle makes soldiers,
during war, be more addicted to riot and expense, than any
other race of men.[a] Present pleasure is always of importance;
and whatever diminishes the importance of all other objects,
must bestow on it an additional influence and value.

The *second* philosophical consideration, which may often
have an influence on the affections, is derived from a comparison of our own condition with the condition of others. This
comparison we are continually making even in common life;

---

[10] [Thucydides, *The Peloponnesian War* II. 39.]
[11] [Boccaccio, *Decameron*, "Preface to the Ladies."]

but the misfortune is, that we are rather apt to compare our situation with that of our superiors, than with that of our inferiors. A philosopher corrects this natural infirmity, by turning his view to the other side, in order to render himself easy in the situation to which fortune has confined him. There are few people who are not susceptible of some consolation from this reflection, though, to a very good-natured man, the view of human miseries should rather produce sorrow than comfort, and add, to his lamentations for his own misfortunes, a deep compassion for those of others. Such is the imperfection, even of the best of these philosophical topics of consolation.[12]

[12] The Sceptic, perhaps, carries the matter too far, when he limits all philosophical topics and reflections to these two. There seem to be others, whose truth is undeniable, and whose natural tendency is to tranquillize and soften all the passions. Philosophy greedily seizes these; studies them, weighs them, commits them to the memory, and familiarizes them to the mind: and their influence on tempers which are thoughtful, gentle, and moderate, may be considerable. But what is their influence, you will say, if the temper be antecedently disposed after the same manner as that to which they pretend to form it? They may, at least, fortify that temper, and furnish it with views, by which it may entertain and nourish itself. Here are a few examples of such philosophical reflections.

1. Is it not certain, that every condition has concealed ills? Then why envy anybody?

2. Every one has known ills; and there is a compensation throughout. Why not be contented with the present?

3. Custom deadens the sense both of the good and the ill, and levels every thing.

4. Health and humor all. The rest of little consequence, except these be affected.

5. How many other good things have I? Then why be vexed for one ill?

6. How many are happy in the condition of which I complain? How many envy me?

7. Every good must be paid for: fortune by labor, favor by flattery. Would I keep the price, yet have the commodity?

8. Expect not too great happiness in life. Human nature admits it not.

9. Propose not a happiness too complicated. But does that depend on me? Yes: the first choice does. Life is like a game: one may choose the game: and passion, by degrees, seizes the proper object.

10. Anticipate by your hopes and fancy future consolation, which time infallibly brings to every affliction.

11. I desire to be rich. Why? That I may possess many fine objects;

I shall conclude this subject with observing, that, though virtue be undoubtedly the best choice, when it is attainable, yet such is the disorder and confusion of human affairs, that no perfect or regular distribution of happiness and misery is ever in this life to be expected. Not only the goods of fortune, and the endowments of the body (both of which are important), not only these advantages, I say, are unequally divided between the virtuous and vicious, but even the mind itself partakes, in some degree, of this disorder; and the most worthy character, by the very constitution of the passions, enjoys not always the highest felicity.

It is observable, that though every bodily pain proceeds from some disorder in the part or organ, yet the pain is not always proportioned to the disorder, but is greater or less, according to the greater or less sensibility of the part upon which the noxious humors exert their influence. A *toothache* produces more violent convulsions of pain than a *phthisis* or a

---

houses, gardens, equipage, etc. How many fine objects does nature offer to every one without expense? if enjoyed, sufficient. If not: see the effect of custom or of temper, which would soon take off the relish of the riches.

12. I desire fame. Let this occur: if I act well, I shall have the esteem of all my acquaintance. And what is all the rest to me?

These reflections are so obvious, that it is a wonder they occur not to every man. So convincing, that it is a wonder they persuade not every man. But, perhaps, they do occur to, and persuade most men, when they consider human life by a general and calm survey: but where any real, affecting incident happens; when passion is awakened, fancy agitated, example draws, and counsel urges; the philosopher is lost in the man, and he seeks in vain for that persuasion which before seemed so firm and unshaken. What remedy for this inconvenience? Assist yourself by a frequent perusal of the entertaining moralists: have recourse to the learning of Plutarch, the imagination of Lucian, the eloquence of Cicero, the wit of Seneca, the gaiety of Montaigne, the sublimity of Shaftesbury. Moral precepts, so couched, strike deep, and fortify the mind against the illusions of passion. But trust not altogether to external aid: by habit and study acquire that philosophical temper which both gives force to reflection, and by rendering a great part of your happiness independent, takes off the edge from all disorderly passions, and tranquillizes the mind. Despise not these helps; but confide not too much in them neither; unless nature has been favorable in the temper with which she has endowed you.

dropsy. In like manner, with regard to the economy of the mind, we may observe, that all vice is indeed pernicious; yet the disturbance or pain is not measured out by nature with exact proportion to the degrees of vice; nor is the man of highest virtue, even abstracting from external accidents, always the most happy. A gloomy and melancholy disposition is certainly, *to our sentiments,* a vice or imperfection; but as it may be accompanied with great sense of honor and great integrity, it may be found in very worthy characters, though it is sufficient alone to embitter life, and render the person affected with it completely miserable. On the other hand, a selfish villain may possess a spring and alacrity of temper, a certain *gaiety of heart,* which is indeed a good quality, but which is rewarded much beyond its merit, and when attended with good fortune, will compensate for the uneasiness and remorse arising from all the other vices.

I shall add, as an observation to the same purpose, that, if a man be liable to a vice or imperfection, it may often happen, that a good quality, which he possesses along with it, will render him more miserable, than if he were completely vicious. A person of such imbecility of temper, as to be easily broken by affliction, is more unhappy for being endowed with a generous and friendly disposition, which gives him a lively concern for others, and exposes him the more to fortune and accidents. A sense of shame, in an imperfect character, is certainly a virtue; but produces great uneasiness and remorse, from which the abandoned villain is entirely free. A very amorous complexion, with a heart incapable of friendship, is happier than the same excess in love, with a generosity of temper, which transports a man beyond himself, and renders him a total slave to the object of his passion.

In a word, human life is more governed by fortune than by reason; is to be regarded more as a dull pastime than a serious occupation; and is more influenced by particular humor, than by general principles. Shall we engage ourselves in it with passion and anxiety? It is not worthy of so much concern. Shall we be indifferent about what happens? We lose all the pleasure of the game by our phlegm and carelessness. While we are reasoning concerning life, life is gone; and death, though *perhaps* they receive him differently, yet treats alike the fool and the philosopher. To reduce life to exact rule and method is commonly a painful, oft a fruitless occupation: and is it not also a proof, that we overvalue the prize for which we contend? Even to reason so carefully concerning it, and to fix with accuracy its just idea, would be overvaluing it, were it not that, to some tempers, this occupation is one of the most amusing in which life could possibly be employed.

Of the Dignity or Meanness of Human Nature

THERE are certain sects which secretly form themselves in the learned world, as well as factions in the political; and though sometimes they come not to an open rupture, they give a different turn to the ways of thinking of those who have taken part on either side. The most remarkable of this kind are the sects founded on the different sentiments with regard to the *dignity of human nature;* which is a point that seems to have divided philosophers and poets, as well as divines, from the beginning of the world to this day. Some exalt our species to the skies, and represent man as a kind of human demigod, who derives his origin from heaven, and retains evident marks of his lineage and descent. Others insist upon the blind sides of human nature, and can discover nothing, except vanity, in which man surpasses the other animals, whom he affects so much to despise. If an author possess the talent of rhetoric and declamation, he commonly takes part with the former: if his turn lie towards irony and ridicule, he naturally throws himself into the other extreme.

I am far from thinking that all those who have depreciated our species have been enemies to virtue, and have exposed the frailties of their fellow-creatures with any bad intention. On the contrary, I am sensible that a delicate sense of morals, especially when attended with a splenetic temper, is apt to give a man a disgust of the world, and to make him consider the common course of human affairs with too much indignation. I must, however, be of opinion, that the sentiments of those who are inclined to think favorably of mankind, are more advantageous to virtue than the contrary principles, which give us a mean opinion of our nature. When a man is prepossessed with a high notion of his rank and character in the creation, he will naturally endeavor to act up to it, and will scorn to do a base or vicious action which might sink him below that figure which he makes in his own imagination. Accordingly we find, that all our polite and fashionable moralists insist upon this topic, and endeavor to represent vice unworthy of man, as well as odious in itself.[a]

We find few disputes that are not founded on some ambiguity in the expression; and I am persuaded that the present dispute, concerning the dignity or meanness of human nature, is not more exempt from it than any other. It may therefore be worth while to consider what is real, and what is only verbal, in this controversy.

That there is a natural difference between merit and demerit, virtue and vice, wisdom and folly, no reasonable man will deny: yet it is evident that, in affixing the term, which denotes either our approbation or blame, we are commonly more influenced by comparison than by any fixed unalterable standard in the nature of things. In like manner, quantity, and extension, and bulk, are by every one acknowledged to be real things: but when we call any animal *great* or *little,* we always form a secret comparison between that animal and others of the same species; and it is that comparison which regulates our judgment concerning its greatness. A dog and a horse may be of the very same size, while the one is admired for the greatness of its bulk, and the other for the smallness. When I am present, therefore, at any dispute, I always consider with myself whether it be a question of comparison or not that is the subject of controversy; and if it be, whether the disputants compare the same objects together, or talk of things that are widely different.

In forming our notions of human nature, we are apt to make a comparison between men and animals, the only creatures endowed with thought that fall under our senses. Certainly this comparison is favorable to mankind. On the one hand, we see a creature whose thoughts are not limited by any narrow bounds, either of place or time; who carries his researches into the most distant regions of this globe, and beyond this globe, to the planets and heavenly bodies; looks backward to consider the first origin, at least the history of the human race; casts his eye forward to see the influence of his actions upon posterity, and the judgments which will be formed of his character a thousand years hence; a creature, who traces causes and effects to a great length and intricacy; extracts general principles from particular appearances; improves upon his discoveries; corrects his mistakes; and makes his very errors profitable. On the other hand, we are presented with a creature the very reverse of this; limited in its observations and reasonings to a few sensible objects which surround it; without curiosity, without foresight; blindly conducted by instinct, and attaining, in a short time, its utmost perfection, beyond which it is never able to advance a single step. What a wide difference is there between these creatures! And how exalted a notion must we entertain of the former, in comparison of the latter.

There are two means commonly employed to destroy this conclusion: *First,* By making an unfair representation of the case, and insisting only upon the weakness of human nature. And, *secondly,* By forming a new and secret comparison between man and beings of the most perfect wisdom. Among the other excellences of man, this is one, that he can form an idea of perfections much beyond what he has experience of in himself; and is not limited in his conception of wisdom and virtue. He can easily exalt his notions, and conceive a degree of knowledge, which, when compared to his own, will make the latter appear very contemptible, and will cause the difference between that and the sagacity of animals, in a manner, to disappear and vanish. Now this being a point in which all the world is agreed, that human understanding falls infinitely short of perfect wisdom, it is proper we should know when this comparison takes place, that we may not dispute where there is no real difference in our sentiments. Man falls much more short of perfect wisdom, and even of his own ideas of perfect wisdom, than animals do of man; yet the latter difference is so considerable, that nothing but a comparison with the former can make it appear of little moment.

It is also usual to *compare* one man with another; and find-

ing very few whom we can call *wise* or *virtuous*, we are apt to
entertain a contemptible notion of our species in general. That
we may be sensible of the fallacy of this way of reasoning, we
may observe, that the honorable appellations of wise and virtuous are not annexed to any particular degree of those qualities of *wisdom* and *virtue*, but arise altogether from the comparison we make between one man and another. When we
find a man who arrives at such a pitch of wisdom as is very
uncommon, we pronounce him a wise man: so that to say
there are few wise men in the world, is really to say nothing;
since it is only by their scarcity that they merit that appellation. Were the lowest of our species as wise as Tully [1] or Lord
Bacon, we should still have reason to say that there are few
wise men. For in that case we should exalt our notions of wisdom, and should not pay a singular homage to any one who
was not singularly distinguished by his talents. In like manner,
I have heard it observed by thoughtless people, that there are
few women possessed of beauty in comparison of those who
want it; not considering that we bestow the epithet of *beautiful* only on such as possess a degree of beauty that is common
to them with a few. The same degree of beauty in a woman is
called deformity, which is treated as real beauty in one of our
sex.

   As it is usual, in forming a notion of our species, to *compare* it with the other species above or below it, or to compare
the individuals of the species among themselves; so we often
compare together the different motives or actuating principles
of human nature, in order to regulate our judgment concerning it. And, indeed, this is the only kind of comparison which
is worth our attention, or decides any thing in the present
question. Were our selfish and vicious principles so much
predominant above our social and virtuous, as is asserted by
some philosophers, we ought undoubtedly to entertain a contemptible notion of human nature.[b]

   There is much of a dispute of words in all this controversy.[c]
When a man denies the sincerity of all public spirit or affec-

1 [That is, Cicero.]

tion to a country and community, I am at a loss what to think of him. Perhaps he never felt this passion in so clear and distinct a manner as to remove all his doubts concerning its force and reality. But when he proceeds afterwards to reject all private friendship, if no interest or self-love intermix itself; I am then confident that he abuses terms, and confounds the ideas of things; since it is impossible for any one to be so selfish, or rather so stupid, as to make no difference between one man and another, and give no preference to qualities which engage his approbation and esteem. Is he also, say I, as insensible to anger as he pretends to be to friendship? And does injury and wrong no more affect him than kindness or benefits? Impossible: he does not know himself: he has forgotten the movements of his heart; or rather, he makes use of a different language from the rest of his countrymen, and calls not things by their proper names. What say you of natural affection? (I subjoin), Is that also a species of self-love? Yes; all is self-love. *Your* children are loved only because they are yours: *your* friend for a like reason: and *your* country engages you only so far as it has a connection with *yourself*. Were the idea of self removed, nothing would affect you: you would be altogether unactive and insensible: or, if you ever give yourself any movement, it would only be from vanity, and a desire of fame and reputation to this same self. I am willing, reply I, to receive your interpretation of human actions, provided you admit the facts. That species of self-love which displays itself in kindness to others, you must allow to have great influence over human actions, and even greater, on many occasions, than that which remains in its original shape and form. For how few are there, having a family, children, and relations, who do not spend more on the maintenance and education of these than on their own pleasures? This, indeed, you justly observe, may proceed from their self-love, since the prosperity of their family and friends is one, or the chief, of their pleasures, as well as their chief honor. Be you also one of these selfish men, and you are sure of every one's good opinion and good-will; or, not to shock your ears with these expressions, the self-love of every one, and mine among the rest, will then incline us to serve you, and speak well of you.

In my opinion, there are two things which have led astray those philosophers that have insisted so much on the selfishness of man. In the *first* place, they found that every act of virtue or friendship was attended with a secret pleasure; whence they concluded, that friendship and virtue could not be disinterested. But the fallacy of this is obvious. The virtuous sentiment or passion produces the pleasure, and does not arise from it. I feel a pleasure in doing good to my friend, because I love him; but do not love him for the sake of that pleasure.

In the *second* place, it has always been found, that the virtuous are far from being indifferent to praise; and therefore they have been represented as a set of vainglorious men, who had nothing in view but the applauses of others. But this also is a fallacy. It is very unjust in the world, when they find any tincture of vanity in a laudable action, to depreciate it upon that account, or ascribe it entirely to that motive. The case is not the same with vanity, as with other passions. Where avarice or revenge enters into any seemingly virtuous action, it is difficult for us to determine how far it enters, and it is natural to suppose it the sole actuating principle. But vanity is so closely allied to virtue, and to love the fame of laudable actions approaches so near the love of laudable actions for their own sake, that these passions are more capable of mixture, than any other kinds of affection; and it is almost impossible to have the latter without some degree of the former. Accordingly we find, that this passion for glory is always warped and varied according to the particular taste or disposition of the mind on which it falls. Nero had the same vanity in driving a chariot, that Trajan had in governing the empire with justice and ability. To love the glory of virtuous deeds is a sure proof of the love of virtue.

Of Superstition and Enthusiasm

THAT *the corruption of the best of things produces the worst,* is grown into a maxim, and is commonly proved, among other instances, by the pernicious effects of *superstition* and *enthusiasm,* the corruptions of true religion.

These two species of false religion, though both pernicious, are yet of a very different, and even of a contrary nature. The mind of man is subject to certain unaccountable terrors and apprehensions, proceeding either from the unhappy situation of private or public affairs, from ill health, from a gloomy and melancholy disposition, or from the concurrence of all these circumstances. In such a state of mind, infinite unknown evils are dreaded from unknown agents; and where real objects of terror are wanting, the soul, active to its own prejudice, and fostering its predominant inclination, finds imaginary ones, to whose power and malevolence it sets no limits. As these enemies are entirely invisible and unknown, the methods taken to appease them are equally unaccountable, and consist in ceremonies, observances, mortifications, sacrifices, presents, or in any practice, however absurd or frivolous, which either folly or knavery recommends to a blind and terrified credulity. Weakness, fear, melancholy, together with ignorance, are, therefore, the true sources of Superstition.

But the mind of man is also subject to an unaccountable elevation and presumption, arising from prosperous success, from luxuriant health, from strong spirits, or from a bold and confident disposition. In such a state of mind, the imagination swells with great, but confused conceptions, to which no sublunary beauties or enjoyments can correspond. Every thing mortal and perishable vanishes as unworthy of attention; and a full range is given to the fancy in the invisible regions, or world of Spirits, where the soul is at liberty to indulge itself in every imagination, which may best suit its present taste and disposition. Hence arise raptures, transports, and surprising flights of fancy; and, confidence and presumption still increasing, these raptures, being altogether unaccountable, and seeming quite beyond the reach of our ordinary faculties, are attributed to the immediate inspiration of that Divine Being who is the object of devotion. In a little time, the inspired person comes to regard himself as a distinguished favorite of the Divinity; and when this phrensy once takes place, which is the summit of enthusiasm, every whimsey is consecrated: human reason, and even morality, are rejected as fallacious guides; and the fanatic madman delivers himself over, blindly and without reserve, to the supposed illapses of the Spirit, and to inspiration from above.—Hope, pride, presumption, a warm imagination, together with ignorance, are therefore the true sources of Enthusiasm.

These two species of false religion might afford occasion to many speculations; but I shall confine myself, at present, to a few reflections concerning their different influence on government and society.

ᵃMy *first* reflection is, *that superstition is favorable to priestly power, and enthusiasm not less, or rather more contrary to it, than sound reason and philosophy.* As superstition is founded on fear, sorrow, and a depression of spirits, it represents the man to himself in such despicable colors, that he appears unworthy, in his own eyes, of approaching the Divine presence, and naturally has recourse to any other person, whose sanctity of life, or perhaps impudence and cunning, have made him be supposed more favored by the Divinity. To him the superstitious intrust their devotions: to his care they recommend their prayers, petitions, and sacrifices: and by his means, they hope to render their addresses acceptable to their incensed Deity. Hence the origin of PRIESTS, who may justly be regarded as an invention of a timorous and abject superstition, which, ever diffident of itself, dares not offer up its own devotions, but ignorantly thinks to recommend itself to the Divinity, by the mediation of his supposed friends and servants. As superstition is a considerable ingredient in almost all religions, even the most fanatical; there being nothing but philosophy able entirely to conquer these unaccountable terrors; hence it proceeds, that in almost every sect of religion there are priests to be found: but the stronger mixture there is of superstition, the higher is the authority of the priesthood.

On the other hand, it may be observed, that all enthusiasts have been free from the yoke of ecclesiastics, and have expressed great independence in their devotion, with a contempt of forms, ceremonies, and traditions. The *Quakers* are the most egregious, though, at the same time, the most innocent enthusiasts that have yet been known; and are perhaps the only sect that have never admitted priests among them. The *Independents*, of all the English sectaries, approach nearest to the *Quakers* in fanaticism, and in their freedom from priestly bondage. The *Presbyterians* follow after, at an equal distance, in both particulars. In short, this observation is founded in experience; and will also appear to be founded in reason, if we consider, that, as enthusiasm arises from a presumptuous pride and confidence, it thinks itself sufficiently qualified to *approach* the Divinity, without any human mediator. Its rapturous devotions are so fervent, that it even imagines itself *actually* to *approach* him by the way of contemplation and inward converse; which makes it neglect all those outward ceremonies and observances, to which the assistance of the priests appears so requisite in the eyes of their superstitious votaries. The fanatic consecrates himself, and bestows on his own person a sacred character, much superior to what forms and ceremonious institutions can confer on any other.

My *second* reflection with regard to these species of false religion is, *that religions which partake of enthusiasm, are, on their first rise, more furious and violent than those which partake of superstition; but in a little time become more gentle and moderate.* The violence of this species of religion, when excited by novelty, and animated by opposition, appears from numberless instances; of the *Anabaptists* in Germany, the *Camisars* in France, the *Levellers,* and other fanatics in England, and the *Covenanters* in Scotland. Enthusiasm being founded on strong spirits, and a presumptuous boldness of character, it naturally begets the most extreme resolutions; especially after it rises to that height as to inspire the deluded fanatic with the opinion of Divine illuminations, and with a contempt for the common rules of reason, morality, and prudence.

It is thus enthusiasm produces the most cruel disorders in human society; but its fury is like that of thunder and tempest, which exhaust themselves in a little time, and leave the air more calm and serene than before. When the first fire of enthusiasm is spent, men naturally, in all fanatical sects, sink into the greatest remissness and coolness in sacred matters; there being no body of men among them endowed with sufficient authority, whose interest is concerned to support the religious spirit; no rites, no ceremonies, no holy observances, which may enter into the common train of life, and preserve the sacred principles from oblivion. Superstition, on the contrary, steals in gradually and insensibly; renders men tame and submissive; is acceptable to the magistrate, and seems inoffensive to the people: till at last the priest, having firmly established his authority, becomes the tyrant and disturber of human society, by his endless contentions, persecutions, and religious wars. How smoothly did the Romish church advance in her acquisition of power! But into what dismal convulsions did she throw all Europe, in order to maintain it! On the other hand, our sectaries, who were formerly such dangerous bigots, are now become very free reasoners; and the *Quakers* seem to approach nearly the only regular body of *Deists* in the universe, the *literati,* or the disciples of Confucius in China.[1]

My *third* observation on this head is, *that superstition is an enemy to civil liberty, and enthusiasm a friend to it.* As superstition groans under the dominion of priests, and enthusiasm is destructive of all ecclesiastical power, this sufficiently accounts for the present observation. Not to mention that enthusiasm, being the infirmity of bold and ambitious tempers, is naturally accompanied with a spirit of liberty; as superstition,

[1] The Chinese literati have no priests or ecclesiastical establishment.

on the contrary, renders men tame and abject, and fits them
for slavery. We learn from English history, that, during the
civil wars, the *Independents* and *Deists,* though the most opposite in their religious principles, yet were united in their
political ones, and were alike passionate for a commonwealth.
And since the origin of *Whig* and *Tory,* the leaders of the
Whigs have either been *Deists* or professed *Latitudinarians* in
their principles; that is, friends to toleration, and indifferent
to any particular sect of *Christians:* while the sectaries, who
have all a strong tincture of enthusiasm, have always, without
exception, concurred with that party in defence of civil liberty. The resemblance in their superstitions long united the
High-Church *Tories* and the *Roman Catholics,* in support of
prerogative and kingly power; though experience of the tol-
erating spirit of the *Whigs* seems of late to have reconciled the
Catholics to that party.

The *Molinists* and *Jansenists* in France have a thousand unintelligible disputes, which are not worthy the reflection of a
man of sense: but what principally distinguishes these two
sects, and alone merits attention, is the different spirit of their
religion. The *Molinists,* conducted by the *Jesuits,* are great
friends to superstition, rigid observers of external forms and
ceremonies, and devoted to the authority of the priests, and to
tradition. The *Jansenists* are enthusiasts, and zealous pro-
moters of the passionate devotion, and of the inward life; little
influenced by authority; and, in a word, but half Catholics.
The consequences are exactly conformable to the foregoing
reasoning. The *Jesuits* are the tyrants of the people, and the
slaves of the court: and the *Jansenists* preserve alive the small
sparks of the love of liberty which are to be found in the
French nation.

On Suicide*

ONE considerable advantage that arises from philosophy, consists in the sovereign antidote which it affords to superstition and false religion. All other remedies against that pestilent distemper are vain, or at least uncertain. Plain good sense, and the practice of the world, which alone serve most purposes of life, are here found ineffectual: history, as well as daily experience, furnish instances of men endowed with the strongest capacity for business and affairs, who have all their lives crouched under slavery to the grossest superstition. Even gaiety and sweetness of temper, which infuse a balm into every other wound, afford no remedy to so virulent a poison, as we may particularly observe of the fair sex, who, though commonly possessed of these rich presents of nature, feel many of their joys blasted by this importunate intruder. But when sound philosophy has once gained possession of the mind, superstition is effectually excluded; and one may fairly affirm, that her triumph over this enemy is more complete than over most of the vices and imperfections incident to human nature. Love or anger, ambition or avarice, have their root in the temper and affections, which the soundest reason is scarce ever able fully to correct; but superstition being founded on false opinion, must immediately vanish when true philosophy has inspired juster sentiments of superior powers. The contest is here more equal between the distemper and the medicine; and nothing can hinder the latter from proving effectual, but its being false and sophisticated.

It will here be superfluous to magnify the merits of Philosophy by displaying the pernicious tendency of that vice of which it cures the human mind. The superstitious man, says Tully,[1] is miserable in every scene, in every incident in life; even sleep itself, which banishes all other cares of unhappy

[1] Cicero, *De Divinatione* [II. 149–50.]

mortals, affords to him matter of new terror, while he examines his dreams, and finds in those visions of the night prognostications of future calamities. I may add, that though death alone can put a full period to his misery, he dares not fly to this refuge, but still prolongs a miserable existence, from a vain fear lest he offend his Maker, by using the power with which that beneficent Being has endowed him. The presents of GOD and nature are ravished from us by this cruel enemy; and notwithstanding that one step would remove us from the regions of pain and sorrow, her menaces still chain us down to a hated being, which she herself chiefly contributes to render miserable.

It is observed by such as have been reduced by the calamities of life to the necessity of employing this fatal remedy, that if the unseasonable care of their friends deprive them of that species of death which they proposed to themselves, they seldom venture upon any other, or can summon up so much resolution a second time, as to execute their purpose. So great is our horror of death, that when it presents itself under any form besides that to which a man has endeavored to reconcile his imagination, it acquires new terrors, and overcomes his feeble courage: but when the menaces of superstition are joined to this natural timidity, no wonder it quite deprives men of all power over their lives, since even many pleasures and enjoyments, to which we are carried by a strong propensity, are torn from us by this inhuman tyrant. Let us here endeavor to restore men to their native liberty, by examining all the common arguments against suicide, and showing that that action may be free from every imputation of guilt or blame, according to the sentiments of all the ancient philosophers.

If suicide be criminal, it must be a transgression of our duty either to God, our neighbor, or ourselves. To prove that suicide is no transgression of our duty to God, the following considerations may perhaps suffice. In order to govern the material world, the almighty Creator has established general and immutable laws, by which all bodies, from the greatest planet to the smallest particle of matter, are maintained in their proper sphere and function. To govern the animal world, he has endowed all living creatures with bodily and mental powers; with senses, passions, appetites, memory, and judgment, by which they are impelled or regulated in that course of life to which they are destined. These two distinct principles of the material and animal world continually encroach upon each other, and mutually retard or forward each other's operation. The powers of men and of all other animals are restrained and directed by the nature and qualities of the surrounding bodies; and the modifications and actions of these bodies are incessantly altered by the operation of all animals. Man is stopped by rivers in his passage over the surface of the earth; and rivers, when properly directed, lend their force to the motion of machines, which serve to the use of man. But though the provinces of the material and animal powers are not kept entirely separate, there results from thence no discord or disorder in the creation; on the contrary, from the mixture, union, and contrast of all the various powers of inanimate bodies and living creatures, arises that sympathy, harmony, and proportion, which affords the surest argument of Supreme Wisdom. The providence of the Deity appears not immediately in any operation, but governs every thing by those general and immutable laws which have been established from the beginning of time. All events, in one sense, may be pronounced the action of the Almighty; they all proceed from those powers with which he has endowed his creatures. A house which falls by its own weight, is not brought to ruin by his providence, more than one destroyed by the hands of men; nor are the human faculties less his workmanship than the laws of motion and gravitation. When the passions play, when the judgment dictates, when the limbs obey; this is all the operation of God; and upon these animate principles, as well as upon the inanimate, has he established the government of the universe. Every event is alike important in the eyes of that infinite Being, who takes in at one glance the most distant regions of space, and remotest periods of time. There is no event, however important to us, which he has exempted from the general laws that govern the universe, or which he has peculiarly reserved for his own immediate action and operation. The revolution of states and empires depends upon the smallest caprice or passion of single men; and the lives of men are shortened or extended by the smallest accident of air or diet, sunshine or tempest. Nature still continues her progress and operation; and if general laws be ever broke by particular volitions of the Deity, it is after a manner which entirely escapes human observation. As, on the one hand, the elements and other inanimate parts of the creation carry on their action without regard to the particular interest and situation of men; so men are intrusted to their own judgment and discretion in the various shocks of matter, and may employ every faculty with which they are endowed, in order to provide for their ease, happiness, or preservation. What is the meaning then of that principle, that a man, who, tired of life, and hunted by pain and misery, bravely overcomes all the natural terrors of death, and makes his escape from this cruel scene; that such a man, I say, has incurred the indignation of his Creator, by encroaching on the office of divine providence, and disturbing the order of the universe? Shall we assert, that the Almighty has reserved to himself, in any peculiar manner, the disposal of the lives of men, and has not submitted that event, in common with others, to the general laws by which the universe is governed? This is plainly false: the lives of men depend upon the same laws as the lives of all other animals; and these are subjected to the general laws of matter and motion. The fall of a tower, or the infusion of a poison, will destroy a man equally with the meanest creature; an inundation sweeps away every thing without distinction that comes within the reach of its fury. Since therefore the lives of men are for ever dependent on the general laws of matter and motion, is a man's disposing of his life criminal, because in every case it is criminal to encroach upon these laws, or disturb their operation? But this seems absurd: all animals are intrusted to their own prudence and skill for their conduct in the world; and have full authority, as far as their power extends, to alter all the operations of nature. Without the exercise of this authority, they could not subsist a moment; every action, every motion of a man, innovates on the order of some parts of matter, and diverts from their ordinary course the general laws of motion. Putting together therefore these conclusions, we find that human life depends upon the general laws of matter and motion, and that it is no encroachment on the office of Providence to disturb or alter these general laws: has not every one of consequence the free disposal of his own life? And may he not lawfully employ that power with which nature has endowed him? In order to destroy the evidence of this conclusion, we must show a reason why this particular case is excepted. Is it because human life is of such great importance, that it is a presumption for human prudence to dispose of it? But the life of a man is of no greater importance to the universe than that of an oyster: and were it of ever so great importance, the order of human nature has actually submitted it to human prudence, and reduced us to a necessity, in every incident, of determining concerning it.

Were the disposal of human life so much reserved as the peculiar province of the Almighty, that it were an encroachment on his right for men to dispose of their own lives, it would be equally criminal to act for the preservation of life as for its destruction. If I turn aside a stone which is falling upon my head, I disturb the course of nature; and I invade the peculiar province of the Almighty, by lengthening out my life beyond the period, which, by the general laws of matter and motion, he had assigned it.

A hair, a fly, an insect, is able to destroy this mighty being whose life is of such importance. Is it an absurdity to suppose that human prudence may lawfully dispose of what depends on such insignificant causes? It would be no crime in me to divert the Nile or Danube from its course, were I able to effect such purposes. Where then is the crime of turning a few ounces of blood from their natural channel? Do you imagine that I repine at Providence, or curse my creation, because I go out of life, and put a period to a being which, were it to continue, would render me miserable? Far be such sentiments from me. I am only convinced of a matter of fact which you yourself acknowledge possible, that human life may be unhappy; and that my existence, if further prolonged, would become ineligible: but I thank Providence, both for the good which I have already enjoyed, and for the power with which I am endowed of escaping the ills that threaten me.[2] To you it belongs to repine at Providence, who foolishly imagine that you have no such power; and who must still prolong a hated life, though loaded with pain and sickness, with shame and poverty. Do not you teach, that when any ill befalls me, though by the malice of my enemies, I ought to be resigned to Providence; and that the actions of men are the operations of the Almighty, as much as the actions of inanimate beings? When I fall upon my own sword, therefore, I receive my death equally from the hands of the Deity as if it had proceeded from a lion, a precipice, or a fever. The submission which you require to Providence, in every calamity that befalls me, excludes not human skill and industry, if possibly by their means I can avoid or escape the calamity. And why may I not employ one remedy as well as another? If my life be not my own, it were criminal for me to put it in danger, as well as to dispose of it; nor could one man deserve the appellation of *hero,* whom glory or friendship transports into the greatest dangers; and another merit the reproach of *wretch* or *miscreant,* who puts a period to his life from the same or like motives. There is no being which possesses any power or faculty, that it receives not from its Creator; nor is there any one, which by ever so irregular an action, can encroach upon the plan of his providence, or disorder the universe. Its operations are his works equally with that chain of events which it invades; and whichever principle prevails, we may for that very reason conclude it to be most favored by him. Be it animate or inanimate; rational or irrational; it is all the same case: its power is still derived from the Supreme Creator, and is alike compre-

---

[2] Agamus Deo gratias, quod nemo in vita teneri potest. Seneca, *Epistles* XII. 10.

hended in the order of his providence. When the horror of pain prevails over the love of life; when a voluntary action anticipates the effects of blind causes; it is only in consequence of those powers and principles which he has implanted in his creatures. Divine Providence is still inviolate, and placed far beyond the reach of human injuries.[3] It is impious, says the old Roman superstition, to divert rivers from their course, or invade the prerogatives of nature. It is impious, says the French superstition, to inoculate for the smallpox, or usurp the business of Providence, by voluntarily producing distempers and maladies. It is impious, says the modern European superstition, to put a period to our own life, and thereby rebel against our Creator: and why not impious, say I, to build houses, cultivate the ground, or sail upon the ocean? In all these actions we employ our powers of mind and body to produce some innovation in the course of nature; and in none of them do we any more. They are all of them therefore equally innocent, or equally criminal. *But you are placed by Providence, like a sentinel, in a particular station; and when you desert it without being recalled, you are equally guilty of rebellion against your Almighty Sovereign, and have incurred his displeasure*—I ask, Why do you conclude that Providence has placed me in this station? For my part, I find that I owe my birth to a long chain of causes, of which many depended upon voluntary actions of men. *But Providence guided all these causes, and nothing happens in the universe without its consent and coöperation.* If so, then neither does my death, however voluntary, happen without its consent; and whenever pain or sorrow so far overcome my patience, as to make me tired of life, I may conclude that I am recalled from my station in the clearest and most express terms. It is Providence surely that has placed me at this present moment in this chamber: but may I not leave it when I think proper, without being liable to the imputation of having deserted my post or station? When I shall be dead, the principles of which I am composed will still perform their part in the universe, and

3 Tacitus, *Annals* I. 74.

will be equally useful in the grand fabric, as when they compose this individual creature. The difference to the whole will be no greater than betwixt my being in a chamber and in the open air. The one change is of more importance to me than the other; but not more so to the universe.

It is a kind of blasphemy to imagine that any created being can disturb the order of the world, or invade the business of Providence? It supposes, that that being possesses powers and faculties which it received not from its Creator, and which are not subordinate to his government and authority. A man may disturb society, no doubt, and thereby incur the displeasure of the Almighty: but the government of the world is placed far beyond his reach and violence. And how does it appear that the Almighty is displeased with those actions that disturb society? By the principles which he has implanted in human nature, and which inspire us with a sentiment of remorse if we ourselves have been guilty of such actions, and with that of blame and disapprobation, if we ever observe them in others. Let us now examine, according to the method proposed, whether Suicide be of this kind of actions, and be a breach of our duty to our *neighbor* and to *society*.

A man who retires from life does no harm to society: he only ceases to do good; which, if it is an injury, is of the lowest kind. All our obligations to do good to society seem to imply something reciprocal. I receive the benefits of society, and therefore ought to promote its interests; but when I withdraw myself altogether from society, can I be bound any longer? But allowing that our obligations to do good were perpetual, they have certainly some bounds; I am not obliged to do a small good to society at the expense of a great harm to myself: why then should I prolong a miserable existence, because of some frivolous advantage which the public may perhaps receive from me? If upon account of age and infirmities, I may lawfully resign any office, and employ my time altogether in fencing against these calamities, and alleviating as much as possible the miseries of my future life; why may I not cut short these miseries at once by an action which is no more prejudicial to society? But suppose that it is no longer in my power to promote the interest of society; suppose that I am a burden to it; suppose that my life hinders some person from being much more useful to society: in such cases, my resignation of life must not only be innocent, but laudable. And most people who lie under any temptation to abandon existence, are in some such situation; those who have health, or power, or authority, have commonly better reason to be in humor with the world.

A man is engaged in a conspiracy for the public interest; is seized upon suspicion; is threatened with the rack; and knows from his own weakness that the secret will be extorted from him: could such a one consult the public interest better than by putting a quick period to a miserable life? This was the case of the famous and brave Strozi of Florence.[4] Again, suppose a malefactor is justly condemned to a shameful death; can any reason be imagined why he may not anticipate his punishment, and save himself all the anguish of thinking on its dreadful approaches? He invades the business of Providence no more than the magistrate did who ordered his execution; and his voluntary death is equally advantageous to society, by ridding it of a pernicious member.

That Suicide may often be consistent with interest and with our duty to ourselves, no one can question, who allows that age, sickness, or misfortune, may render life a burden, and make it worse even than annihilation. I believe that no man ever threw away life while it was worth keeping. For such is our natural horror of death, that small motives will never be able to reconcile us to it; and though perhaps the situation of a man's health or fortune did not seem to require this remedy, we may at least be assured, that any one who, without appar-

4 [Filippo Strozzi (1488–1538), wealthy Florentine merchant, captured after organizing an abortive revolt against Cosimo de' Medici. He was not strong, and incapable of withstanding torture; one day he was found dead in his cell, lying between two bloodstained swords, with a note that read in part: "If I have not hitherto known how to live, I will know how to die." Unfortunately for Hume's argument, it is now believed that Cosimo staged the "suicide" to rid himself of his enemy.]

ent reason, has had recourse to it, was cursed with such an incurable depravity or gloominess of temper as must poison all enjoyment, and render him equally miserable as if he had been loaded with the most grievous misfortunes. If Suicide be supposed a crime, it is only cowardice can impel us to it. If it be no crime, both prudence and courage should engage us to rid ourselves at once of existence when it becomes a burden. It is the only way that we can then be useful to society, by setting an example, which, if imitated, would preserve to every one his chance for happiness in life, and would effectually free him from all danger or misery.[5]

[5] It would be easy to prove that suicide is as lawful under the Christian dispensation as it was to the Heathens. There is not a single text of Scripture which prohibits it. That great and infallible rule of faith and practice which must control all philosophy and human reasoning, has left us in this particular to our natural liberty. Resignation to Providence is indeed recommended in Scripture; but that implies only submission to ills that are unavoidable, not to such as may be remedied by prudence or courage. *Thou shalt not kill*, is evidently meant to exclude only the killing of others, over whose life we have no authority. That this precept, like most of the Scripture precepts, must be modified by reason and common sense, is plain from the practice of magistrates, who punish criminals capitally, notwithstanding the letter of the law. But were this commandment ever so express against suicide, it would now have no authority, for all the law of *Moses* is abolished, except so far as it is established by the law of nature. And we have already endeavored to prove that suicide is not prohibited by that law. In all cases Christians and Heathens are precisely upon the same footing; *Cato* and *Brutus*, *Arrea* and *Portia* acted heroically; those who now imitate their example ought to receive the same praises from posterity. The power of committing suicide is regarded by *Pliny* as an advantage which men possess even above the Deity himself. "Deus non sibi potest mortem consciscere si velit, quod homini dedit optimum in tantis vitae poenis." [*Natural History*, II. 5.]

On the Immortality of the Soul

By the mere light of reason it seems difficult to prove the immortality of the soul; the arguments for it are commonly derived either from metaphysical topics, or moral, or physical. But in reality it is the gospel, and the gospel alone, that has brought *life and immortality to light.*

I. Metaphysical topics suppose that the soul is immaterial, and that it is impossible for thought to belong to a material substance. But just metaphysics teach us, that the notion of substance is wholly confused and imperfect; and that we have no other idea of any substance, than as an aggregate of particular qualities inhering in an unknown something. Matter, therefore, and spirit, are at bottom equally unknown; and we cannot determine what qualities inhere in the one or in the other. They likewise teach us, that nothing can be decided *à priori* concerning any cause or effect; and that experience, being the only source of our judgments of this nature, we cannot know from any other principle, whether matter, by its structure or arrangement, may not be the cause of thought. Abstract reasonings cannot decide any question of fact or existence. But admitting a spiritual substance to be dispersed throughout the universe, like the ethereal fire of the Stoics, and to be the only inherent subject of thought, we have reason to conclude from *analogy,* that nature uses it after the manner she does the other substance, *matter.* She employs it as a kind of paste or clay; modifies it into a variety of forms and existences; dissolves after a time each modification, and from its substance erects a new form. As the same material substance may successively compose the bodies of all animals, the same spiritual substance may compose their minds: their consciousness or that system of thought which they formed during life, may be continually dissolved by death, and nothing interests them in the new modification. The most positive assertors of the mortality of the soul never denied the immortality of its substance; and that an immaterial substance, as well as a material, may lose its memory or consciousness, appears in part from experience, if the soul be immaterial. Reasoning from the common course of nature, and without supposing any new interposition of the Supreme Cause, which ought always to be excluded from philosophy, *what is incorruptible must also be ingenerable*. The soul therefore, if immortal, existed before our birth; and if the former existence noways concerned us, neither will the latter. Animals undoubtedly feel, think, love, hate, will, and even reason, though in a more imperfect manner than men: are their souls also immaterial and immortal?

II. Let us now consider the moral arguments, chiefly those derived from the justice of God, which is supposed to be further interested in the future punishment of the vicious and reward of the virtuous. But these arguments are grounded on the supposition that God has attributes beyond what he has exerted in this universe, with which alone we are acquainted. Whence do we infer the existence of these attributes? It is very safe for us to affirm, that whatever we know the Deity to have actually done is best; but it is very dangerous to affirm that he must always do what to us seems best. In how many instances would this reasoning fail us with regard to the present world? But if any purpose of nature be clear, we may affirm, that the whole scope and intention of man's creation, so far as we can judge by natural reason, is limited to the present life. With how weak a concern from the original inherent structure of the mind and passions, does he ever look further? What comparison either for steadiness or efficacy, betwixt so floating an idea and the most doubtful persuasion of any matter of fact that occurs in common life? There arise indeed in some minds some unaccountable terrors with regard to futurity; but these would quickly vanish were they not artificially fostered by precept and education. And those who foster them, what is their motive? Only to gain a livelihood, and to acquire power and riches in this world. Their very zeal and industry, therefore, are an argument against them.

What cruelty, what iniquity, what injustice in nature, to confine all our concern, as well as all our knowledge, to the present life, if there be another scene still waiting us of infinitely greater consequence? Ought this barbarous deceit to be ascribed to a beneficent and wise Being? Observe with what exact proportion the task to be performed, and the performing powers, are adjusted throughout all nature. If the reason of man gives him great superiority above other animals, his necessities are proportionably multiplied upon him: his whole time, his whole capacity, activity, courage, and passion, find sufficient employment in fencing against the miseries of his present condition; and frequently, nay, almost always, are too slender for the business assigned them. A pair of shoes, perhaps, was never yet wrought to the highest degree of perfection which that commodity is capable of attaining; yet it is necessary, at least very useful, that there should be some politicians and moralists, even some geometers, poets, and philosophers among mankind. The powers of men are no more superior to their wants, considered merely in this life, than those of foxes and hares are, compared to *their* wants and to their period of existence. The inference from parity of reason is therefore obvious.

On the theory of the soul's mortality, the inferiority of women's capacity is easily accounted for. Their domestic life requires no higher faculties either of mind or body. This circumstance vanishes and becomes absolutely insignificant on the religious theory: the one sex has an equal task to perform as the other; their powers of reason and resolution ought also to have been equal, and both of them infinitely greater than at present. As every effect implies a cause, and that another, till we reach the first cause of all, which is the Deity; every thing that happens is ordained by him, and nothing can be the object of his punishment or vengeance. By what rule are punishments and rewards distributed? What is the Divine standard of merit and demerit? Shall we suppose that human sentiments have place in the Deity? How bold that hypothesis! We have no conception of any other sentiments. According to human sentiments, sense, courage, good-manners, industry, prudence, genius, etc. are essential parts of personal merits. Shall we therefore erect an elysium for poets and heroes like that of ancient mythology? Why confine all rewards to one species of virtue? Punishment, without any proper end or purpose, is inconsistent with *our* ideas of goodness and justice; and no end can be served by it after the whole scene is closed. Punishment, according to *our* conception, should bear some proportion to the offence. Why then eternal punishment for the temporary offences of so frail a creature as man? Can any one approve of Alexander's rage, who intended to exterminate a whole nation because they had seized his favorite horse Bucephalus? [1]

Heaven and hell suppose two distinct species of men, the good and the bad; but the greatest part of mankind float betwixt vice and virtue. Were one to go round the world with an intention of giving a good supper to the righteous and a sound drubbing to the wicked, he would frequently be embarrassed in his choice, and would find the merits and demerits of most men and women scarcely amount to the value of either. To suppose measures of approbation and blame different from the human confounds every thing. Whence do we learn that there is such a thing as moral distinctions, but from our own sentiments? What man who has not met with personal provocation (or what good-natured man who has) could inflict on crimes, from the sense of blame alone, even the common, legal, frivolous punishments? And does any thing steel the breast of judges and juries against the sentiments of humanity but reflection on necessity and public interest? By the Roman law, those who had been guilty of parricide, and confessed their crime, were put into a sack along with an ape, a dog, and a serpent, and thrown into the river. Death alone was the punishment of those who denied their guilt, however fully proved. A criminal was tried before Augustus, and condemned after a full conviction; but the humane emperor, when he put the last interrogatory, gave it such a turn as to lead the wretch into a denial of his guilt. "You surely (said the prince) did not

[1] Quintus Curtius [*History of Alexander,* VI. 5.]

kill your father?" [2] This lenity suits our natural ideas of *right* even towards the greatest of all criminals, and even though it prevents so inconsiderable a sufferance. Nay, even the most bigoted priest would naturally without reflection approve of it, provided the crime was not heresy or infidelity; for as these crimes hurt himself in his *temporal* interest and advantages, perhaps he may not be altogether so indulgent to them. The chief source of moral ideas is the reflection on the interests of human society. Ought these interests, so short, so frivolous, to be guarded by punishments eternal and infinite? The damnation of one man is an infinitely greater evil in the universe than the subversion of a thousand millions of kingdoms. Nature has rendered human infancy peculiarly frail and mortal, as it were on purpose to refute the notion of a probationary state; the half of mankind die before they are rational creatures.

III. The physical arguments from the analogy of nature are strong for the mortality of the soul; and are really the only philosophical arguments which ought to be admitted with regard to this question, or indeed any question of fact. Where any two objects are so closely connected that all alterations which we have ever seen in the one are attended with proportionable alterations in the other; we ought to conclude, by all rules of analogy, that, when there are still greater alterations produced in the former, and it is totally dissolved, there follows a total dissolution of the latter. Sleep, a very small effect on the body, is attended with a temporary extinction, at least a great confusion in the soul. The weakness of the body and that of the mind in infancy are exactly proportioned; their vigor in manhood, their sympathetic disorder in sickness, their common gradual decay in old age. The step further seems unavoidable; their common dissolution in death. The last symptoms which the mind discovers, are disorder, weakness, insensibility, and stupidity; the forerunners of its annihilation. The further progress of the same causes increasing, the same effects totally extinguish it. Judging by the usual

2 Suetonius, *The Deified Augustus*, II. 3.

analogy of nature, no form can continue when transferred to a condition of life very different from the original one in which it was placed. Trees perish in the water, fishes in the air, animals in the earth. Even so small a difference as that of climate is often fatal. What reason then to imagine, that an immense alteration, such as is made on the soul by the dissolution of its body, and all its organs of thought and sensation, can be effected without the dissolution of the whole? Every thing is in common betwixt soul and body. The organs of the one are all of them the organs of the other; the existence, therefore, of the one must be dependent on the other. The souls of animals are allowed to be mortal; and these bear so near a resemblance to the souls of men, that the analogy from one to the other forms a very strong argument. Their bodies are not more resembling, yet no one rejects the argument drawn from comparative anatomy. The Metempsychosis is therefore the only system of this kind that philosophy can hearken to.

Nothing in this world is perpetual; every thing, however, seemingly firm, is in continual flux and change: the world itself gives symptoms of frailty and dissolution. How contrary to analogy, therefore, to imagine that one single form, seeming the frailest of any, and subject to the greatest disorders, is immortal and indissoluble? What theory is that! how lightly, not to say how rashly, entertained! How to dispose of the infinite number of posthumous existences ought also to embarrass the religious theory. Every planet in every solar system, we are at liberty to imagine peopled with intelligent mortal beings, at least we can fix on no other supposition. For these then a new universe must every generation be created beyond the bounds of the present universe, or one must have been created at first so prodigiously wide as to admit of this continual influx of beings. Ought such bold suppositions to be received by any philosophy, and that merely on the pretext of a bare possibility? When it is asked, whether Agamemnon, Thersites, Hannibal, Varro, and every stupid clown that ever existed in Italy, Scythia, Bactria, or Guinea, are now alive; can any man think, that a scrutiny of nature will furnish arguments strong enough to answer so strange a question in the affirmative? The want of argument without revelation sufficiently establishes the negative. *Quanto facilius,* says Pliny,[3] *certiusque sibi quemque credere, ac specimen securitatis antigene tali sumere experimento.* Our insensibility before the composition of the body seems to natural reason a proof of a like state after dissolution. Were our horrors of annihilation an original passion, not the effect of our general love of happiness, it would rather prove the mortality of the soul: for as nature does nothing in vain, she would never give us a horror against an impossible event. She may give us a horror against an unavoidable event, provided our endeavors, as in the present case, may often remove it to some distance. Death is in the end unavoidable; yet the human species could not be preserved had not nature inspired us with an aversion towards it. All doctrines are to be suspected which are favored by our passions; and the hopes and fears which gave rise to this doctrine are very obvious.

It is an infinite advantage in every controversy to defend the negative. If the question be out of the common experienced course of nature, this circumstance is almost if not altogether decisive. By what arguments or analogies can we prove any state of existence, which no one ever saw, and which no way resembles any that ever was seen? Who will repose such trust in any pretended philosophy as to admit upon its testimony the reality of so marvellous a scene? Some new species of logic is requisite for that purpose, and some new faculties of the mind, that they may enable us to comprehend that logic.

Nothing could set in a fuller light the infinite obligations which mankind have to Divine revelation, since we find that no other medium could ascertain this great and important truth.

---

[3] ["But how much easier and safer for each to trust in himself, and for us to derive our idea of future tranquillity from our experience of it before birth!" Pliny, *Natural History* VII. 55, tr. H. Rackham (Cambridge, Mass.: "Loeb Classical Library," 1947).]

Textual Notes
and
Variants

Textual Notes and Variants

The editions of Hume's works prior to that from which the present volume is taken contain textual variations which are noted below. These earlier editions are designated by letters, as follows:

A. *Essays, Moral and Political.* Edinburgh, Kincaid, 1741. 12mo.

B. *Essays, Moral and Political.* Vol. II. Edinburgh, Kincaid, 1742. 12mo. pp. 105.

C. *Essays, Moral and Political.* 2d Edition, corrected. Edinburgh, Kincaid, 1742. 12mo. pp. 189.

D. *Essays, Moral and Political.* By D. Hume, Esq. 3d Edition, corrected, with additions. London, Millar, 1748. 12 mo.

E. *Three Essays, Moral and Political, never before published, which completes the former Edition, in two volumes octavo.* By D. Hume, Esq. London, Millar, 1748. 12mo.

F. *Political Discourses.* By D. Hume, Esq. Edinburgh, Kincaid, 1752. Small 8vo. *To this Edition there is sometimes added "a List of Scotticisms."*

G. *Political Discourses.* By D. Hume, Esq. 2d Edition. Edinburgh, Kincaid, 1752. 12mo. *Merely a reprint of the preceding.*

H. *Essays and Treatises on several Subjects.* By D. Hume, Esq. Vol. IV. containing Political Discourses. 3d Edition, with Additions and Corrections. London, Millar, 1754.

I. *Four Dissertations: 1st, Natural History of Religion: 2d, of the Passions: 3d, of Tragedy: 4th, of the Standard of Taste.* By D. Hume, Esq. London, Millar, 1757. 12mo.

K. *Philosophical Essays concerning Human Understanding.*

By the Author of the Essays Moral and Political. London, Millar, 1748. 12mo.

L. *Philosophical Essays concerning Human Understanding.* By D. Hume, Esq. 2d Edition, with Additions and Corrections. London, Millar, 1750. 12mo.

M. *An Enquiry concerning the Principles of Morals.* By D. Hume, Esq. London, Millar, 1751.

N. *Essays and Treatises on several Subjects.* By D. Hume, Esq. London, Millar, 1768. 2 vols. 4to.

O. *Essays and Treatises on several Subjects.* By D. Hume, Esq. London, Cadell, 1777. 2 vols. 8vo.

The above list includes all the editions which vary substantially from each other. Those which are mere reprints are not included.

Of the Delicacy of Taste and Passion

Note *a*, p. 26. Editions A, C, D, N: How far the delicacy of taste, and that of passion are connected together in the original frame of the mind, it is hard to determine. To me there appears to be a very considerable connection betwixt them. For we may observe that women, who have more delicate passions than men, have also a more delicate taste of the ornaments of life, of dress, equipage, and the ordinary decencies of behavior. Any excellency in these hits their taste much sooner than ours; and when you please their taste, you soon engage their affections.

Of Essay Writing

Note *a*, p. 38. Taken from Edition B.

Of Simplicity and Refinement in Writing

Note *a*, p. 43. Note in Editions B and D: *Naïveté,* a word which I have borrowed from the French, and which is much wanted in our language.

Of Refinement in the Arts

Note *a*, p. 48. In Editions F, G, and H, this essay is entitled "Of Luxury."

Note *b*, p. 58. Edition N: Prodigality is not to be confounded with a refinement in the arts. It even appears that vice is much less frequent in the cultivated ages. Industry and gain beget this frugality among the lower and middle ranks of men, and in all the busy professions. Men of high rank, indeed, it may be pretended, are more allured by the pleasures, which become more frequent; but idleness is the great source of prodigality at all times; and there are pleasures and vanities in every age, which allure men equally when they are unacquainted with better enjoyments, not to mention that the high interest paid in rude times quickly consumes the fortunes of the landed gentry, and multiplies their necessities.

Of Eloquence

Note *a*, p. 67. This paragraph is not in the first editions; it occurs in Edition N.

Note *b*, p. 68. In the early editions the sentence begins: "Had such a cultivated genius as *my Lord Bolingbroke* arisen. . . ."

Note *c*, p. 68. I have confessed that there is something accidental in the origin and progress of the arts in any nation; and yet I cannot forbear thinking, that if the other learned and polite nations of Europe had possessed the same advantages of a popular government, they would probably have carried eloquence to a greater height than it has yet reached in Britain. The French sermons, especially those of Flechier and Bourdaloue,[1] are much superior to the English in this particular; and in Flechier there are many strokes of the

1 [Esprit Flechier (1632–1710), bishop of Nîmes; Louis Bourdaloue (1632–1704), Jesuit known for the rationality and moral strictness of his sermons.]

most sublime poetry. His funeral sermon on the Marechal de Turenne, is a good instance. None but private causes in that country, are ever debated before their Parliament or Courts of Judicature; but, notwithstanding this disadvantage, there appears a spirit of eloquence in many of their lawyers, which, with proper cultivation and encouragement, might rise to the greatest heights. The pleadings of Patru [2] are very elegant, and give us room to imagine what so fine a genius could have performed in questions concerning public liberty or slavery, peace or war, who exerts himself with such success, in debates concerning the price of an old horse, or the gossiping story of a quarrel betwixt an abbess and her nuns. For it is remarkable, that this polite writer, though esteemed by all the men of wit in his time, was never employed in the most considerable causes of their courts of judicature, but lived and died in poverty; from an ancient prejudice industriously propagated by the *Dunces* in all countries, *That a man of genius is unfit for business.* The disorders produced by the ministry of Cardinal Mazarine,[3] made the Parliament of Paris enter into the discussion of public affairs; and during that short interval, there appeared many symptoms of the revival of ancient eloquence. The Avocat-General, Talon,[4] in an oration, invoked on his knees the spirit of St. Louis to look down with compassion on his divided and unhappy people, and to inspire them, from above, with the love of concord and unanimity.[5] The members of the French Academy have attempted to give us models of eloquence in their harangues at their admittance; but having no subject to discourse upon, they have run altogether into a fulsome strain of panegyric and flattery, the most barren of all subjects. Their style, however, is commonly, on these occasions, very elevated and sublime, and might reach

[2] [Olivier Patru (1604–81), lawyer, and friend of Boileau. The tradition of newly-admitted Academy members giving speeches, which Hume goes on to mention, was begun by the admittance speech of Patru.]

[3] [Giulio Mazarini (1602–61), Italian Cardinal, Prime Minister under Louis XIII and Louis XIV.]

[4] [Omer Talon (1595–1652), French magistrate; during the Fronde, he defended the rights of Parliament against the royalty.]

[5] De Retz's Memoirs.

the greatest heights, were it employed on a subject more favorable and engaging.

There are some circumstances of the English temper and genius, which are disadvantageous to the progress of eloquence, and render all attempts of that kind more dangerous and difficult among them, than among any other nation in the universe. The English are conspicuous for *good sense,* which makes them very jealous of any attempts to deceive them, by the flowers of rhetoric and elocution. They are also peculiarly *modest;* which makes them consider it as a piece of arrogance to offer any thing but reason to public assemblies, or attempt to guide them by passion or fancy. I may, perhaps, be allowed to add, that the people in general are not remarkable for delicacy of taste, or for sensibility to the charms of the Muses. Their *musical parts,* to use the expression of a noble author, are but indifferent. Hence their comic poets, to move them, must have recourse to obscenity; their tragic poets to blood and slaughter. And hence, their orators, being deprived of any such resource, have abandoned altogether the hopes of moving them, and have confined themselves to plain argument and reasoning.

These circumstances, joined to particular accidents, may, perhaps, have retarded the growth of eloquence in this kingdom; but will not be able to prevent its success, if ever it appear amongst us. And one may safely pronounce, that this is a field in which the most flourishing laurels may yet be gathered, if any youth of accomplished genius, thoroughly acquainted with all the polite arts, and not ignorant of public business, should appear in Parliament, and accustom our ears to an eloquence more commanding and pathetic. And to confirm me in this opinion, there occur two considerations, the one derived from ancient, the other from modern times.

Of the Rise and Progress of the Arts and Sciences

Note *a*, p. 78. Editions B, D, and N: According to the necessary progress of things, law must precede science. In republics, law may precede science, and may arise from the very nature of the government. In monarchies, it arises not from the nature of the government, and cannot precede science. An absolute prince, that is barbarous, renders all his ministers and magistrates as absolute as himself: and there needs no more to prevent, for ever, all industry, curiosity, and science.

Note *b*, p. 85. Immediately after this passage, we find in the early Editions B, D, and N: There is a very great connection among all the arts, that contribute to pleasure; and the same delicacy of taste which enables us to make improvements in one, will not allow the others to remain altogether rude and barbarous.

Note *c*, p. 87. Editions B, D, and N: And it is remarkable, that Cicero, being a great sceptic in matters among the different sects of philosophy, introduces his friends disputing concerning the being and nature of the gods, while he is only a hearer, because, forsooth, it would have been an impropriety for so great a genius as himself had he spoke, not to have said something decisive on the subject, and have carried every thing before him, as he always does on other occasions. There is also a spirit of dialogue observed in the charming books *de Oratore,* and a tolerable equality maintained among the speakers; but then these speakers are the great men of the age preceding our author, and he recounts the conference as only from hearsay.

It is but a very indifferent compliment which Horace pays to his friend Grosphus, in the ode addressed to him. *No one, says he, is happy in every respect. And I may, perhaps, enjoy some advantages, which you are deprived of. You possess great riches: your bellowing herds cover the Sicilian plains: your chariot is drawn by the finest horses: and you are arrayed in the richest purple. But the indulgent Fates, with a small inheritance have given me a fine genius, and have endowed me with a contempt for the malignant judgments of the vulgar.*[6]

---

[6] ——Nihil est ab omni
　　　　Parte beatum.
　Abstulit clarum cita mors Achillem,
　Longa Tithonum minuit senectus,

Phaedrus says to his patron, *Eutychus, if you design to read my works, I shall be pleased: if not, I shall, at least, have the advantage of pleasing posterity.*[7] I am apt to think, that a modern poet would not have been guilty of such an impropriety, as that which may be observed in Virgil's address to Augustus, when, after a great deal of extravagant flattery, and after having deified the emperor, according to the custom of the times, he at last places this god on the same level with himself. *By your gracious nod,* says he, *render my undertaking prosperous; and taking pity, along with me, of the swains ignorant of husbandry, bestow your favorable influence on this work.*[8] Had men in that age been accustomed to observe such

---

Et mihi forsan, tibi quod negarit,
   Porriget hora.
Te greges centum, Siculaeque circum
Mugiunt vaccae: tibi tollit hinni-
Tum apta quadrigis equa: te bis Afro
   Murice tinctae
Vestiunt lanae: mihi parva rura, et
Spiritum Graiae tenuem Camoenae
Parca non mendax dedit, et malignum
   Spernare vulgus. [II, 16.]

[7] Quem si leges, laetabor; sin autem minus, habebunt certe quo se oblectent posteri.

[8] Ignarosque viae mecum miseratus agrestes
Ingredere, et votis jam nunc assuence vocari.

One would not say to a prince or great man, *When you and I were in such a place, we saw such a thing happen.* But *when you were in such a place, I attended on you; and such a thing happened.*

Here I cannot forbear mentioning a piece of delicacy observed in France, which seems to me excessive and ridiculous. You must not say, *That is a very fine dog, Madam,*—But, *Madam, that is a very fine dog.* They think it indecent that those words *Dog* and *Madam* should be coupled together in the sentence, though they have no reference to each other in the sense.

After all, I acknowledge, that this reasoning from single passages of ancient authors may seem fallacious, and that the foregoing arguments cannot have great force, but with those who are well acquainted with these authors, and know the truth of the general position. For instance, what absurdity would it be to assert that Virgil understood not the force of the terms he employs, and could not choose his epithets with propriety; because, in the following lines addressed also to Augustus, he has

niceties, a writer so delicate as Virgil, would certainly have given a different turn to this sentence. The court of Augustus, however polite, had not yet, it seems, wore off the manners of the republic.

Note *d*, p. 92. Editions B and D: I must confess that my own particular choice rather leads me to prefer the company of a few select companions, with whom I can calmly and peaceably enjoy the feast of reason, and try the justness of every reflection, whether gay or serious, that may occur to me. But as such a delightful society is not every day to be met with, I must think that mixed companies without the fair sex, are the most insipid entertainment in the world, and destitute of gaiety and politeness, as much as of sense and reason. Nothing can keep them from excessive dulness but hard drinking, a remedy worse than the disease.

Note *e*, p. 92. Editions B, D, and N: The point of *honor* is a modern invention, as well as *gallantry;* and by some esteemed equally useful for the refining of manners: but how it has contributed to that effect, I am at a loss to determine. Conversation among the greatest rustics, is not commonly infested with such rudeness as can give occasion to duels, even according to the most refined laws of this fantastic honor; and as to the other smaller indecencies, which are the most offensive, because the most frequent, they can never be cured by the practice of duelling. But these notions are not only useless but pernicious. By separating the man of honor from the man of virtue, the greatest profligates have got something to value themselves upon, and have been able to keep themselves in countenance, though guilty of the most shameful and most dangerous vices. They are debauchees, spendthrifts, and never pay a farthing they owe; but they are men of honor, and therefore are to be received as gentlemen in all companies.

---

failed in that particular, and has ascribed to the Indians a quality which seems, in a manner, to turn his hero into ridicule!

———Et te, maxime Caesar,

Qui nunc, extremis Asiae jam victor in oris,

Imbellem avertis Romanis arcibus Indum.   [*Georgics* II.]

There are some of the parts of modern honor which are the most essential parts of morality, such as fidelity, the observing promises, and telling truth. These points of honor Mr. Addison had in his eye, when he made Juba say,

Honor's a sacred tie, the law of kings,
The noble mind's distinguishing perfection,
That aids and strengthens virtue, when it meets her,
And imitates her actions where she is not:
It ought not to be sported with.

These lines are very beautiful; but I am afraid that Mr. Addison has here been guilty of that impropriety of sentiment with which he has so justly reproved other poets. The ancients certainly never had any notion of *honor* as distinct from *virtue*.

Of the Study of History

Note *a*, p. 95. This essay is found in Editions A, C, and D.

The Sceptic

Note *a*, p. 135. Editions B and D: And it is observable, in this kingdom, that long peace, by producing security, has much altered them in this particular, and has quite removed our officers from the generous character of their profession.

Of the Dignity or Meanness of Human Nature

Note *a*, p. 141. Editions A, C, D, and N: Women are generally much more flattered in their youth than men, which may proceed from this reason among others, that their chief point of honor is considered as much more difficult than ours, and requires to be supported by all that decent pride which can be instilled into them.

Note *b*, p. 143. Editions A, C, D, and N: I may perhaps treat more fully of this subject in some future Essay. In the mean time I shall observe, what has been proved beyond question by several great moralists of the present age, that the social passions are by far the most powerful of any, and that even all the other passions receive from them their chief force and influence. Whoever desires to see this question treated at large, with the greatest force of argument and eloquence, may consult my Lord Shaftesbury's Enquiry concerning Virtue.

Note *c,* p. 143. This passage is not in the early editions. It is found in Edition N.

Of Superstition and Enthusiasm

Note *a,* p. 147. In Editions A and C, the next four paragraphs are replaced by the following: My first reflection is, that religions which partake of enthusiasm are, on their first rise, much more furious and violent than those which partake of superstition; but in a little time become much more gentle and moderate. The violence of this species of religion, when excited by novelty, and animated by opposition, appears from numberless instances: of the *Anabaptists* in *Germany,* the *Camisars* in *France,* the *Levellers,* and other fanatics in *England,* and the *Covenanters* in *Scotland.* As enthusiasm is founded on strong spirits and a presumptuous boldness of character, it naturally begets the most extreme resolutions; especially after it rises to that height as to inspire the deluded fanatics with the opinion of Divine illuminations, and with a contempt of the common rules of reason, morality, and prudence.

It is thus enthusiasm produces the most cruel desolation in human society: but its fury is like that of thunder and tempest, which exhaust themselves in a little time, and leave the air more calm and serene than before. The reason of this will appear evidently, by comparing enthusiasm to superstition, the other species of false religion, and tracing the natural consequences of each. As superstition is founded on fear, sorrow, and a depression of spirits, it represents the person to himself in such despicable colors, that he appears unworthy, in his own eyes, of approaching the Divine presence, and naturally has recourse to any other person whose sanctity of life, or perhaps impudence and cunning, have made him be supposed to be more favored by the Divinity. To him they intrust their devotions; to his care they recommend their prayers, petitions, and sacrifices: and by his means hope to render their addresses acceptable to their incensed Deity. Hence the origin of Priests,[9] who may justly be regarded as proceeding from one of the grossest inventions of a timorous and abject superstition, which, ever diffident of itself, dares not offer up its own devotions, but ignorantly thinks to recommend itself to the Divinity by the mediation of his supposed friends and servants. As superstition is a considerable ingredient of almost all religions, even the most fanatical, there being nothing but philosophy able to conquer entirely these unaccountable terrors; hence it proceeds, that in almost every sect of religion there are priests to be found. But the stronger mixture there is of superstition, the higher is the authority of the priesthood. Modern Judaism and Popery, especially the latter, being the most barbarous and absurd superstitions that have yet been known in the world, are the most enslaved by their priests. As the Church of England has a strong mixture of Popish superstition, it partakes also, in its original constitution, of a propensity of priestly power and dominion, particularly in the respect it exacts to the priest. And though, according to the sentiments of that church, the prayers of the priest must be accompanied with those of the laity, yet is he the mouth of the congregation; his person is sacred, and without his presence few would think their public devotions, or the sacraments and other rites, acceptable to the Divinity.

On the other hand, it may be observed, that all enthusiasts have been free from the yoke of Ecclesiastics, and have expressed a great independence in their devotion; with a con-

[9] By priest, I understand only the pretenders to power and dominion, and to a superior sanctity of character, distinct from virtue and good morals. These are very different from *clergymen,* who are set apart to the care of sacred matters, and the conducting our public devotions with greater decency and order. There is no rank of man more to be respected than the latter.

tempt of forms, traditions, and authorities. The *Quakers* are the most egregious, though at the same time the most innocent enthusiasts that have been yet known; and are, perhaps, the only sect that have never admitted priests amongst them. The *Independents,* of all the English sectaries, approach nearest to the Quakers in fanaticism, and in their freedom from priestly bondage. The *Presbyterians* follow after at an equal distance in both these particulars. In short, this observation is founded on the most certain experience; and will also appear to be founded on reason, if we consider, that as enthusiasm arises from a presumptuous pride and confidence, it thinks itself sufficiently qualified to approach the Divinity without any human mediator. Its rapturous devotions are so fervent, that it even imagines itself *actually* to *approach* him by the way of contemplation and inward converse,—which makes it neglect all those outward ceremonies and observances, to which the assistance of the priest appears so requisite in the eyes of their superstitious votaries. The fanatic consecrates himself, and bestows on his own person a sacred character, much superior to what forms and ceremonious institutions can confer on any other.

It is therefore an infallible rule that superstition is favorable to priestly power, and enthusiasm as much, or rather more, contrary to it, than sound reason and philosophy. The consequences are evident. When the first fire of enthusiasm is spent, man naturally, in such fanatical sects, sinks into the greatest remissness and coolness in sacred matters; there being no body of men amongst them endowed with sufficient authority, whose interest is concerned, to support the religious spirit. Superstition, on the contrary, steals in gradually and insensibly; renders men tame and submissive; is acceptable to the magistrate, and seems inoffensive to the people: till at last the priest, having firmly established his authority, becomes the tyrant and disturber of human society, by his endless contentions, persecutions, and religious wars. How smoothly did the *Romish* church advance in their acquisition of power! But into what dismal convulsions did they throw all Europe, in order to maintain it! On the other hand, our sectaries, who were formerly such dangerous bigots, are now become our greatest freethinkers; and the *Quakers* are perhaps the only regular body of *Deists* in the universe, except the literati, or disciples of *Confucius* in *China*.

My second observation with regard to these species of false religion is, that superstition is an enemy to civil liberty, and enthusiasm a friend to it, &c. . . .

On Suicide

Note *a*, p. 151. This essay and the next, *On the Immortality of the Soul*, are taken from the edition printed at London under the title "Essays on Suicide, and the Immortality of the Soul, ascribed to the late David Hume, Esq. Never before published. With Remarks, intended as an Antidote to the Poison contained in these Performances, by the Editor. To which is added, two Letters on Suicide, from Rousseau's Eloisa. London, 1783."

The Library of Liberal Arts

SCHILLER, J., Wilhelm Tell

SCHLEGEL, J., On Imitation and
    Other Essays

SCHNEIDER, H., Sources of
    Contemporary
    Philosophical Realism
    in America

SCHOPENHAUER, A., On the Basis
    of Morality
    Freedom of the Will

SELBY-BIGGE, L., British Moralists

SENECA, Medea
    Oedipus
    Thyestes

SHAFTESBURY, A., Characteristics

SHELLEY, P., A Defence of Poetry

SMITH, A., The Wealth of Nations
    (Selections)

Song of Roland, Terry, trans.

SOPHOCLES, Electra

SPIEGELBERG, H., The Socratic
    Enigma

SPINOZA, B., Earlier Philosophical
    Writings
    On the Improvement of the
    Understanding

TERENCE, The Brothers
    The Eunuch
    The Mother-in-Law
    Phormio
    The Self-Tormentor
    The Woman of Andros

Three Greek Romances, Hadas,
    trans.

TOLSTOY, L., What is Art?

VERGIL, Aeneid

VICO, G. B., On the Study Methods
    Our Time

VOLTAIRE, Philosophical Letters

WHITEHEAD, A., Interpretation of
    Science

WOLFF, C., Preliminary Discourse
    on Philosophy in General

XENOPHON, Recollections of
    Socrates *and* Socrates'
    Defense Before the Jury

THE AMERICAN HERITAGE SERIES

THE COLONIAL PERIOD

THE REVOLUTIONARY ERA

THE YOUNG NATION

TOPICAL VOLUMES

The Library of Literature